Praise for V. M. Burns and

MURDER ON TOUR

"A much-hated author's publicist is offed by a poisoned cocktail doubtless designed for his client. Who had the guts to do what everyone wished they could've done? . . . The remarkable heroine's refreshing lack of aspirations adds to the charm of this mystery."
—*Kirkus Reviews*

KILLER WORDS

"Charming. . . . Newcomers will have fun, while established fans will relish the evolution of the characters and welcome Samantha's bright new future." —*Publishers Weekly*

A TOURIST'S GUIDE TO MURDER

"Colorful characters and just enough mystery trivia boost the fast-moving plot. Cozy fans are sure to have fun." —*Publishers Weekly*

BOOKMARKED FOR MURDER

"This two-in-one mystery satisfies on so many levels, with this fifth in the series being as fresh and unique as the first."
—*Kings River Life Magazine*

"In the end, *Bookmarked for Murder* is a fantastic bookstore cozy murder book, and the 'Mystery Bookshop' series is an enthralling read that makes me smile and has me hoping my retirement will be just like Nana Jo's and the other characters. This book is beyond entertaining. It's a page-turner that is filled with remarkable characters that have readers coming back for more." —The Cozy Review

READ HERRING HUNT

"As good as any Jessica Fletcher story could be, Burns has a way with words and her characters are absolutely riveting. There is no doubt this is one series that will continue for a good, long time to come." —*Suspense Magazine*

THE PLOT IS MURDER

"This debut cleverly integrates a historical cozy within a contemporary mystery. In both story lines, the elder characters shine; they are refreshingly witty and robust, with formidable connections and investigative skills." —*Library Journal* (Starred Review)

Books by Valerie Burns

Baker Street Mysteries
TWO PARTS SUGAR, ONE PART MURDER
MURDER IS A PIECE OF CAKE
A CUP OF FLOUR, A PINCH OF DEATH

Books by Valerie Burns writing as V. M. Burns

Mystery Bookshop Mysteries
THE PLOT IS MURDER
READ HERRING HUNT
THE NOVEL ART OF MURDER
WED, READ & DEAD
BOOKMARKED FOR MURDER
A TOURIST'S GUIDE TO MURDER
KILLER WORDS
BOOKCLUBBED TO DEATH
MURDER ON TOUR
THE NEXT DEADLY CHAPTER

Dog Club Mysteries
IN THE DOG HOUSE
THE PUPPY WHO KNEW TOO MUCH
BARK IF IT'S MURDER
PAW AND ORDER
SIT, STAY, SLAY

Published by Kensington Publishing Corp.

The Next Deadly Chapter

V. M. BURNS

Kensington Publishing Corp.
kensingtonbooks.com

KENSINGTON BOOKS are published by

Kensington Publishing Corp.
900 Third Avenue
New York, NY 10022

All Kensington titles, imprints, and distributed lines are available at special quantity discounts for bulk purchases for sales promotion, premiums, fund-raising, and educational or institutional use.

Special book excerpts or customized printings can also be created to fit specific needs. For details, write or phone the office of the Kensington Sales Manager: Kensington Publishing Corp., 900 Third Avenue, New York, NY 10022. Attn. Sales Department. Phone: 1-800-221-2647.

ISBN: 978-1-4967-5080-8
First Trade Paperback Printing: March 2025

ISBN: 978-1-4967-5081-5 (e-book)

10 9 8 7 6 5 4 3 2 1

Printed in the United States of America

In loving memory of my parents, Benjamin and Elvira Burns.
Together again for eternity.

Acknowledgments

While writing this book, I faced some extremely tough times. I would not have gotten through that season in my life, let alone finished this book, without the help of family, friends, and a fantastic team of people.

Thanks to my friend Debra H. Goldstein for the pep talks, legal insight, and for listening to me whine and complain. You deserve a medal. Thanks to Kellye Garrett for the sprints and the encouragement. I'm so thankful to have you all in my life.

Thanks to my family: Jackie, Jillian, Christopher, Carson, Drew, Marcie, William, Crosby, and Cameron. We had a rough ride, but we made it. I love you all.

Special thanks to my agent, Jessica Faust at BookEnds Literary Agency; Mary Lasher for the great covers; the best P.A., Kelly Fowler; and my wonderful team at Kensington (John Scognamiglio, Larissa Ackerman, Michelle Addo, Carly Sommerstein, et. al.).

Acknowledgments

Chapter 1

"Good afternoon. My name's Samantha Washington and I write murder mysteries," I said with a big grin on my face.

"Women shouldn't be writing books about murder. You should be home raising a family and taking care of your husbands," a gravel-filled voice yelled from the back of the room.

My grandmother, Nana Jo, was seated in the front row. Even though I was standing over six feet away, I heard a growl rise from her gut to her throat.

The crowd of mostly women at the Pontolomas Senior Citizens Center who came to hear me talk about my book, *Murder at Wickfield Lodge*, shushed and murmured. There was a good amount of shuffling and moving of chairs. This event wasn't getting off to a good start.

I craned my neck to see where the disruption originated. It didn't take a genius to see that my heckler was a short white-haired elderly man. He chomped on an unlit cigar in the corner with a smirk on his face that left no doubt that he was the one whose views were still mired in the early twentieth-century quicksand. He had a short neck that reminded me of a toad. He sat with his arms folded across his chest and leaned back in his chair. I wasn't sure if he reminded me of an antique because of his outdated mindset or because of the years etched on his face like growth rings on a tree.

I took a deep breath and swallowed hard. *Pull it together, Sam.* I reminded myself that before I'd quit my job to open my mystery bookshop and write full-time, I had been a high school English teacher. I'd endured far more creative hecklers and insurgents than this guy. *So why is this guy getting under my skin?* As a teacher, I'd mastered the art of bringing teenage dissidents to a screeching halt with a raised eyebrow and a look. All teachers, the good ones who stood the test of time, have a look. Maybe I was rusty. It had been quite some time since I'd taught and last had to employ *the look*. I gazed out at the sea of faces, the people who had come out to see me. The event was on land belonging to the Pontolomas. The vast majority of those present were female with features indicating they were indigenous.

The Pontolomas were a Native American tribe that had populated Southwestern Michigan long before any settlers arrived from Europe. The expressions they wore were kind. These were people who had left the comfort of their homes to make their way to the community center to listen to me talk about and read from my book. This wasn't me spouting off about dangling participles or sentence structure. This was my book. It was personal.

I cleared my throat and started again. "*Murder at Wickfield Lodge* is the first book in a historical cozy mystery series that features—"

"What a lot of claptrap."

I didn't need to look up to know that the comment came from the same person. The gravel-throated toad.

The crowd rustled. Most shushed. Some pleaded for silence.

If at first you don't succeed, try, try again. "*Murder at Wickfield*

Lodge is set in England in 1939. It's right before the start of World War II and—"

"Ha. Women always get their facts wrong. World War II didn't start until December 1941, after the bombing of Pearl Harbor. Every fool knows that. That's why women should stick to things they know, like cooking, cleaning, and babies. Leave the important facts like war to a man," Toad Throat said.

The booing and the shushing volume increased. Unlike the last time, the response was more vocal and charged with anger and included more words.

"Chauvinist."

"Quiet."

"Silence."

"Actually, World War II officially started in September 1939. After the Germans invaded Poland, Great Britain and France declared war on Germany. The Soviet Union joined the war in June 1941. The United States declared war on Japan after the bombing of Pearl Harbor in December, later that same year. In support of Japan, Hitler declared war on the U.S., and so you are partially correct if you are only talking about when the United States joined the war." I flashed a big smile to soften the correction, but based on the grunt I received in response, it didn't matter.

A few women applauded.

"So, this is a cozy mystery that—"

"What the heck is that anyway? A cozy mystery?" Toad Throat yelled. "Never heard of it. Sounds like some made-up word, a *cozy mystery*."

"There are enough things a Neanderthal like you have never heard before to fill an entire planet. But maybe if you'd shut up and listen you'll learn something," Nana Jo yelled.

"Yeah."

"Let her talk."

"I came to hear the author, not you."

The crowd was getting rowdy.

"A cozy mystery is a subgenre of crime fiction. Has anyone ever watched *Murder, She Wrote*?" I asked.

There were lots of head nods.

"That's a perfect example of a cozy mystery. Jessica Fletcher is an amateur sleuth. She's a retired teacher who turns to writing mysteries after her husband dies. She doesn't get paid to solve crimes like the police." The similarities between Jessica Fletcher and myself weren't lost on me. I too had turned to writing murder mysteries after Leon, my late husband, died. But that wasn't part of the presentation.

A young woman in the front row raised her hand. "Is that the only thing that makes it cozy?"

"No. Experts within publishing will disagree on the exact criteria for a cozy mystery. Some people think you have to have a theme or a pet. But the thing that pretty much everyone agrees on is that a cozy mystery doesn't have any violence on the page. No explicit sex, and no severe bad words."

"No violence? I thought you said it was a murder mystery. How can you have a murder mystery without violence?" Toad Throat asked.

This time, the crowd wasn't as vocal in their opposition to the heckler. Many of them probably had the same question.

"I said there's *no violence on the page*. So, you don't see the gruesome grisly deed. When you read a cozy, the author won't describe the murder in graphic detail. There won't be detailed descriptions of the body decomposition or any of the other nastiness that comes along with murder and dead bodies. If you think about Jessica Fletcher in *Murder, She Wrote*, she always just stumbled across a dead body. The important thing wasn't the body. The important thing was the puzzle. It's about figuring out the clues to determine whodunit."

"Pshaw! Nonsense. Leave it up to a woman to create something so completely ridiculous. Murders aren't cozy. Murders are brutal and bloody. They are horrific. Men know this. A woman has to soften it and turn the most vicious of actions into something warm and cozy. Geez! You've taken away the core of the thing and turned it into something cheerful and fuzzy with cats and recipes. That's not serious literature. That's just fluff."

The crowd's reaction was no longer polite and friendly. Several of the women turned around and yelled at the toad. Things were getting out of control.

Nana Jo was on her feet. At five foot ten and over two hundred pounds, my grandmother was no lightweight. She towered over the crowd and narrowed her gaze at the toad-throated heckler. "Now, you listen here. If you say one more word, I'm going to put my foot up your rear and drop-kick you like a bad habit."

"Bring it on, old woman." Blood rushed up the heckler's neck and flooded his face. He stood up, knocking his chair over in the process.

Nana Jo walked slowly around the crowd so she was nearly toe to toe with the heckler. She spread her legs so her feet were shoulder-width apart. Left foot forward and pointed toward her opponent. Her right foot was slightly back and pointed at a forty-five-degree angle. Her knees were slightly bent and her hands were up, with her fingers pointed upward. If the heckler didn't know my grandmother held a black belt in aikido and jujitsu, her stance must have given him a clue. She extended one hand like Morpheus in *The Matrix* and beckoned for the heckler to make the first move.

A tall thin man with long gray hair pulled back into a ponytail hurried from a back room and into the central area set up for my talk and reading. He wore a dark suit with a white shirt. He walked over to my heckler and whispered something in his ear.

"I'm entitled to my opinions. It's in the First Amendment," Mr. Toad Throat erupted. "It's supposed to be a free country, even on a reservation."

I was too far away to hear the exchange, but whatever my ponytailed helper said, it doused the flames. The heckler appeared to have had a change of heart. He forced his lips to curl upward. It didn't reach his eyes, and what was likely intended to be a smile looked more like a grimace in the end. Still, even a grimace was better than the fire-breathing dragon he'd unleashed moments earlier.

The heckler grunted, turned, and marched out of the room.

The cheers and applause were so loud that even if Toad Throat wanted to say something more, he would have had to shout.

After he left, the atmosphere in the room changed completely. Instead of the tense, highly charged space that existed moments earlier, the air was calm and peaceful. The sun shone. Birds chirped. People relaxed and smiled.

Nana Jo watched as her opponent walked away for a few moments before she turned, shrugged, and returned to her seat.

The group gave her a standing ovation.

Nana Jo turned to face the group. "Too bad. I've been practicing my crane kick and was looking forward to giving it a try." She stood on one leg with both hands raised in the air like the kid in *The Karate Kid* movie.

The crowd burst into laughter.

Nana Jo made a dramatic bow and took her seat.

The remainder of the presentation went without a hitch and surprisingly fast. I read a passage from my book, answered questions, and then signed copies. It turned out to be a great event.

Afterward, the staff thanked me for coming and apologized profusely for the unpleasantness. The activities coordinator, Enola Nightingale, a small middle-aged woman with dark eyes and a big smile, pulled me aside.

"I'm so sorry that you experienced such a rude personality. The manager was appalled when I told him what happened."

"It's okay. I know it wasn't your fault." I smiled. "I'm just glad my grandmother didn't get into a physical fight with him." I glanced around and saw Nana Jo talking to the man who'd evicted the heckler earlier. They seemed to be having a friendly conversation and both were smiling.

"Just between you and me," Mrs. Nightingale leaned forward and whispered, "I would have enjoyed seeing that man taken down by a woman."

We both chuckled.

Since I'd published my first book and started promoting it, I'd purchased a plastic tote on wheels, which is where I stored all the things I hauled to book events. It contained a few books, bookmarks, pens, candy, and other swag that I carted around to book readings and signings. It made life easy to have the tote packed and ready to go. When I had everything loaded into the tote, I looked around for Nana Jo.

She finished her conversation with the manager in time to help me load the tote in the back of my SUV. Then, she surprised me by handing me an envelope.

"What's this?" I asked.

"That man I was talking to, the one who tossed that heckler out, his name is Kai Strongbow. Nice man. He's one of the tribal leaders with the Pontolomas and I think he manages the community center. Mr. Strongbow was horrified by the way you were treated by that sawed-off troll who had the nerve to heckle you."

"Is that what he called him?" I laughed.

"No, that's what I called him. Anyway, Mr. Strongbow is also a member of the tribal council."

"It sounds impressive, but what does that mean?" I asked.

"It means he's one of the big muckety-mucks connected with the Four Feathers. When I found that out, I dropped a few hints about how you were getting married soon and your soon-to-be mother-in-law is coming tomorrow and that you were stressed out about that and didn't need this toad-faced sexist adding to your stress level."

"Nana Jo!"

"It's the truth."

"I know, but none of that was Mr. Strongbow's fault. Besides, it all worked out in the end."

"Once Strongbow threatened him. He just should have let me drop-kick him into the middle of next week. I would have enjoyed putting that backward-thinking Neanderthal in his place. That—"

"Wait. What? He threatened him? I was too far away to hear what he said to him."

"Well, I was up close and personal. Mr. Strongbow said, '*If you don't leave these premises immediately, you will regret it. I will personally make it my mission to destroy you. Now, get off our land.*'"

Chapter 2

"Wow. That sounds serious. I almost feel sorry for him." I backed out of the parking lot and headed toward the interstate.

"I don't feel sorry for the little troll," Nana Jo said. "He was rude and deserved to be taught a lesson, and I was just itching to be the one to do the teaching."

"I said *almost*." I focused on merging onto Interstate 94 and back to North Harbor.

North Harbor was a small town located on the shores of Lake Michigan in Southwestern Michigan. It was only about thirty minutes away from the Pontoloma reservation. The Pontoloma Nation was one of the newer tribes to be recognized by the United States Government. Since receiving their official tribal designation, they had bought a substantial amount of land, built a school, a medical facility, and the community center. They'd also built residential homes and established the highly successful Four Feathers Casino and Resort.

"Anyway, Mr. Strongbow and I got to talking and he wanted to do something to make up for the way Oscar Pembrook treated you."

"Oscar Pembrook? Is that Toad Throat's name? I mean—"

"I know what you meant, and yes, that's his name according to Mr. Strongbow."

"That was nice, but it wasn't necessary."

"Sam, he wanted to do it."

"Do what?"

"He's offering a complimentary stay at the casino resort for an entire four-day weekend. All expenses paid." Nana Jo pulled a business card out of the envelope she'd handed me earlier but that I had barely glanced at. "For you and five friends."

"Wow. I've heard the rooms at the Four Feathers are nice, but I've never seen them," I said. "Six rooms? That's really nice."

"Yeah, so I was thinking it would be a nice little excursion for Frank's mother," Nana Jo said.

"I don't know if she likes to gamble," I said. "She's rather conservative."

"She doesn't have to gamble. There are plenty of other things she can do." Nana Jo pulled out her phone and swiped until she found the Four Feathers website. "The website lists tons of activities, like hiking, fishing, golf, a pool, shops, and a world-class spa. Surely she can find something to do, even if it's just sitting in the bar and reading a book."

"Really? They have a spa? And golf?"

"That's what their website says. I don't know if the golfing is on the property or if you have to take a shuttle, but they list it under the activities section. Personally, I don't think I'd want to go hiking around there. At least not without my peacemaker." Nana Jo patted her purse. "They've got bears, coyotes, and bobcats in all that wooded land surrounding the casino."

My grandmother barely went anywhere without her *peacemaker*. She was a good shot, but that just made matters worse.

The last thing I wanted was for my grandmother to whip out her gun and shoot someone. There were too many people packing guns, in my opinion. The last thing I needed was for Nana Jo to end up in an old-fashioned gunfight. Still, she usually carried the gun with her. Fortunately, my sister Jenna had gotten her a permit so she could legally carry her gun to most places. The Four Feathers wasn't technically on United States soil, so our gun laws didn't apply and she would have to leave it in the car.

I drove to Nana Jo's house at Shady Acres Retirement Village. She'd bought her house—or villa, as the staff called them—when the senior community was just starting. She'd seen the potential in a community for active seniors right on Lake Michigan and bought one of the first lots. The retirement village was restricted to people over the age of fifty-five. It included individual homes, and the Homeowners Association took care of the yard work. There were also apartments for people who didn't want the hassle of upkeep on a single-family home. The residents of Shady Acres enjoyed world-class cuisine from a Michelin chef in the main dining room. Set on the shores of Lake Michigan, Shady Acres had breathtaking water views with plenty of activities. Residents enjoyed all of the benefits of an active lifestyle, with classes that covered everything from martial arts to yoga, scuba diving, bicycling, and belly dancing.

Most days, Nana Jo stayed with me in the home I created above the mystery bookshop that I bought after my late husband died. Leon and I had both been avid mystery lovers. We dreamed about one day quitting our jobs and opening a bookshop that specialized in mysteries. Leon's battle with cancer was short, and it taught me that life is too short not to spend it doing what you love. So, I stopped waiting for the planets to align perfectly. I quit my job as a high school English teacher and used the insurance money to buy the building that we used to walk by and talk about *one day*. The upstairs of the building had been converted into residential apartments. Leon and I had planned on renting them out to help supplement the bookstore. Before he died, Leon made me promise that I would sell the house that we lived in together and move into the upstairs. He knew that I would have a hard time letting go of the past and moving on with a new future if I stayed in the house. It was a good call. I converted the upstairs into a large two-bedroom apartment, and it was perfect for me and my two poodles, Snickers and Oreo.

Nana Jo spent most of the week with me working in the bookstore. After all, she was the one who first got me started with my love of mysteries. She was also an expert at helping people find the perfect genre of mystery by merely asking them a series of questions. When Nana Jo learned that my fiancé's mother was coming for a visit, she offered her the use of her house.

"I realize the point is for you two to get acquainted, but it's possible to have too much togetherness. You and I are family. If we get on each other's nerves, we can have a good old-fashioned fight and then hug and make up. You and Mrs. Patterson aren't ready for that yet."

"*Dr.* Patterson."

"Whatever." Nana Jo waved away my correction. "She's a medical doctor, not the queen. I'm going to clean for her royal highness and I'll pack a bag and have Freddie drop me at your place after our date."

Freddie Williams was a retired police officer and Nana Jo's boyfriend.

I dropped off Nana Jo and continued toward downtown North Harbor and home. I loved looking at the lake as I drove. North Harbor and its twin city, South Harbor, both shared the same breathtaking views of Lake Michigan. Separated by the St. Thomas River, the two towns should have been mirror images of each other. However, they were almost exact opposites. Up until the midtwentieth century, North Harbor was the more prosperous of the two towns, as evidenced by the large Victorian homes that still dotted the community. North Harbor was once a thriving town with a booming economy spurred by manufacturing jobs connected to the auto industry. After those manufacturing jobs moved South and the civil rights struggle in the 1960s, the town underwent an urban and economic decline. A recent report from the governor described the city of North Harbor as suffering from *extreme generational poverty, corruption, and mismanaged finances*. North Harbor was almost 90 percent minority and more than half of the population lived below the poverty line.

South Harbor's demographics were almost exactly the opposite. Formerly a working-class community, it had transformed into a picturesque tourist town. South Harbor lacked the old Victorian homes of its twin city but managed to showcase its best features for maximum impact. Perched on a bluff overlooking the lake, the city offered horse-drawn buggy rides through its cobblestoned streets and quaint brick-fronted shops. In the summer months tourists flocked to the pristine beaches.

Leon and I were idealistic believers that North Harbor could be turned around, so when we dreamed of opening our specialty bookshop, North Harbor was the only possible location. Market Street Mysteries was located on a corner lot. I shared a small parking lot with the church next door. The bookstore was closed on Sundays, so it worked out well. There was a detached garage at the back of the lot, which I accessed through an alley. I'd had a fence installed when I moved in. The fence ran from the side of the building to the garage and created a small courtyard enclosure that worked well for containing my dogs.

I pulled into the garage and went through the side door of the bookstore. From the moment my key went into the lock I heard barking. Two chocolate toy poodles rushed down the stairs to greet me. Snickers, my female poodle, was almost fifteen. Her muzzle was more white than brown. She was eight pounds of pure feistiness, although she had mellowed considerably in her old age. Despite congenital heart failure, she was doing remarkably well thanks to the marvels of modern medicine and a great vet. Oreo, my ten-pound male, was only two years younger than Snickers, but you would never know it by the way he acted. He still had a lot of puppy exuberance. His dorkiness never failed to put a smile on my face.

True to form, Snickers hurried to a corner, squatted, and took care of business while Oreo pounced on leaves and barked at a bird perched on the fence. Snickers and I stood and watched him play until he eventually remembered why he was there. He hiked his leg on the corner of the garage and then ran inside as though he were being chased by the hounds of hell. He skidded to a halt inside just before colliding with the wall.

The aroma of chocolate, vanilla, and sugar drifted down from the kitchen and drew me up the stairs. Dawson Alexander was baking. If my nose was correct, chocolate chip cookies were waiting for me upstairs. Nothing soothed the nerves like chocolate chip cookies, and between the heckler and the anxiety I felt about meeting Frank's mother face-to-face, I needed plenty of soothing.

I raced the poodles upstairs. Dogs couldn't have chocolate, but they knew Dawson would make sure they got plenty of dog-friendly treats.

"Chocolate chip cookies. I knew it." I grabbed a cookie from a nearby platter, bit into the warm gooey goodness, and let the chocolate work its magic.

"I knew you'd like them. I even put nuts in some of them. I know you like nuts in your cookies." He pointed to a Tupperware container filled with cookies.

I swallowed the cookie I'd just tasted and reached for the others. One bite and I was in heaven. I must have moaned because when I opened my eyes, Dawson was chuckling. "What?" I asked around a mouthful of the nutty chocolatey gooeyness.

"Nothing. I just haven't seen many people enjoy a cookie the way you do." He poured a glass of milk and handed it to me.

"There's more than nuts in these. It tastes like . . . butter and chocolate and . . . caramel?"

He nodded. "I tried something a little different. I know how much you like turtle candy, so that's my version of a turtle cookie."

"Yum. These are delicious." I savored the flavors in my mouth before washing it down with the milk.

The kitchen table was littered with textbooks and papers. Dawson was a college student, but whenever he was stuck, baking helped him work through his problems. Based on the looks of the tables and the vast amount of cookies, he must have been stuck fairly well.

Dawson Alexander was a local kid, one of my students at North Harbor High School. Raised by his father, an abusive alcoholic, Dawson might have become another statistic of poverty, a broken home, and abuse. Fortunately for him, his athletic ability provided an escape, gaining him recognition with the local media and catapulting him to stardom. As a local star on the gridiron, Dawson received a golden ticket out of the vicious cycle of poverty when he landed a full scholarship to play football for the Michigan Southwest University Tigers. Locals referred to the school as MIS-U. Academics weren't Dawson's strong suit. After a challenging freshman year that placed him on academic probation and a beating from his father, he ended up hiding out in the bathroom of my bookshop. I converted the area above my garage into a studio apartment and Nana Jo and I tutored him so that he was now in great shape both academically and mentally. When he wasn't playing football he earned extra money working in the bookstore. Plus, I got to enjoy a lot of amazing baked goods.

I sat on the barstool and ate chocolate chip turtle cookies while Dawson told me about his day. The upstairs was large and open. It had oak hardwood floors, exposed brick walls, seventeen-foot ceilings, and windows stretching from floor to ceiling. Originally the space had been sectioned off, but I renovated the 2,000-square-foot space and added track lighting and skylights, making the space bright and inviting. Despite the industrial décor, the space still felt warm and cozy.

One glance at the vast amount of cookies lining the counter in my kitchen told me that he had a lot to work through.

"Do you want to talk about it?" I asked.

Dawson put a cookie sheet in the oven and wiped his hands. He turned around slowly to face me. "No . . . yes . . ." He shrugged. "I heard from my dad. He's out of jail. And he wants to see me."

Chapter 3

Dawson's dad, Alex Alexander, or A-Squared, was often in and out of jail for various offenses. Most stemmed from his battle with alcohol and anger. Their relationship was complicated by the fact that even though Dawson recognized his dad's flaws and shortcomings, he still loved him and wanted his approval. Those were emotions I knew something about.

"Okay." I wanted to tread lightly. I'd grown fond of Dawson in the time since he'd taken up residence in the studio over my garage. He wasn't just a tenant, a baker, and my assistant. Leon and I had not been blessed with children and Dawson was the son I'd never had. Still, he wasn't my son. "Did he want anything in particular?"

"He said he wants to talk." Dawson shrugged. "I don't suppose it would hurt to see him. Do you?"

I wanted to scream at him not to fall for his father's manipulation. A-Squared only reached out when he wanted something, usually money. For Dawson's sake I hoped that this time would be different. I hoped that time in jail had helped A-Squared to realize what a treasure his son was. I prayed that he wanted to apologize for the years of abuse and neglect. But I didn't believe it. I gazed at Dawson and knew that he didn't believe that his dad had changed either.

"Would you like me to go with you?" I asked.

Dawson shook his head. "Naw. I haven't decided if I'm going to go yet." He paused. "What do you think? Should I meet him?"

Inside my head I was screaming, *Noooo! No way. Stay as far away from him as possible. He's only going to use you and then toss you aside like a dirty tissue. Don't put yourself in that position. Don't let him hurt you. He doesn't deserve your love.* What came out of my mouth was completely different. "I think you should follow your heart. What do you want to do? Do you want to see him?"

Please say no.

He paused too long before answering. "I don't know. I guess so. I mean, he's my dad. I haven't seen him in almost a year. Maybe he's changed."

Not likely.

He shrugged. "I guess it won't hurt just to talk to him. Would it?"

Yes, if he breaks your heart.

"People can change a lot in a year. Maybe you should take him some cookies."

Not my special turtle cookies, but maybe the ones that are burned on the bottom to match his soul. "When does he want to meet?"

"Tonight." He glanced at his watch. "I've got about two hours."

"Where are you meeting?"

Maybe I can cruise the parking lot with Nana Jo and her peacemaker in case you need backup.

"He wanted to come here, but I didn't think that was a good idea."

Not unless you want me to sic Oreo on him.

"Your friends and family are always welcome."

I'll just need to make sure the security cameras are turned on so nothing gets stolen.

Dawson shook his head. "Jillian didn't think that was a good idea."

Jillian Clark was Dawson's girlfriend and the granddaughter of Nana Jo's best friend, Dorothy Clark. She was a level-headed girl who was a talented singer and dancer.

"She didn't think we should go on campus in case . . . you know."

In case your dad tried to use the fact that his son was a star football player to steal, manipulate, and take advantage of you or your friends?

"She suggested we go to Silver Beach Pizza. It's sort of neutral."

"Do you need money?" I asked. Although money was one thing Dawson would not have to worry about anymore, thanks to my stepfather Harold Robertson's generosity. Harold was a nice man who loved and adored my mom, Grace. He was also extremely wealthy. His family had once owned one of the nicest department stores in the area. Harold had been an aeronautical engineer with NASA for forty years before he retired. Although he hadn't followed in his ancestors' footsteps and gone into retail, he had inherited a ton of money, from the stores and savvy investments, which he loved to lavish on my mom and her family. Before he and Mom packed up and moved to Australia on a crazy mission to save koalas, he'd put a pile of money in trust funds for my sister's twins, Christopher and Zaq.

Even though Dawson wasn't technically a member of the family, Harold had made provisions for him also. As far as I knew, A-Squared didn't know that Dawson had a trust fund.

If he had, he would undoubtedly have figured out a way to access the money, although my sister Jenna had used every legal technique she could to make sure that A-Squared wouldn't be able to get his hands on a dime of the money. The weakest link in this chain was Dawson. A-Squared might not be able to get to the trust, but Dawson certainly could.

"Naw. I'm good." Dawson pulled a Visa gift card from his pocket and held it up. "She also suggested that I take this. It's one hundred dollars. That way if . . . when he asks for money, I can honestly say all I have is this gift card."

Jillian was a smart young woman.

"That's a great idea."

"It's okay with you? I mean, does it bother you if I go? I don't have to go. I can cancel. I can say something came up. If it bothers you."

I walked around the counter and pulled Dawson into a hug. I was worried about him meeting with his dad and here he was worrying that I would be upset about it. When I pulled away I looked into his eyes. "Dawson, I'm perfectly fine with you meeting with your dad. I would be lying if I said I didn't worry about you. I do. I worry that you'll get hurt, but I'll probably always worry about you. You're a part of my family and I love you. Worrying comes with the territory. Alex is your dad and you should see him."

We talked for a few more minutes. Dawson's shoulders relaxed, and this time when he smiled, it went to his eyes. He was okay.

My phone vibrated, and my fiancé's face popped on the screen. I could feel the smile form on my face without looking in the mirror. I grabbed a cookie and made my way to my bedroom so we could talk privately.

"Hello, beautiful," Frank Patterson said. "I have a proposition for you."

"Okay, fire away. No one has propositioned me in years," I joked.

"That's sad and I'll need to make sure to fix that in the future."

I giggled. "What's the proposition?"

"How about we hop on a flight to Vegas? We don't even need to pack. We can buy clothes when we get there. What do you say?"

"Vegas? Why Vegas?"

"We can get married by Elvis."

I chuckled. "Elvis? I had no idea you were a fan."

"I'm not, but that's not the point. The point is we can get married in two hours in Vegas. What do you say?"

"Your mother would kill you. Then she'd kill me. Considering she's a doctor, she'd probably bring us back to life just so she could kill us again. No way."

"Small price to pay," Frank said.

"Sorry, but your mom wants to see you get married. Heck, my mom is still angry that Leon and I eloped and she didn't get to see us get married. She's planning to fly back from Australia for the wedding. So, I'm sorry, but Elvis is a no."

"We could get married again after we get back. Vegas would just be the real wedding. We could stage a fake wedding for later. They would never have to know."

"A fake wedding? Frank Patterson, what are you talking about? You can't possibly be nervous about your mother coming? Do you think she'll object to you marrying me?" I tried to make my voice sound as though I was joking although I wasn't.

"I couldn't care less whether my mother objects or not. I'm a grown man. I don't need my mother's approval to marry the woman of my dreams."

I released the breath I'd been holding.

"Besides, what's to object about? You're smart, funny, beautiful, honest, loving, the kindest person I know, and you make me incredibly happy."

I grinned. "Then why do you want to elope?"

"I'm not worried about my mom meeting you. I'm worried that once you meet my mom, you might want to back out."

I laughed out loud. We spent a few minutes talking nonsense. It had been years since I flirted with anyone when we first met. Even before Leon died I'd allowed myself to get rusty. But I was back in the saddle and knew exactly what to say to get Frank hot and bothered. I knew I'd been successful when he said he'd be over in five minutes. However, before the words were out of his mouth, I could hear someone in the background at the restaurant he owned calling for him.

Frank swore. "If you'd agreed to Vegas, we would have been gone by now."

"You wouldn't have been able to enjoy the trip knowing the oven wasn't working."

"Wanna bet?"

I wasn't willing to take that bet, so we said our goodbyes. I sat for a few minutes thinking about how lucky I was to find Frank. After Leon died I couldn't conceive of ever being in love again. Let alone sharing my life with anyone else. When Frank retired from his top-secret work in the military to follow his dream of opening a restaurant, I was as surprised as anyone to find that my heart had expanded and made room for someone new. I was glad that I had.

Frank loved me. That thought brought a smile to my face. If only I could be sure that his mother would at least like me. Was that asking too much of a mother-in-law? I had had a wonderful relationship with Leon's mother. I was the daughter she never had but always wanted. And she was the nonjudgmental nonmeddling loving mother-in-law of my dreams.

I suspected that Dr. Camilia Patterson wasn't cut from the same cloth.

Baking was how Dawson reduced stress and worked through his problems. My stress reliever was writing. I sat down at my laptop and took a trip back in time to 1939 and the British countryside to relieve my own stress.

Shoulder of Mutton Pub, Village of Bletchley, Buckinghamshire, 1939

"It's not too late. Say the word and we can be on a train to Gretna Green in a flash," Detective Inspector Peter Covington whispered.

Lady Clara snuggled closer to her fiancé. "Darling, we're both of legal age. We don't have to go to Scotland to get married."

"Then let's apply for a license and get married here. It'll take three days, but we could be married and sneak away for our honeymoon before either of our families are the wiser."

Lady Clara pulled away to look into the eyes of the man she loved. "Why? My mother loves you. And if I can ever convince your mother to forget about the fact that I have a title, I think she'll learn to love me too."

Detective Inspector Peter Covington was tall, lean, and gangly with thick curly hair.

"My mother already thinks you're beautiful, intelligent, and far too good for me."

"Good." Clara chuckled. "But she has to realize that just because I inherited a title for something a great great distant relative did eons ago, that doesn't make me better than anyone else."

Lady Clara was tall, slim, and stately. She had light brown curly hair, intelligent eyes, and a quick smile.

"Good luck disavowing her of that notion. Mum has been poring over the latest copy of Debrett's, while my aunt Ida is memorizing Burke's."

The owner, a red-faced publican, had seated the couple in an alcove set off from the rest of the pub. He brought two tankards to the table and made a hasty retreat.

Lady Clara rolled her eyes. "I wished she'd just forget about that."

"Not likely. You, my love, are related to the king. And she has convinced herself that there is a chance, no matter how slim, that His Majesty, George the Sixth, by the Grace of God of Great Britain, Ireland, and the British Dominions beyond the Seas King, Defender of the Faith, Emperor of India, will attend our wedding."

"Good Lord." Clara stared.

"She's been practicing her curtsies. Just in case."

Lady Clara shook her head. "Britain is on the brink of war. I doubt very seriously if His Majesty will be attending the wedding of a poor and distant relation like me. I do think Cousin Winnie is going to try to come. Although I expect he's even busier than the King."

"Cousin Winnie? Would that be Winston Churchill, who also just happens to be a Member of Parliament? Winston Churchill, the newly appointed First Lord of the Admiralty? And Winston Churchill, the man many believe is destined to one day be the

Prime Minister of Great Britain? That Winston Churchill?" Peter asked.

"Yes, but Cousin Winnie isn't at all stuffy and formal. He used to sneak me peppermints when I was little." Clara smiled.

"I'm sure that will put Mum at ease." Peter pulled Clara close and gazed into her eyes. "All joking aside. Are you sure you want to go through with this? You know if things get bad, and it looks like they will, I won't be waiting to be called up. I've already signed up for military service. You know there's a chance that I won't—"

"Darling, we've been through this before. But let me be clear. I love you and I intend to marry you if I have to club you over the head and drag you to the altar." She chuckled. "All joking aside. If England goes to war, I know you'll do your part. And so will I. I'll do my bit at Bletchley Park. But I can be as stubborn and bullheaded as the enemy. I refuse to allow Hitler to ruin my future and prevent me from marrying the man I love." She leaned over and kissed her fiancé passionately.

When the two came up for air Detective Inspector Covington took a deep breath. "Wow. I guess I've got to adapt to the fact that I'm marrying into a very old, established, noble, and stubborn family."

Clara laughed. "And don't you forget it. Now, we'd better be on our way to Wickfield Lodge. You're going to motor down and pick up your mother, aunt, and two cousins. I've convinced Dilly and Jean to take the train down with me."

"Dilly?"

"Debrett's will refer to him as Lord Reginald

Dilworth, son of the Baron of Shepley. And you can tell your mother that, like me, Dilly doesn't have a bean. But he is loads of fun. He'll dance with your cousins and keep the laughs going. He looks great in tails. He's great laughs, which gets him invitations to all the aristocratic balls, soirees, and house parties." Lady Clara took a drink of ale. "Jean is Lady Jean Groverton. Unlike Dilly and me, her family is positively swimming in money. She's a wizard with maths and is already distinguishing herself at Bletchley. She's got a major grade A crush on Dilly, and I was hoping that . . ."

"Doing a bit of matchmaking?" Peter glanced at Clara.

"Honestly, it's just a matter of time before Dilly realizes that Jean is the answer to his prayers. He has a title and no money. She's got a title and gobs of money. Plus, she's got brains, a great personality, and a mammoth-sized crush on the ninny."

"I noticed you didn't mention her looks." Peter raised a brow.

Clara squirmed. "She has potential. She's not unattractive, but she just doesn't put forth the effort to showcase herself. With the right clothes, makeup, and a more flattering hairstyle, she would be stunning."

"And you're going to provide this assistance?"

"Actually, I was hoping to get some help from your cousins. I asked Beryl . . . or was it Beatrice? Whichever one, I indicated that I might be interested in purchasing a few outfits for my trousseau. I asked if she wouldn't mind bringing a few samples that I might try on." Clara avoided making eye contact.

"What exactly were you planning to use for money for these outfits?" Peter asked.

"If my plan works the way I want, I won't have to buy them. Jean will."

Peter started to object, but Clara interrupted him. "Look, we don't have time to argue. Everything's all set. Honestly, my plan is foolproof. What could possibly go wrong?"

Chapter 4

"Famous last words." I saved the file and closed the lid on my laptop. It was late and I was tired. Tomorrow was D–Day, and I was going to need all of my strength and mental acuity for meeting with Frank's mother.

Despite my desire to rest, sleep eluded me. My mind wouldn't shut off. I spent quite a bit of time tossing and turning.

What if Frank's mother doesn't like me?

It wouldn't matter to Frank if she didn't. But it would matter to me. I'd talked to her on the phone, of course, and we'd planned to meet several times, but something always came up to prevent a face-to-face meeting. Honestly, what did I know about her?

Frank's mother was a medical doctor, highly respected within her field and her community, if the number of advisory boards and volunteer organizations she supported was any indication. I reached over and grabbed my phone from the nightstand. I'd been stalking my future mother-in-law on social media for months, so I didn't have to swipe long to find her in my browser history.

Her hair, makeup, and clothes were perfect in every photo I found. Even in the photos when she was wearing scrubs, she looked as though she was photo ready and smiling. "I'll bet her nail polish isn't chipped and her cuticles are perfectly shaped half-moons."

Snickers didn't bother lifting her head. We both knew my cuticles hadn't seen the light of day in months. Not so Dr. Camilia Patterson.

"I wonder if I have time to get a mani-pedi before her flight lands?" I checked the airline site again to confirm that nothing was canceled. "It would be cutting things close, but if I could get into the salon first thing, as soon as the doors opened in the morning, and everyone was on time and the planets were perfectly aligned and . . . never mind." There was no way. She was flying into the airport in Chicago. I'd suggested she fly into River Bend, Indiana, which was only thirty miles away. But Dr. Patterson chose to fly into O'Hare. Chicago was ninety miles from North Harbor. Chicago was on central time, which would help, but traffic in the windy city was unpredictable. And going to O'Hare required driving through busy Chicago traffic, which was even more harrowing than if she had chosen Midway. I would need all of my wits about me to navigate through that.

"Thanks to the kind gift from my friends at the Four Feathers, we're going to get a weekend at the Four Feathers Casino and Resort. Plus, Nana Jo said they had a spa." I scrolled to the Four Feathers website and looked for the hotel amenities. Sure enough, they did have a spa, and it looked luxurious enough to please even the pickiest of guests. "If these prices are any indication of quality, it should be top-of-the-line."

Snickers opened an eye and then closed it and continued snoring.

"If we went to the spa, that would be something we could

do together. We could have some bonding time." I quickly reserved two late afternoon slots and refused to look at the hit that my credit card would take. Surely the all-expenses-paid pass wouldn't include spa services. Would it?

More site surfing showed the hotel also had afternoon tea. I booked a table for that too. Camilia looked well-preserved and classy. She would fit right in with the photographs of cultured individuals sipping tea and eating scones in the pictures. "OMG. Dr. Patterson will fit in perfectly, but what will I wear?"

I grabbed my phone from the nightstand and called my sister. I startled Snickers, who had been lying next to me, and kicked off a domino effect. Startled, Snickers started barking. The barking woke up Oreo, who joined in on the barkfest. Nana Jo burst through the door carrying her gun just as my sister Jenna answered.

"What's happened?" Nana Jo glanced wildly around the room.

"Someone better be dead," Jenna mumbled.

"Sorry," I apologized to both my sister and my grandmother. "I had a panic attack. I have to pick up Frank's mom tomorrow and I have no idea what to wear."

Neither Nana Jo nor Jenna thought my wardrobe was important at two in the morning. Nana Jo turned and walked back to her room without a word.

Jenna mumbled a few words that I hadn't realized she even knew. I certainly had never heard her use them before. Then, the phone went silent as she hung up.

I shushed the poodles, but once they were awake, I decided to make the most of the time and took them outside to take care of business.

When they were done I went back to my panic attack. *What to wear for a luxurious weekend with Dr. Camilia Patterson?*

My closet wasn't vast and it didn't take long before I realized that practically everything I owned was old, stained, or torn. When I started dating Frank, I'd purchased a few *date outfits*. Nothing too risqué, but I didn't exactly feel comfortable wearing a dress that showcased my curves, or one with a plunging neckline, for dinner with my soon-to-be mother-in-law. Recently, I purchased a few dresses that made me look *authory* for book events. These were a step down from a formal business suit, but not exactly a let's-go-have-tea-at-the-resort appropriate.

Trying on practically everything in my closet brought me to the realization that I needed a completely new wardrobe. "Ugh, I need to shop." However, even the wonders of the Internet couldn't get a brand-new wardrobe delivered to my door in just a few hours.

I went into the kitchen and got the largest garbage bags I had. I tossed out all of the items that were stained or torn. Then I discarded all of the items that not only didn't fit but, short of major surgery, would never fit again. The last items to go were the ones that weren't damaged but were so outdated or ugly that I wouldn't be caught dead wearing. Five contractor-sized garbage bags later, my closet was sparse.

"What on earth?" Nana Jo stared at the mounds of discarded clothes.

"I did a little decluttering."

"A little?" Nana Jo looked at the few items that remained in my closet. "Sam, do you have any clothes left?"

"Not many. I did go online and ordered a few items, but they won't arrive in time for this weekend."

"Sounds like a shoppertunity, and you definitely deserve it, but don't you think maybe you should have waited a bit before the big purge?"

"If I waited, I wouldn't have done it."

"Maybe we can stop off at Water Tower or Michigan Avenue after we pick up Frank's mom. We could do a little shopping and then have lunch."

"That's a good idea, but . . . "

"What? We should have plenty of time. Besides, I can run into Garrett's and grab some popcorn."

"I don't know if Dr. Patterson likes shopping. Besides, I don't know that I want her standing beside me and judging . . ."

"Who says she'll judge? Sam, I don't think you're being fair. You haven't even given the poor woman a chance. Just because she's a medical doctor doesn't mean that she's not the same as you and me. Now, unless you want to be late, you'd better find something to wear and get showered. I'll help you take these bags downstairs."

"Showered? What time is it?" I glanced at the time and had another panic attack. "I had no idea it was so late. I've been at this all night."

"I know. I heard you." Nana Jo grabbed two of the garbage bags and headed downstairs.

I grabbed two and followed, although slower than Nana Jo.

Nana Jo offered to take the last bag down to the dumpster while I hopped in the shower. When I was done and presentable I allowed the aroma of freshly brewed coffee to pull me into the kitchen. Nana Jo had filled my travel mug with coffee and was waiting for me. I allowed the aroma to seep into my body. I sipped the warm elixir and felt the warmth spread through my body. "I love you."

Nana Jo laughed. "I'm not sure if you're talking to me or that cup of coffee."

I wasn't sure either, but I kept my mouth shut and continued to sip.

Chapter 5

Christopher and Zaq arrived just as we went downstairs to let the poodles out.

"Hey Aunt Sammy." Christopher leaned down and hugged me.

I got on my tiptoes and returned the hug. Then repeated the maneuver for Zaq.

My twin nephews moved to Chicago after graduating from nearby Jesus and Mary University, or JAMU. The boys were identical twins, but when it came to their personalities, they couldn't be more different. Both were tall and slender. That's really where the similarities ended. Christopher was the preppy business-minded marketing guru, while Zaq was my edgy tech nerd. Neither of them inherited a love for mysteries from Nana Jo like I did. But, thankfully for me, they were both willing to use their skills to benefit me. While I picked up Frank's mother from the airport, they would be in town running Market Street Mysteries. Zaq's girlfriend, Emma Lee, was visiting for the week. The two were getting serious, but Emma was also serious about finishing medical school. I couldn't believe that the boys I once bounced on my knee were both now over six feet tall and that I was even considering the possibility of a wedding. It just didn't seem possible. Where had the time gone?

I gave the boys a quick rundown, but they didn't need it. They had helped me out many times before. Plus, they knew how to reach me if anything urgent came up before I got back. Still, it eased my anxiety a bit to review the basics.

"Yeah. Yeah. We got this," Christopher said. "I'm going to redo your front display to attract more foot traffic."

"I'm going to upgrade your POS system while you're gone. It's outdated. Plus, I'm going to install this new security software to help prevent cyberattacks," Zaq said.

"All of my passwords are in a book in my office if you need to get into anything," I said.

"You know that's really not safe. You shouldn't write down your passwords. Anyone could get that book, and then they'd have access to all of your systems," Zaq said.

"True, but some of these places make you change your password every three months. How am I supposed to remember all of those passwords and PINs?"

They shook their heads but listened in silence while I went over things that I'd told them hundreds of times before. They listened impatiently and then hustled out Nana Jo and me so they could change the radio station that I piped into the store away from the smooth jazz that I like to the hip-hop station they preferred.

Once in the car I pointed the car west, put the pedal to the metal, and hit the interstate. The drive to Chicago wasn't bad. It was the traffic once you hit the city that was the problem. As I anticipated, there was construction on the interstate that slowed my progress to a crawl in spots. Years of experience taught me that no matter how fast I drove, I would barely keep up with yellow school buses in the slow lane.

"Did that nun just flip you the bird as she passed you?" Nana Jo asked.

"Beats me. I have to stay focused. I'm going seventy and the speed limit is only fifty-five."

"We both know that in Chicago the speed limit is merely a suggestion," Nana Jo said.

I navigated through the congestion and eventually made my way to O'Hare, which was also undergoing construction. After circling the arrivals area eight times, I eventually saw my target.

"There she is." I swerved and pulled up to the curb beside Dr. Patterson. Next to her stood a porter with a cart with a mountain of matching Louis Vuitton bags.

"How long is she staying?" Nana Jo climbed out.

I released the rear gate of my SUV and hurried to help load luggage before the policeman directing traffic at the end of the block made his way down to me.

Dr. Patterson didn't look like a woman who had just flown a few hundred miles in a cramped plane. She looked as though she'd just stepped out of a high-class salon. Her make-up was flawless. Her salt and pepper hair was perfectly pulled back into a bun. In a pale pink skirt set and Louboutin heels that matched her outfit perfectly, she looked as fresh as a daisy.

I walked over to Dr. Patterson and immediately felt awk-ward.

Do I hug her?

I extended my arms to pull her into a hug, but Dr. Camilia Patterson wasn't a hugger. She took one step backward and extended her arm. "You must be Samantha?"

I shook. "Please, call me Sam."

She sniffed.

What did that mean? Did she have a cold? Did I smell? I re-sisted the urge to check my armpits to determine if my deodorant had failed. Instead, I forced my lips into an upward curl and prayed it didn't look like a gargoyle grimace, and then I helped the porter, who was undoubtedly a Tetris master, get all of the luggage into the back of the SUV.

It took a bit of manipulation, but between me, the porter, and eventually a Chicago policeman, we got it in.

Nana Jo offered Dr. Patterson the front passenger seat, but she declined, stating she preferred the back.

I suppose she was accustomed to being chauffeured around.

I glanced at her in my rearview mirror as I pulled away from the curb. Dr. Patterson still looked fresh and relaxed while I was sweating like a sumo wrestler. Nana Jo turned on the air and directed the vents in my direction. Again, I wondered if my shower had been sufficient and vowed to purchase the full-body deodorant that was flooding my social media as soon as I got home.

"How was your flight?" Nana Jo asked.

Driving in Chicago is not for the timid or easily distracted driver, so I focused on the traffic as I navigated onto the interstate and made my way toward downtown. I barely heard the small talk between the two women. When I was able to simply cruise I tuned in to the conversation.

"Now that Sam's a published author and doing book tours and speaking engagements, I suggested she pick up some new clothes for the news and all of her media events."

Nana Jo was laying it on thick. Apart from the book launch party at my bookstore, which was heavily attended by friends and family, my book tour wasn't exactly newsworthy. Mostly my book tour had been virtual thanks to Lori Caswell at Dollycas and some Zoom appearances at book clubs. My publicist had managed to get me booked at a prestigious local book festival after one of the authors canceled at the last minute. Otherwise my media events involved me dropping into regional bookstores and signing any stock copies of my book they had on hand.

"Francis told me Samantha had written a book," Dr. Patterson pursed her lips and touched up her lipstick.

Francis? How did I not know that his first name was Francis?

"Sam's book is selling great and it's gotten a lot of positive reviews. Have you read it?" Nana Jo asked.

"Francis sent me a copy, but I have to admit I haven't read it yet," Dr. Patterson said. "I don't have a lot of spare time for reading *novels*. If I can find the time in my busy schedule to sit down and read, it's usually medical journals."

Should I be happy or sad that my soon-to-be mother-in-law hasn't read my book? I'm going with happy.

"I don't think we've ever had an *author* in the family."

Is it just me or did she say author *in the same way she would have said* serial killer*?*

"There's a first time for everything," Nana Jo said.

Dr. Patterson didn't look convinced.

I was thankful to get off the interstate even though avoiding double-parked vehicles, daredevil cyclists, cellphone-distracted pedestrians with a death wish who think they're made of rubber, and city buses jamming their brakes every half block could be just as tricky. I breathed a sigh of relief when I finally pulled down into the underground parking lot.

Once we were out of the car I got a moment to breathe. Despite Water Tower Place's premium location on Michigan Avenue, the parking garage smelled of urine, rotten food, and gasoline.

Nana Jo climbed out of the car and stretched. "The last time we were here we came on a bus trip with three friends. It was fantastic. We went to the theater, did a lot of shopping, and partied like it was 1999." She chuckled.

Dr. Patterson didn't respond. She was focused on her cell phone and was texting as she walked toward the elevator.

Moments later my phone vibrated. I glanced at the screen and saw it was Frank.

Did U Introduce Nana Jo 2 my mom?

I wracked my brain, but I think in all the excitement I missed that part.

Umm. Not sure. Y?

Some days my elevator moves very slowly to the top floor, but eventually it dawned on me that Dr. Patterson must have texted Frank to complain. I had been walking slightly in front of Nana Jo, but I stopped abruptly and she bumped into me.

"What's wrong?"

I showed her the text.

"Geez Louise. She was in the same car with us. She talked to us, but rather than speaking to us directly, she sent a text message to Frank, who's ninety miles away? How rude. Why, I'm going to give her a piece of my mind. I'm going to—"

I took a firm hold of my grandmother's sleeve to stop her from whatever she planned to say or do. "Please, Nana Jo. Don't."

She stopped. "What's the matter?"

Tears stung the back of my eyes and threatened to fall. The last thing I needed was to burst into tears here in the parking garage. I blinked them away. "Please. I just want to get this over with. Besides, she's my problem. I'm too old to have my grandmother fighting my battles."

Nana Jo hugged me. "Fine, but if she steps out of line, I can't promise that I won't teach Dr. Bad Manners a lesson."

"Are you two coming?" Dr. Patterson yelled from the elevator.

We hurried on and got inside. We stood in awkward silence for a few moments while we waited for the doors to close. When the elevator started I turned to Dr. Patterson and forced a smile. "We've talked on the phone, but we've never been formally introduced. I'm terribly sorry that I didn't do this at the airport. I was flustered by the traffic at O'Hare. Dr. Camilia Patterson, I'm Samantha Washington." I stuck out my hand. "Please call me Sam."

She shook it.

"This is my grandmother, Josephine Thomas. Although I call her Nana Jo." I turned to my grandmother, "Nana Jo, this is Frank's mother, Dr. Camilia Patterson."

"Call me Josephine." Nana Jo extended her hand and the two women shook.

"What should we call you?" Nana Jo asked.

"Dr. Patterson is fine."

Nana Jo's brows furled and I could see a response welling up inside her. I preempted it. "I hope you don't mind if we do a little shopping. I don't come to Chicago often and I really do need some new clothes. Plus, there's a lovely restaurant at the Ritz. I thought we could meet for lunch."

"Perfect; why don't we split up and then meet back at say, noon?" Dr. Patterson said.

I guess she prefers to shop alone.

"Great."

The elevator doors opened and Dr. Camilia Patterson took off as though she were entering a speed walking race.

Nana Jo and I watched her leave and then she wrapped her arm around my shoulders. "Let's not let Dr. Cruella de Vil ruin our day. We're in Chicago and you need some outfits befitting a best-selling author."

She was right. It was a lovely morning. Most of the time I went shopping in Chicago on the weekends. The stores were always jam-packed. Today was Thursday and the foot traffic was much lighter. We had two hours until we needed to meet up for lunch and I was determined to make the best of the time.

Water Tower Place was located on a street referred to as the Magnificent Mile. Most of the high-end department stores like Nordstrom, Bloomingdale's, and Neiman Marcus were located within easy walking distance. When we came to Chicago on the bus trip we also learned about some less expensive stores, too.

With no time for dawdling, we power shopped. Nana Jo was a martinet when it came to ordering salesclerks around. She pushed me into a dressing room and sent the clerks to find ensembles that would look great on network television. When I reproached her for lying she said she never told them that I was going to actually *be* on network television, she merely told them to find outfits *for* television. Which they did.

Three dresses, two pairs of straight-legged slacks, a cashmere sweater, a silk blouse, and a pair of black slingback kitten heel shoes later, I was exhausted and ready for fortification in the form of lunch.

Dr. Patterson was waiting for us in the lobby of the Ritz-Carlton.

Nana Jo leaned close and whispered, "Something must be wrong."

"Why?"

"Because Cruella de Vil's smiling."

Dr. Patterson hopped up from her seat and came over to us. "Looks like you failed to make reservations and the restaurants are all booked."

"Excuse me." Nana Jo went over to the maître d' stand and had a quick, whispered conversation.

After a few moments the tall distinguished man smiled broadly, grabbed three menus, and hurried over to our group. "Mrs. Washington. I'm terribly sorry. I had no idea that the other woman was referring to you when she asked about a reservation. Of course we have a table for you. Please forgive me."

It took me a half second before I realized my mouth was open and closed it. Then I followed the gentleman to a table that was strategically placed in between a large window and a fireplace.

He pulled out my chair. I sat. He placed a napkin on my lap and handed me a menu. Then he snapped his fingers and another waiter hurried over. "Check Mrs. Washington's bags."

"My name is Lucas. Please don't hesitate to reach out to me if you need anything. Anything at all. Your waiter, Phillipe, will take excellent care of you and your guests." The maître d' bowed, turned, and walked away.

Phillipe collected my bags and dashed away. In record time he returned and handed me a claim check ticket. Then he bowed, filled our water glasses, and stood nearby waiting for requests.

We received so much attention that the other diners glanced our way.

Dr. Patterson was dazed. She glanced from me to Nana Jo and then back to me. She turned to the hovering waiter. "Can you point me to the ladies' room?"

When she was gone I leaned over to Nana Jo. "What did you promise him, a kidney?"

She pulled a wad of money from her purse and slipped it inside her dessert menu. Then she asked Phillipe if he would take the menu to the maître d'.

I watched Lucas slip the money from the menu and into his pocket without glancing up from his tasks.

"That was smooth. How much did this royal treatment cost?"

"Didn't Grace teach you that it's rude to ask what something costs?" Nana Jo sipped her water. "But I'll tell you it was worth every single dime to see the look on Cruella's face."

"Nana Jo!"

"Excuse me. Dr. Cruella de Vil."

I hated to admit it, but I agreed with her.

Nana Jo nodded toward the maître d' stand. "Look, she's trying to find out what happened from Lucas."

I casually glanced at the stand where Dr. Patterson was chatting. Based on the frustrated look on her face as she walked toward the table, he hadn't given us away.

Dr. Patterson returned to her seat and opened her menu. After a few moments she said, "Based on the prices, you must be selling quite a few books."

Nana Jo was right. Talking about how much something costs was rude.

"Don't worry about the cost. Lunch is on me," Nana Jo said.

A red flush rose up Dr. Patterson's neck. "That won't be necessary. I'm certainly able to afford to pay for my own meal."

Nana Jo smiled broadly and waved away Dr. Patterson's objections. "It's no problem at all. We want you to enjoy yourself this weekend. We've got some exciting things planned."

We ordered lunch and sat quietly for several moments.

"You mentioned plans for the weekend. Francis didn't mention anything to me."

"When we get back to North Harbor I'll take you to Nana Jo's house. It's right on Lake Michigan with amazing views," I said.

Dr. Patterson turned to Nana Jo. "Thank you. I appreciate you giving up your home for me. That was very thoughtful. Francis offered to let me stay at his place, but . . . he is getting it ready for sale and has contractors renovating the place. He says it's a disaster zone."

"That's true. He bought an old Victorian and started renovating and updating it, but he spends so much time at the restaurant that he never has time to get everything finished," I said.

"Well, thank you for the use of your home."

"It makes sense. I spend most of my time with Sam anyway, helping with the bookstore. No point in my house sitting empty."

"I had hoped to get to know Samantha better," Dr. Patterson said. "And her family, of course. Families are so important."

"You'll have plenty of time for that. We're going to have a family dinner at Frank's restaurant. You'll get to meet most of my family tonight."

"Most of your family?" Dr. Patterson said.

"My mother and stepfather are still in Australia."

"She's doing something with animals?"

"Saving the koala," I said. "My sister, my brother-in-law, and my nephews will be there. Plus, Nana Jo, Dawson, and friends from the retirement village. Mom and Harold will be here for the wedding next month."

"Lovely." Dr. Patterson sipped her water.

Our waiter, Phillipe, came and took our orders. Then another waiter brought us a large charcuterie platter.

"We didn't order this. I think you have the wrong table," I said.

"On the house." He grinned.

"Isn't that nice." Nana Jo added a sample of the various cheese, olives, fruits, and crackers to her plate.

"Does this type of thing happen to you often?" Dr. Patterson gave me a suspicious look.

"All the time," Nana Jo added. "Why, just yesterday Sam gave a book reading at the Pontolomas community center. The Pontolomas are the indigenous people in our area. When she finished one of the tribal leaders wanted to show his appreciation and gave her a free weekend at the Four Feathers Casino and Resort, not only for herself but for five friends."

"Really?" Based on the tone of her voice and the smirk on

her face, Dr. Patterson clearly didn't believe her. "How generous. I've never heard of the Pontolomas. Are they a small tribe?"

"The Citizen Pontolomas Nation is the federally recognized government of the Pontolomas Nation. They have over thirty-eight thousand tribal members and offer services like housing, education, healthcare, veteran and career services for their citizens, and other Native Americans throughout their tribal jurisdiction." I was grateful that I took the time to read the brochures they have around the casino when I was waiting there one night.

"The Pontolomas have a variety of businesses, including the Four Feathers Casino and Resort. It's a lovely place."

"It was very generous and kind of Mr. Strongbow to offer the weekend at the resort. I hoped that we could get spa treatments."

"The girls from the retirement village are planning a little surprise for Sam, but if you don't want to come . . ." Nana Jo shrugged and stuffed a cracker in her mouth.

I was just about to take a bite of the creamiest cheese that smelled amazing but stopped. "What kind of surprise?" I asked.

"If I tell you, then it won't be a surprise, will it?" Nana Jo grinned.

The girls from Shady Acres Retirement Village, Irma Starczewski, Dorothy Clark, and Ruby Mae Stevenson, were wonderful and I loved them dearly. However, they could also be unpredictable and quite the handful.

I glared but then remembered Dr. Patterson was watching, so I unfurled my brow.

"Actually, I don't really know. When I told the girls about the free weekend they said they wanted to do something nice for you for a change." Nana Jo looked at Dr. Patterson. "Sam is always doing nice things for others and they wanted to return the favor."

Dr. Patterson raised a brow and turned to look at me more closely. "That's very kind. Francis mentioned that you did a lot with your grandmother and others in the community."

I'm not sure serving as the designated driver and wheelman for my grandmother and their friends as they bar-hopped and hung out at the casino was what Dr. Patterson was thinking, but she didn't frown nearly as much and actually seemed to enjoy the appetizers.

The rest of our lunch was cordial and delicious. Even Dr. Patterson couldn't say anything negative about the cuisine or the service. Nana Jo picked up the tab and left a tip that had our waiter fawning over us even more than before.

After picking up my bags I went to the garage. I'd forgotten that the back was full of Dr. Patterson's luggage, so I had to slip my bags onto the back seat. I brought the car around and picked up Nana Jo and Dr. Patterson and then started back toward the interstate.

The drive home was uneventful and relatively peaceful. I pulled up to Nana Jo's house and dropped off Dr. Patterson.

Nana Jo showed her around while I hauled her luggage into the house. By the time I'd finished I was exhausted and in desperate need of another shower.

Nana Jo and I left with promises to return in three hours to collect her and the girls for dinner.

My intention was to relieve Christopher and Zaq from bookstore duty, but they had everything in hand. All of the stress from a sleepless night, plus the stress of driving through Chicago piled on top of my first face-to-face meeting with Frank's mother caught up with me all at once. It took all of my strength to climb the stairs. Nana Jo was the first to notice and ordered me to take a shower and a nap.

"Sam, you're exhausted. Now march," she ordered.

I couldn't have argued with her if I'd wanted to.

Chapter 6

I nearly fell asleep in the shower but dragged myself out before my skin shriveled up and turned into prunes. Still wrapped in a towel, I crashed on the bed and fell asleep. When I awoke I was refreshed, alert, and rejuvenated. I checked the time, afraid that Nana Jo had allowed me to miss dinner. That was when the realization hit me. I'd only slept for forty minutes.

There was no way that I'd be able to go back to sleep, so I decided to write. Maybe a stroll through the English countryside would put me in a good mood before my next encounter with Dr. Patterson.

Lady Elizabeth Marsh sat in her favorite spot in the drawing room at Wickfield Lodge. She loved sitting on the sofa in front of the fireplace, especially when the fireplace was lit and the flames crackled and filled the room with warmth, light, and the earthy aroma of bark and leaves. Wickfield Lodge was the ancestral home of her husband, Lord William Marsh. Lady Elizabeth had loved the home from the moment she entered as a new bride. Over the years, she'd learned to love the estate even more.

Lady Elizabeth knitted a pale pink baby blanket for the newest addition to the family, Lady Helene Elizabeth Henrietta Browning. Lady Elizabeth and Lord William had never been blessed with children of their own, but after her brother-in-law, Lord Peregrine Marsh, and his wife, the former Lady Henrietta Pringle, were both killed, she and William had raised their two nieces, Penelope and Daphne, as their own. Elizabeth was thankful that both girls had grown up to be healthy, intelligent, and kind. She was also thankful that both had married kind men of good character. Lady Penelope was happily married to Lord Victor Carlston and Lady Daphne was married to Lord James FitzAndrew Browning, the 15th Duke of Kingsfordshire. Victor and Penelope had a son, Lord William Carlston. Daphne and James had now been blessed with a daughter. If Lady Elizabeth had any regrets, it was that Lady Helene wasn't as close, so she wouldn't get to see her as much.

Lord William sat nearby in his favorite chair with his legs propped up on the ottoman that he shared with Cuddles, a King Charles spaniel. Lord William puffed on his pipe while Cuddles napped. It was a peaceful scene.

There was a soft knock on the door and Thompkins, the Marsh family butler, entered. He pushed a tea cart to Lady Elizabeth. Then he gave a discreet cough.

"I beg your pardon, but Lady Clara phoned to say we should expect at least two more for the weekend."

"Did she say who she was bringing?" Lady Elizabeth asked. "I hope we don't end up with an odd number."

Thompkins coughed again. "I believe she called them Dilly and Jean."

"That will be Lord Reginald Dilworth and Lady Jean Groverton." Lady Elizabeth set aside her knitting and picked up a notepad and pen that were on a nearby table. She reviewed the list and added the two names.

"How many does that make?" Lord William asked.

"Clara and Peter, of course." She looked through the list.

"Can't have an engagement party without the bride and groom-to-be," Lord William mumbled around the stem of his pipe.

"I believe Peter's invited four people. His mother, Rosemary Covington, and her sister, Ida Smythe. He's also invited Ida's twin daughters, his cousins, Beryl and Beatrice Smythe."

"Beryl and Beatrice? That sounds like the names of one of those singing sister duos that are all the rage on the wireless," Lord William grumbled.

"Actually, dear, Beryl and Beatrice are fashion designers. They've started a business designing smart fashions that I hear are all the rage," Lady Elizabeth said.

"Hmm, probably trousers and skirts so short they leave nothing to the imagination." Lord William puffed.

Lady Elizabeth smiled indulgently at her husband but continued her count. "Clara's mother, Mildred."

She frowned. "Counting us, that makes eleven. I don't like having an odd number."

"What's wrong with that?" Lord William asked.

"It's unlucky. I wish Victor could have come, but of course he couldn't leave Penelope alone. In her condition, she needs her husband." Lady Elizabeth smiled at the thought of the new edition to the family that would join Wills, their firstborn.

"Poor girl is having a rough go of it this time around," Lord William said.

"It'll get easier as she gets further along, but right now she needs rest. Hopefully, she'll feel up to coming over sometime during the weekend. Clara had always been more like a sister to Penelope and Daphne than a cousin."

The telephone rang. Thompkins excused himself and went to answer it. When he returned he coughed discreetly. "That was Lady Mildred Trewellen-Harper."

"Mildred? What could she possibly want?" Lord William scowled.

Thompkins coughed. "Lady Mildred telephoned to say that she was going to be bringing a guest. She said she has a friend who is going to be in the area on business and hoped you wouldn't mind putting him up."

"Did she mention the name of this *friend*?" Lord William asked.

"I'm sorry, your lordship, but Lady Mildred has rung off. I asked her to wait while I called you to the telephone, but she said she didn't have time to wait and that she'd talk to you tomorrow," Thompkins said.

"I don't suppose she would invite anyone disagreeable. It's probably fine." Lady Elizabeth gave a reassuring smile to the butler.

Thompkins bowed and quietly left.

Lord William grumbled, "I don't like this. Who could Mildred possibly know to invite?"

"Dear, mind your blood pressure," Lady Elizabeth said. "I'm sure whoever she brings it will be fine." She sighed. "Besides, we'll have a detective handy. Whoever she brings, he'll need to be on his best behavior with Peter here. No one can get into too much trouble with a detective inspector from Scotland Yard on the premises."

"Hmm," Lord William grumbled.

"I'm sure whoever Mildred invites will be well-spoken. Well-read. And with any luck he'll also be a good dancer. Plus, he'll balance out the numbers for dinner. So there's some good that will come of Mildred's last-minute invitation for the weekend. I'm going to be positive. This weekend will be important for Clara and Peter. It'll be the first time that they're bringing their families together. And with the state of the world, who knows when . . ."

"Now, don't get sentimental. This is supposed to be a happy time."

"You're right." Lady Elizabeth took a handkerchief and dabbed at her eyes. "I want everything to be perfect for Clara. It's just a weekend. What could possibly go wrong?"

Chapter 7

"What could go wrong?" I glanced at Snickers. "Everything. That's what."

Nana Jo said that writing helped my subconscious figure out perplexing problems. I'm not sure what my subconscious was trying to tell me, but my stomach was fluttering. "This can't be good."

"Who are you talking to?" Nana Jo stood in the doorway.

"No one."

She walked over and put a hand on my forehead. "Are you sure you're alright?"

"I'm fine."

"Good. Then get dressed. We have thirty minutes."

"Thirty minutes?" I hopped up and ran to my closet. "I have to get dressed. Put on my makeup. Drive to Shady Acres and pick up Dr. Patterson and the—"

"Calm down. I sent the twins to get the girls, and Frank is bringing his mother." Nana Jo held my shoulders to help settle me. "It's alright. You're not alone. You don't have to take care of everything yourself. You have family and we are here to help. That's what families do."

"Thank you." I took a deep breath.

"Now, you get dressed."

I slipped into one of the dresses that I bought that day. This one was purchased specifically for the party. Nana Jo had given one of the salesclerks the task of finding a dress to impress my fiancé's bougie mother and she'd nailed it. It was an off-the-shoulder tea-length navy blue A-line dress that reminded me of Audrey Hepburn. I wore navy-blue heels and a string of pearls that Frank gave me for my birthday along with matching pearl earrings. The dress fit like a glove and made me feel like a princess.

I took special care with my makeup. My hair was always a challenge. However, I recently found a great new hairstylist. She was located quite near the Four Feathers casino and was a wiz with curly hair. She'd given me a great cut and her homemade conditioner that made my curls pop and minimized frizz. I pulled it into a messy ponytail that allowed some of my curls to cascade down my neck and the side of my face. It was a surprisingly good look. I loved it because no matter how hard I tried, my ponytail would end up messy anyway. This was deliberate, and for some reason it worked.

When I went into the living room Nana Jo was dressed in a dusty blue pantsuit with wide-legged pants, a matching tunic with sheer sleeves, and a gold belt. She had gold pumps and looked regal and classy.

Nana Jo whistled. "You look beautiful. Frank is going to love that."

"It's not too much?"

"Definitely not. You look stunning."

"You clean up pretty nice yourself. Is Freddie coming?" I asked.

"No, Marc's wife is due with their second any day now and he's watching the two-year-old." Nana Jo applied her lipstick. "His loss. I might just send him a picture and let him know what he's missing."

I let out Snickers and Oreo and then turned on the television and took out the special treats that they only get when I have to leave them home alone. Whenever Oreo saw the bag he immediately ran for his crate and waited anxiously. Snickers was less impressed with the treats than her brother. Still, she knew the routine and made her way to the crate. I closed the door and gave them each a treat.

"I shouldn't be long. You poodles behave yourselves and I'll be home soon."

I said the same thing every time. Neither poodle paid me any attention. Instead, they both settled down to nibble on their treat.

Nana Jo and I gathered our coats and headed downstairs. Frank's restaurant was only a few doors down from my bookstore. So we walked the short distance rather than driving and taking up a parking space.

Frank's restaurant had gotten a reputation for good food and a great atmosphere and was nearly always packed. We moved around the guests waiting for seats to the hostess stand.

The hostess recognized us. She smiled and was just about to lead us upstairs when Frank and his mother entered.

"I've got this," Frank said.

Normally, Frank wore jeans and a nice shirt when he was working. He loved to cook and didn't want to risk ruining his nicer outfits when he was at the restaurant. Tonight, he'd stepped up his game. He was wearing a dark blue suit that looked as though it was custom-made. Frank gave me an approving look that brought the heat up my neck. Then he leaned close and kissed me. He whispered, "You look amazing."

"Thank you. You look rather nice yourself. Plus, you smell good."

Frank chuckled. "I know, Irish soap, coffee, and bacon."

"All of my favorite things."

"Samantha," Dr. Patterson drew my attention away from Frank, which was probably a good thing.

"Dr. Patterson, you look lovely. I hope you got a chance to get some rest," I said.

"Actually, I did. Your grandmother's home is very nice," she said with just the slightest hint of surprise in her voice.

"What's with this Samantha and Dr. Patterson?" Frank looked from me to his mom.

"Yes, please call me Sam."

Dr. Patterson looked anxious and her ears were flushed. "Yes, I—"

"I saw on an episode of *Murder, She Wrote*, that whenever Seth Hazlitt, the doctor in Cabot Cove, used his title, he didn't have any problems getting restaurant reservations," Nana Jo said.

"I saw that episode. Of course, being a doctor got him into a lot of trouble." Dr. Patterson laughed.

"You watch *Murder, She Wrote*?" Nana Jo hooked her arm through Dr. Patterson's, and the two ladies climbed the steps to the upstairs, leaving Frank and me staring.

Frank gave me his arm and escorted me upstairs. "Is it just me or was there a chill between you, Nana Jo, and my mom?"

"There was a nip in the air earlier, but there may be hope for sunny days ahead."

Many of the buildings in downtown North Harbor were connected brownstones with storefronts on the ground level. Many buildings, like mine, had the upper levels converted to residential space. Frank's building was one of the few exceptions. He planned to renovate the upper level for additional seating, but for now it was closed off and only used for our private gatherings.

Frank leaned close and whispered, "My offer still stands. One word and we can be on a plane to Vegas in no time."

Thankfully, we reached the top of the stairs, so I didn't have to respond. I might have been tempted to take Frank up on his offer. I stopped and turned to him. "I didn't know your name was Francis. What other secrets have you been hiding from me?" I joked.

Frank sighed. "My name isn't Francis. It's Frank. My mother wanted to name me Francis, but my dad refused. They compromised on Frank. My mom just calls me Francis because she knows it irritates me."

"I'll have to keep that in mind. In case I want to irritate you."

Frank didn't get a chance to respond because a loud cheer erupted from our family and friends.

Frank clasped my hand and directed me toward the center of the room, where we were surrounded by the people we loved. He grabbed two glasses of champagne from a passing waiter. He handed one to me and then raised his glass. "Sam and I want to thank all of you for coming out to share our happiness. I am the luckiest man in the world to have met this remarkable, talented, and beautiful woman, and to know that I get to spend the rest of my life with her. Please eat, drink, and enjoy yourselves."

Everyone cheered and then drank. Afterward, Frank and I shared a brief moment before splitting up and mingling with our guests.

My sister, Jenna Rutherford, and her husband, Tony. Christopher and Zaq with their plus-ones. Christopher's date was new to me, but Emma Lee, Zaq's,date, was a friend from when she was a student at MISU. Dawson looked uncomfortable in a dark suit, but Jillian Clark was tall, slender, and as elegant as a dancer. Nana Jo was introducing Dr. Patterson to her friends from Shady Acres, Dorothy Clark, Irma Starczewski, and Ruby Mae Stevenson.

Jenna moved next to me. "What's this I hear about a bridal party at the Four Feathers?"

"I got a complimentary weekend from one of the tribal leaders. I don't know anything more. Nana Jo said it's supposed to be a surprise."

"Are you sure that's a good idea? Frank's mom seems very . . . conservative. Are you sure you want to expose her to that rowdy bunch?"

The same thought had been floating through my mind, but whether it was due to the champagne, the feeling of safety as I gazed at the faces of our friends and family, or the influence that writing had given me, I let the anxiety slip away. I was going to enjoy every moment of this time. "It's a weekend at a world-class resort and casino. In the words of Lady Clara Trewellen-Harper and Lady Elizabeth Marsh, what could possibly go wrong?"

Chapter 8

Jenna narrowed her gaze and tilted her head to the side. "Aren't those characters in your book?"

"So, what's your point?"

"Not real."

"Doesn't matter. Just because someone isn't real doesn't mean it isn't true."

For the second time today someone felt my forehead for a temperature.

I swiped away her hand. "Sherlock Holmes said, 'Once you eliminate the impossible, whatever remains, no matter how improbable, must be the truth.' Just because he wasn't a *real* person doesn't mean it isn't true."

"Crazy." Jenna shook her head and mumbled, "My whole family's crazy."

"I've said the same thing for years." Tony Rutherford sidled up to his wife and received a poke in the ribs. "Ouch."

We chatted a bit longer, then Emma Lee came over and hugged me. "Mrs. Washington, I'm so happy for you."

"I'm so glad you were able to come. How is medical school?" I asked.

"It's hard, but I love it." She spent a few minutes telling me about her teachers, classes, and fellow medical students at Northwestern University School of Medicine.

Emma Lee was Asian American, with dark hair and dark eyes, and at five feet tall and barely one hundred pounds, was a big contrast to my more than six foot tall nephew. She was also from the South and spoke with a Southern drawl, which was more prominent whenever she was angry or stressed. Tonight, her drawl was minimal, which was a good sign.

"Are you going to be able to come to the Four Feathers? I think the girls are planning a surprise shower of some type."

"I wish I could, but I've got too much studying to do. And any free time I have I'm going to hang out with Zaq." She glanced lovingly at my nephew.

"I understand completely."

"But nothing is going to keep me from the wedding."

Zaq came over and claimed his girlfriend's attention.

Christopher brought over his date and introduced me. "Aunt Sammy, I'd like to introduce you to Jade. Jade, this is my aunt, Samantha Washington."

Jade was tall, almost as tall as Christopher. Her hair was dark blue and shaved on one side.

I recognized Jade from the bookstore. She was a fan of classic noir detective novels. She and my late husband, Leon, would have gotten along famously.

We talked detective fiction for a few moments and then they moved on.

I had a moment alone, which was nice, but then I noticed Dawson and Jillian standing in a corner and wandered over to them.

"Thank you both for coming." I hugged Jillian. "We haven't had a chance to talk since you got back from New York. How was the Bolshoi?"

Jillian had spent six weeks in the summer in New York,

where she received training from teachers from the prestigious Bolshoi Ballet Academy.

Her face lit up as she talked about the hours spent dancing, and how badly her feet and legs ached at the end of it. Her enthusiasm put a smile on my face.

"Geez! It sounds like you enjoyed the pain. Should I be worried?" Dawson joked.

Jillian chuckled. "I'm not a masochist, but it truly was wonderful to dance and learn from the best dancers in the world. I learned so much about how the smallest movement can completely change your silhouette. The tilt of your head. The point of your fingers. It was crazy sick."

I was fairly sure *crazy sick* was a good thing, so I smiled. "Dorothy mentioned that you might be going to Moscow," I said.

"I was invited. That was the coolest thing ever." She frowned. "I wanted to go so badly. I mean, it would have been so fire. My parents left the decision up to me. I really, really, really wanted to go. I mean . . . it would have been amazing, but with everything going on in the world, I just didn't think it would be a good idea."

"I hate to say it, but I agree. I think you made a wise decision."

"Maybe, but I just want to dance and I wish politics would stay out of it." She pouted.

I pulled her into a hug. "I know, dear. Politics is making its way into a lot of things that it shouldn't. But that's a discussion for another time."

We moved on to Jillian's plans for the school year. The school was finally, according to Jillian, putting on *A Chorus Line*. She was excited to audition and had her fingers crossed for a good role.

"You'll get the lead. You're the best singer and dancer at MISU," Dawson said.

"You're my boyfriend; you have to say that."

"I don't have to say anything." Dawson grinned. After receiving a playful punch on the arm he admitted, "However, it does happen to be true."

"How did the meeting go with your dad?" I asked.

Dawson sighed. "About the way you would expect. He wanted money." He shrugged. "I gave him the gift card. He left." Pain and disappointment flashed across his face.

"Are you okay?" I asked.

He hesitated. "He'll never change. Will he?"

The odds that A-Squared would change were slim to none. Dawson knew that. He didn't need me to state the obvious. Instead, I pulled him into a hug. "Never say never."

By the time I left them, they were back to their playful flirting. Jillian was good for him. She kept him grounded. No matter how successful he was on the football field, she would make sure he kept both feet firmly placed on the ground. Dawson was good for her, too. Jillian was talented. Dawson provided a solid dose of reality and a strong shoulder to lean on. They were young, but I hoped they would beat the odds and stay together.

Nana Jo and Dr. Patterson were having a heated conversation in the corner. I wandered over in case I needed to protect the doctor from my grandmother.

"Camilia, you're out of your mind. There's no way Michael Haggerty is a better sleuth than Dennis Stanton," Nana Jo said.

"If anyone is out of their mind, it's you, Josephine. Michael Haggerty was a member of British intelligence. He was a far superior sleuth than that Raffleslike charlatan, Dennis Stanton. Everyone knows that."

Ruby Mae Stevenson was sitting in a chair nearby. She'd pulled out her knitting. Like my favorite sleuth, Agatha Christie's Miss Marple, Ruby Mae always had her knitting. "Those two have been arguing like that for thirty minutes. You would think they were talking about real people," she said in the Southern Alabama drawl that, even after fifty years living in the north, she'd never lost.

Ruby Mae Stevenson was the youngest of my grandmother's friends and by far my favorite. She was a Black woman who was born and raised in a small town in Alabama. She had long salt-and-pepper hair that she wore pulled back into a bun. Nana Jo said Ruby Mae's hair was so long she could sit on it. Sadly, I'd never seen it down, so I couldn't say. I can say that Ruby Mae was one of the strongest women I have ever known. She was also one of the most connected. She raised nine children and had a massive extended family that we often ran into. She was one of those people who never met a stranger. Within minutes of seeing her face, people talked to her as though they'd known her their entire life.

"Wait . . . Michael Haggerty. Isn't he the—"

Ruby Mae was nodding before the words were out of my mouth. "That character from *Murder, She Wrote.*"

"And Dennis Stanton is the guy who used to be a thief?"

Ruby Mae nodded.

"I guess they've found common ground . . . sort of."

"At least they're on a first-name basis," Frank whispered.

I turned to glance at him. "How did you manage that?"

Frank shrugged. "I wish I could take the credit for it, but I can only say, 'Thank God for Angela Lansbury.' "

"I don't know who that fine specimen of a man is that you brought to the party, Frank, but you may want to save him from Irma." Dorothy Clark joined our group.

If Ruby Mae was Nana Jo's youngest friend, Dorothy Clark was her oldest. Not in age. That distinction went to Irma Starczewski. Dorothy Clark had known Nana Jo the longest of the three. She was also the one most like Nana Jo in appearance. At nearly six feet tall and just shy of three hundred pounds, the two women resembled each other. Both were widows and shameless flirts. Unlike Nana Jo, Dorothy had a wonderful voice and sang like an angel.

Frank turned to look in the direction that Dorothy had pointed. In a corner was a tall dark stranger who reminded me of Idris Elba. Like a pride of lions surrounding a gazelle, Irma Starczewski had cornered her prey and was going in for the kill. Even though Irma was knocking on eighty's door, five feet tall and one hundred pounds sopping wet with a jet-black beehive, she was what Nana Jo called *a brazen hussy*. Sixty years ago, Irma had been a beauty queen. Like Tina Turner, she had amazing legs that she liked to showcase to their fullest advantage by wearing short skirts and six-inch heels.

"Who is that?" I asked.

"That's Cooper Garrett," Frank said.

"That's Cooper? Your best friend?" I leaned close and whispered. "I thought he was undercover on some secret government mission and wasn't going to be able to make it to the wedding."

"Things got hot and they pulled him back. They thought it would do him good to hide out in a place where no one would come looking for him."

"Aren't you going to help him? You have to save him."

Frank grinned and shook his head. "He's good at extricating himself from difficult situations."

"True, but he's never met Irma."

The rest of the evening went by splendidly. We ate. We talked. And we got better acquainted. As the party was drawing to a close, Nana Jo rapped on her glass to get everyone's attention.

"My daughter Grace couldn't be here tonight, but I

wanted to say how happy we are for Sam and Frank. They are a lovely couple, and from the moment I met Frank, I knew he would be a perfect fit for Sam. I'm proud to welcome him into our family. Please raise your glasses and join me in wishing them both health and happiness as they prepare to enter into this next chapter of their lives together. To Sam and Frank."

Chapter 9

The next morning Nana Jo surprised me with the news that the Four Feathers was sending a limousine to pick us up.

"Really? A limousine? What about Dr. Patterson and—"

"All of us. Now get a move on. The limo will be here in ten minutes."

Fortunately, I had already showered and dressed, but I hadn't bothered packing last night and ten minutes wasn't enough time to put together a thoughtful bag for the weekend. I felt paralyzed by the magnitude of packing. Nana Jo watched me flutter around for a few moments.

"Sam, you're not going to see the queen. You're going to a local resort for a long weekend. You're not going overseas. Make sure you have underwear, pajamas, and a nice dress for the party tonight. If you forget something, we'll have Frank or Jenna bring it to you. Or you can just buy another one. Now, move!"

Perspective. That's what I needed. I finished packing, and when the limousine pulled up to the side of the building I was ready and waiting.

Dawson came down from his apartment over my garage to see me off. He whistled at the limo. "Fancy."

"I know, right."

"I hope you have a wonderful time. Don't worry about the bookstore. We've got plenty of cookies, and Christopher and Zaq should be here in an hour."

"I'm just going to be a few miles down the road. If anything comes up. Or if you need anything, call me."

"What could possibly come up? We'll be fine."

Why does that keep coming up?

Nana Jo and I climbed into the limo and gave directions to the driver to Shady Acres.

Dr. Patterson, Irma, Dorothy, and Ruby Mae were eagerly waiting when the limousine pulled up to the main building. They climbed into the limo, and we took off for the Four Feathers.

The six of us all fit comfortably in the luxurious vehicle.

"I wish it wasn't so early in the morning so we could take advantage of this bar," Dorothy said.

Ruby Mae turned on the television. "I missed my stories this morning. Roberto was just about to find out that Marguerite was lying when she said she hadn't been embezzling money from his family's trust fund for the past thirty years because she was the illegitimate daughter of his grandfather and was actually his birth mother and entitled to the money."

"Wow! How is that possible? Isn't Marguerite younger than Roberto?" Nana Jo asked.

"Yep. I have no idea how the writers plan to make that one work. That's why I want to see it."

"Marguerite was placed on a spaceship by Porshia, her half sister, when she was a baby. Supposedly, she traveled on some secret government mission that took her out of our solar system. It traveled at the speed of light, so when she came back to earth she was younger," Dr. Patterson said.

I don't know if I was more shocked by the crazy storyline

or the fact that Dr. Patterson actually knew who these people were.

Everyone sat in silence watching *As the Beat of Our Heart* play out. Everyone except Irma, who found the controls for the limo's sunroof and kept opening it, standing on the seat and whistling whenever she saw a hot guy. That worked fine when we were traveling through the city, at a moderate speed and stopping at stop signs and stop lights. Once we hit the interstate and the limo got up over seventy miles per hour, Irma was in danger of losing the hairpiece that thickened her beehive and she had to sit down.

By the time we pulled up to the resort we still didn't have the answers about Marguerite and Roberto. However, I was happy to see that Dr. Patterson was getting along well not only with Nana Jo but with Dorothy and the others too.

Our driver pulled up to the resort, and a valet hurried to open our doors.

"Mrs. Washington?" the concierge asked.

"Yes."

"You're all checked in and your rooms are waiting for you." The concierge was a young man with red hair and freckles. He reminded me of Opie from *The Andy Griffith Show*, but he knew his job. He directed us to the elevators. He handed keys to each of the women and directed them to their rooms. Everyone was on the third floor except me. I was taken to the top floor, which required inserting my key into the elevator.

My room was the executive suite, and it was the most luxurious room I'd ever seen. At nearly five thousand square feet, it had a spacious living room, a dining room, three bedrooms, a kitchen, and three bathrooms.

"Are you sure this room is for me and not for all of us?" I asked.

The concierge chuckled. "I'm sure. Mr. Strongbow wanted

you to have an extraordinary stay. If there is anything I can do to make your stay better, please don't hesitate to ask."

I rummaged in my purse for a tip, but he waved away my efforts. "No tipping. You are a VIP."

He left, and I stood in the middle of that luxury and stared. One wall of the living room was all glass and looked out on the nature preserve at the back of the property. My phone vibrated and Nana Jo's picture popped up on screen.

"Where are you?" she asked.

"I think it's the penthouse. Meet me at the elevator and I'll bring you up." I hurried to the elevator.

Everyone was waiting at the elevator, and I took them up to my floor. When they saw the opulence of my room they were in awe.

"Wow. I didn't know they had places like this here in Michigan. Las Vegas, yes. New Buffalo, Michigan, no way," Nana Jo said.

"I wonder who stays here," Ruby Mae whispered.

"Why are you whispering?" Nana Jo asked.

"Beats me, but I feel like a kid who's wandered into an area where I'm not supposed to be," Ruby Mae said.

"Exactly. I feel the same way. Maybe I should ask for something a bit more . . . I mean less . . . this is just too much," I said.

There was a knock on the door.

"Maybe they realized they put me in the wrong room and they've come to ask me to leave." I hurried to open the door.

It was a porter bringing up my luggage.

He put my bag in the main bedroom. Again, when I tried to tip him, he waved away the tip, smiled, and quietly left.

"I don't think I'm cut out for anything this . . . grand." I glanced around. "I wouldn't even want to sleep here. I think I'm going to ask for a different room."

"Sam, don't you think that would be rude? You were given

this room . . . this weekend, as a gift. It would be a slap in the face of the person who gave it to you," Dr. Patterson said. "You wouldn't want to insult them by seeming ungrateful."

That was when lightning struck. "Dr. Patterson, would you switch rooms with me? You're right. I don't want to insult the tribal leaders or Mr. Strongbow. I just don't think I would enjoy myself in a room like this. It would make me happy if you would switch with me."

It didn't take much convincing. Dr. Patterson was thrilled to switch. In fact, by the time we had swapped keys and moved her luggage to the suite, she was laughing and insisting that I call her Camilia.

I left her and moved to the room that had been assigned to her. It was a nice spacious room. It had a large king-size bed, a desk, and a comfortable reclining chair near the window. Unlike the suite I'd just vacated, this view overlooked the parking lot instead of a woodland nature preserve, but that was fine with me.

I unpacked my suitcase and set up my laptop near the window. I was going to sneak in a little writing before we were going to meet for tea.

Lady Elizabeth and Lord William Marsh waited for their guests. Lady Clara Trewellen-Harper, Lord Reginald Dilworth, and Lady Jean Groverton were the first to arrive.

"Clara, it's so wonderful to see you." Lady Elizabeth hugged her cousin warmly. "I just wish Daphne and Penelope could be here."

"Oh, me too. I do plan to make my way over to Bidwell Cottage while I'm here to see Victor and

Penelope. The Earl and Countess of Lochloren won't be able to avoid me that easily. Plus, I brought a toy for Lord William." Lady Clara laughed.

"Lady Elizabeth and Lord William Marsh, I want you to meet my friends, Lord Reginald Dilworth and Lady Jean Groverton."

They all shook hands.

"Please, call me Dilly. Everyone does," Lord Dilworth said.

"And I'm Jean. When my mum found out I was coming she told me to be sure to thank you for the invitation and to remind you that you promised to come by Caringford Hall the next time you're in Kingsfordshire."

"I don't travel as much as I used to, but I always look forward to Caringford Hall. Now, how is Lady Catherine?"

The Lord William and Lord Dilworth chatted about hunting while the women chatted about the latest fashions.

Thompkins entered. He coughed and announced, "Lady Mildred Trewellen-Harper."

Lady Mildred was a short, thin, nervous woman of middle age. She rushed into the room and sat. "Elizabeth I can't believe the status of the British railway. Why, that had to be the bumpiest, most uncomfortable ride that I've had in years."

Lady Elizabeth was familiar with her cousin's nerves, as well as her personality. Disagreeing with her cousin would lead to tears and apologies for being sensitive and causing trouble. While agreeing with her would lead to hours of talk about illnesses only impacting those plagued with nerves. She therefore made a noncommittal clicking sound.

Thompkins returned and announced Detective Inspector Peter Covington, Mrs. Rosemary Covington, Mrs. Ida Smythe, Miss Beatrice Smythe, and Miss Beryl Smythe. He opened the door wide and the remainder of the party entered.

Lady Elizabeth hurried forward.

Rosemary Covington, like her son, was tall and lean, with thick curly hair. Her eyes were light and she looked frightened. Upon seeing Lady Elizabeth she made a quick curtsy. "Your ladyship."

Lady Elizabeth smiled. "Please call me Elizabeth. And your name is Rosemary, correct?"

Rosemary Covington gawked but quickly recovered and nodded.

"We're so pleased you were able to come." She turned to face a short, plump woman. "You must be Ida, Peter's aunt?"

Ida Smythe smiled, exposing a missing tooth. "That's right, your ladyship. Pleased, I'm sure."

Lady Elizabeth turned to the two younger women. Both were thin and stylishly dressed. The women were twins, with dark hair, dark eyes, and lean figures. One, Beryl, wore a lot of makeup and bright red lipstick. She was outgoing and confident. She shook hands with Lady Elizabeth but quickly zoned in on Lord Dilworth and made her way to make his acquaintance.

Beatrice was quiet, barely able to make eye contact. She muttered a greeting, flushed, and immediately stepped backward.

Lady Clara introduced her soon-to-be-mother-in-law to her mother and her friends. The group sat down, and Lady Elizabeth rang the bell for tea.

Despite Lady Elizabeth's best efforts to draw Peter's mother, aunt, and Cousin Beatrice into conversation, talk was strained. They responded in as few words as possible. Even Jean Groverton remained mute and stared at her shoes. When Lady Elizabeth gave up on forcing everyone into the conversation, the atmosphere improved. Beryl and Dilly were both lively and kept up a steady stream of amusing antidotes. The only thing that loosened Beatrice's tongue was when Lady Elizabeth complimented her outfit.

"Your suit is stunning and fits you perfectly," Lady Clara said. "Please tell me you designed this."

Beatrice flushed. "Yes, I did. We did." She nodded toward her sister.

"Beatrice does all of the designing. I just add my two cents in here and there," Beryl said.

"I love the lapels on that suit. It's very smart," Lady Elizabeth added. "Don't you agree, Mildred?"

"I never was a fan of women dressing like men." Mildred sniffed. "However, that cut is very nice for women who must work."

Lady Clara rolled her eyes. "Which is most of us these days, and I for one love it. Please tell me you brought some samples. Jean and I are going to try everything."

"Beatrice's trunk is packed full of everything you could possibly want. Except a husband." Beryl laughed and then winked at Lord Dilworth. "Although I guess you've already got that. Haven't you?"

"If what you're wearing is an indication of the outfits that you've brought, I'm sure everyone in our set would appreciate your designs. Don't you agree, Jean?"

Lady Jean Groverton pulled her gaze from her shoes and stared at her friend. However, before she could respond Thompkins appeared at the door.

"Mr. Maximilian Chesterton," Thompkins said.

Beatrice gasped.

Lord William blustered. "What is that . . . traitor doing here?"

The door burst open and in sauntered a short white-haired elderly man. Max Chesterton wore a navy pinstripe suit with a bright pink shirt, an ascot, shoes, and gloves. "Sorry I'm late, but my driver couldn't find this place. You dear folk really should move closer to civilization. How else do you expect people to find you?"

"Family's been here three hundred years. The people we *want* to see don't have a problem." Lord William clamped down on the stem of his pipe and scowled.

Max Chesterton threw back his head and laughed.

"Mr. Chesterton, this is indeed a surprise. We had no idea you were coming." Lady Elizabeth cast a surprised expression in Lady Mildred's direction. "Your dislike of the countryside is well-known. What could possibly have gotten you to come down this weekend?" Lady Elizabeth asked.

"I heard you were entertaining England's hottest new fashion sensation." He smiled at Beatrice and Beryl. "Sadly, I haven't been successful convincing the ladies to come to me, so Muhammad must come to the mountain."

Beryl laughed.

Shy quiet Beatrice on the other hand was enraged. She stood up and glared at Maximilian Chesterton. Her face was flushed and her eyes flashed.

"Mr. Chesterton, I thought I made myself clear that we aren't interested. Not now. Not ever. And this is hardly the time or the place—"

"Agreed. Mr. Chesterton, this is my engagement party, not a business meeting. Perhaps you should plan on conducting your business someplace else," Lady Clara fumed.

Peter Covington hadn't seen his fiancée or his cousin so enraged. He stood. "Mr. Chesterton, it would appear that you came to conduct business, and my cousin and my fiancée—"

"Ah, yes. You're Lady Clara's betrothed—the Scotland Yard copper. Of course when I heard about the engagement party I wanted to come and extend all of my best to the couple." Chesterton walked over to Mildred Trewellen-Harper. He bowed with a flourish, took Lady Mildred's hand, and kissed it.

Lady Mildred giggled. "Oh, Maxy."

"Maxy?" Lady Clara stared from her mother to Maximilian Chesterton. "Please don't tell me that you . . ."

"Yes, dear. Max is my escort for the weekend. I invited him."

Chapter 10

My phone vibrated and I stepped from the British countryside and back to the present. It was a text from Nana Jo.

Going to the high-limit room with Camilia

I thought we were going to the spa. I guess not. I waited for a few minutes for a follow-up text inviting me to join them. None came.

Okay

Meet you at 7 in the lobby

I glanced at my watch. I had three hours.

Okay

It only makes sense that Nana Jo and Camilia would get along. They're closer in age. After all, I wanted them to get along, right? It's much better not to have to be concerned that my grandmother is going to body slam my soon-to-be mother-in-law. This is a good thing.

I paced around in my room. It was a nice room, but not the greatest for pacing. Maybe I should go outside. Get some fresh air. Go on a nature walk? I grabbed my jacket and headed outside.

It was nippy, but the sun was shining and that lifted my

spirits. The nature trail was well-marked. I shook off the jealousy and headed down the path.

"Mrs. Washington?"

I turned when I heard my name. "Mr. Strongbow."

The gentleman from the senior center walked up to me. He was wearing jeans and a denim shirt. "I thought that was you. Are you enjoying your stay?"

I assured him that I was enjoying my stay. I also thanked him profusely for his generosity.

He waved away my thanks. "I'm just sorry you had such a negative experience while on our lands."

"That wasn't your fault, Mr. Strongbow."

"Still, I felt horrible that you were treated so poorly. Please, call me Kai."

"Samantha."

We chatted a little longer and then he cautioned me against leaving the path.

"Is it dangerous?" I asked.

He gave me a mystical look. "There are lots of different types of danger."

I shivered. Then we said our goodbyes and parted ways. Kai went back toward the resort and I headed down the nature path.

Fortunately, I didn't see anything more dangerous than a few squirrels, chipmunks, and a bunny. There was a footbridge that crossed a creek. I stood on the bridge and watched the water crashing against the stones and rushing under the wooden bridge for several minutes. It was the mental readjustment I needed to get back into myself and put life back into perspective. So I turned around and walked back.

In my room, I thought about writing again, but . . . . I wasn't in the mood. I sat and looked at the parking lot out of the window. Then I paced around the room for a few minutes.

Television. I can watch television.

I turned on the television and flipped through what felt like two hundred stations, most of which stated they weren't available, before I landed back where I started. I watched a program called *How the Universe Works*, where I learned a lot of miscellaneous details that I'd probably never use. After one episode I went through the channels again. I stopped when I landed back where I started, watching the hotel's promo video that showcased the highlights of the Four Feathers resort, the casino, and all of the amenities. That was when it dawned on me. I could enjoy my stay at this luxurious resort just like the people in that video. I turned off the television and made my way to the spa. I needed a massage.

The Four Feathers Spa was just as luxurious as the video indicated. Soft lighting, trickling water, and soothing music. The receptionist escorted me back to a private massage room where I undressed and wrapped myself in a large fluffy ultra-luxurious bathrobe. There was a bathrobe in my room too, but it wasn't nearly as luxurious as this one, and there were four red feathers embroidered on it.

When the masseuse entered I was sitting on the table stroking my robe.

"I'm sorry, but this is the softest robe I've ever seen."

"We get that a lot." She introduced herself as Nina. "We splurged on the nicest most luxurious robes, towels, and slippers for our guests. We had to get the Four Feathers logo embroidered on them to separate them from the others. That way if a guest takes one to their rooms, we can differentiate it from the others"

"I might have to buy one of those. Are they for sale?" I asked.

"They are. When we're done I'll show you the price list."

I climbed on the table and lay face down. Nina's magical

fingers kneaded my shoulders and neck and then she worked on my back and legs. I must have fallen asleep because at one point she had to shake my arm to get me to turn over.

The ninety-minute massage was over way too quickly, and I found myself wondering why I didn't do this more often.

Once I was dressed Nina came back in the room and showed me the price list to buy the oils, exfoliating creams, lotions, and robes.

I stared at the list open-mouthed. "You have got to be joking."

Nina smiled and shook her head. "We don't sell many of these robes, although everyone who wears them comments about how wonderful they are."

"It's over eleven hundred dollars. What's it made of?"

"One hundred percent cotton."

"Seriously? Is this some exotic cotton that is only grown in the Brazilian rainforest and picked by Buddhist monks during a full moon when all eight planets in our solar system are perfectly aligned, which happens every three hundred ninety-six billion years?"

Nina chuckled. "I have no idea about all that, but I believe there are twenty-two karat gold threads interspersed throughout."

I gave the robe one final stroke before bidding it and Nina a fond farewell.

Back at my room I showered and put on another of my new dresses and headed downstairs.

In the lobby I met the women, who all appeared to have started the evening with a few cocktails.

We were escorted by one of the staff to one of the restaurants. We walked through a door at the back of the restaurant to a private dining area.

"I never knew this was here," I said.

I wasn't surprised when Nana Jo said, "Ruby Mae's great-niece snagged us this private dining room."

Platters of appetizers were brought in and a waitress took our drink orders. I was hungry, so I piled my plate full. The others had eaten sandwiches in Camilia's suite before coming down.

There was a band playing in the main dining room. If we opened the door to our dining room, we could hear it quite clearly. We ate, drank, and danced. After an hour or so a man dressed like a policeman entered the dining room.

"Is there a Samantha Washington here?" the policeman asked.

This was not good. No way was this good. This absolutely *could not* be happening.

I turned to Nana Jo. "Please tell me you didn't do what I think you did."

Nana Jo shrugged. "Don't blame me. This was Irma's idea."

I turned to glare at Irma, but it was no use. She was waving twenty dollars in the air and whistling.

My face was hot and I didn't need a mirror to see that I was blushing. I glanced at Dr. Patterson. "Dr. Patterson, I'm so sorry. I had no idea." To my utter surprise Dr. Patterson was smiling and waving money in the air too.

"Loosen up, Samantha, and call me Camilia."

The policeman had a boom box and cranked up the music. He removed his shirt and with one quick snatch pulled off his pants. He then gyrated around the room in the tiniest of briefs while the girls screamed and stuffed money down the front.

When the stripper turned his attention in my direction I had had enough. That was when I marched out of the room.

Chapter 11

I paced around my room for nearly an hour. I couldn't believe my friends and family arranged for a stripper. In front of my soon-to-be-mother-in-law. I tried calling Nana Jo to express my displeasure, but she could barely hear me over the music and shouting.

My next call was to Jenna. I needed a sympathetic ear. Unfortunately, she couldn't stop laughing long enough to talk, let alone provide sympathetic pearls of wisdom. Eventually, I gave up and let her go.

I picked up my phone to text Frank several times, *but what if he asked about his mother? What was I going to tell him? I couldn't tell him that when I left his mother was shoving twenty dollars down the front of a stripper's underpants.*

When all else fails I go for my lifelong comfort provider—food. I ordered a club sandwich and a Diet Coke from room service. When it came I ate and went back to the place where things made sense. In my book.

"What could you possibly have been thinking? Inviting Maximilian Chesterton here?" Lady Clara paced in front of the fireplace in Lady Mildred's bedroom.

Mildred Trewellen-Harper sat in a chair near the fireplace sniffing into a handkerchief. "I don't know what the big fuss is about. I've known Max for years."

Lady Clara stopped pacing and turned to stare at her mother. "You don't know what the fuss is about? Maximilian Chesterton is the lowest, most despicable man on the planet."

"Pishposh." Mildred waved her handkerchief.

"Pishposh?" Lady Clara shook her head at her mother and appealed to Lady Elizabeth.

"Mildred, surely you realize that Max Chesterton has done some rather contemptible things."

"Like what?" Mildred cast a puzzled glance at her cousin.

"Like speaking out in favor of Hitler and the Nazis," Lady Elizabeth said.

"But that's just politics. I never concern myself with politics," Mildred said.

"Politics? Mother, England is on the verge of war. Hitler is a malicious despot. He's guilty of atrocious acts of cruelty and violence. He's invaded innocent countries. Violated treaties. Killed innocent men, women, and children. He spews hatred against Jews, Africans, Roma, and Sinti people. I've heard he's even killing the disabled. This is more than just politics. This is a question of humanity and decency."

"I haven't heard about the killing of innocent people. It's not been on the wireless. How can you possibly know this?" Mildred asked.

Lady Clara exchanged a brief glance with her cousin. Lady Elizabeth knew that Lady Clara's work at Bletchley Park involved more than merely translating documents. She was one of the few who knew the truth of the work that Clara was doing. "I just know."

"I'm sure that Max isn't guilty of any of those things," Mildred argued.

"Maybe not directly, but when you align yourself with evil you're condoning it. Honestly, Mildred, I can't believe you share in any of those beliefs." Lady Elizabeth frowned at her cousin.

"I don't know much about what's happening in Germany or in the rest of Europe. But whatever is going on over there, I don't think that England should get involved. We got involved in the last war and look what happened. So many men died. That wasn't our war. I think we should just stay here on our island and mind our own business," Lady Mildred huffed.

Lady Clara kneeled in front of her mother and took her hands. "Mother, war is awful. None of us want another war, but we can't allow Hitler to run rampant, killing and destroying innocent people. It isn't right. Surely you see that."

"But aren't you worried about Peter? He'll be forced to go to war, just like your father. He could be killed and buried in Europe fighting in some other country for people he doesn't even know. He could—" Mildred sobbed into her handkerchief.

"Mother, Peter won't be *forced* to enlist. He'll volunteer," she said with pride. "He will fight and he may die." Clara choked back a sob. She took a deep breath. "But he will be fighting for people like you and me. He'll fight for right."

"But why England? Why him?" Mildred asked.

"If Hitler and the Nazis aren't checked, this won't be a war that's contained to a few countries on the continent. It will spread like a virus. Eventually, that virus will cross the Channel and the White Cliffs of Dover," Lady Elizabeth said. "It's just a matter of time. A great man said, 'The only thing necessary for evil to triumph in the world is that good men do nothing.'"

"You're right. I wasn't thinking," Lady Mildred cried. "I shouldn't have invited Max to come." She turned to her cousin. "Oh, Elizabeth, I'm terribly sorry, but it's too late. He's here. What do you want me to do?"

Lady Elizabeth sighed. "I think we just need to get through dinner. It's getting dark and it's raining. We can't send him packing now. As much as I hate the idea of that man sitting at my dinner table, I wouldn't send a hungry dog out in a storm. However, first thing tomorrow we'll pack his bags and I'll have Thompkins drive him to the train station."

"Thank you, Elizabeth." Lady Mildred dabbed at her eyes.

"Stop worrying, Mildred. It's just one night. I'll just need to make sure William doesn't throttle him between now and tomorrow morning. Then we can all relax and enjoy the weekend."

I awoke to the vibration of my cell. It took several moments before I got my bearings and remembered where I was. I glanced at the time. My first instinct was to ignore the cell. Jenna was probably getting back at me for the other day, when I called her in the wee hours of the morning. But the vibration didn't stop, and when my brain fog lifted I remembered that Jenna would never be up at five in the morning unless something horrible had happened.

I grabbed for the phone without looking to see who it was. "Jenna, if this is payback for me calling—"

"Samantha, this is Camilia."

I instantly sat up, wide awake. "Dr. Patterson . . . Camilia, I'm sorry. I thought it was my sister. I—"

"I need you to come up to my room."

"Sure. Just let me get dressed and I'll be—"

"I don't have time for that. Please. I need you to come now."

"Of course, but I don't have a key. I can't take the elevator to your floor." I pulled on a pair of sweatpants and a T-shirt.

"I'll meet you in the elevator in two minutes."

"Dr. Patterson, if something is wrong, maybe I should—"

"Two minutes." She disconnected the call.

Chapter 12

Two minutes didn't leave much time. So I took care of the call of nature and splashed water on my face. Then I hurried into the hall. When I got to the elevators Camilia was waiting.

One look at her face told me that what had driven her call for help this early in the morning wasn't your average run-of-the-mill problem.

"Camilia, what's happened?"

She was shaking and struggled to get the key into the slot in the elevator. After the third attempt I took the card and inserted it. I turned to face her. "You look . . . tell me what's happened."

She glanced around the elevator like a nervous rabbit. Then she put her finger to her lips and whispered, "I don't think we should talk in public."

Okay, this is weird.

I waited until we were at the door to her room. I inserted the key and opened the door. I walked into the suite and that's when I saw it.

Lying on the floor was a man.

"Who is he?" I asked.

Dr. Patterson shook her head. "No idea. I've never seen him before."

"Was he at the party last night?" I asked.

"I don't know. I don't think so."

"So what's he doing on the floor?"

"I have no idea."

It took a few moments before I realized we'd been whispering and the man on the floor hadn't budged. I walked over to him and looked more closely.

He was lying face down on the floor. Apart from the white bathrobe he was wearing he appeared to be completely naked. I tapped him with my shoe. Still no movement.

"What's he doing on the floor?" I wasn't sure I wanted to know the answer to that question.

"I have no idea why he's on the floor. Who he is. Or why he's here. I told you. I've never seen him before."

I squatted down and reached out to shake the stranger. His arm was stiff and he was cold.

"OMG." I stared into her eyes. "He's . . ."

"Dead."

Chapter 13

This wasn't my first time seeing a dead body, but that didn't make it any easier. I walked around the room while I tried to avoid hyperventilating. "Dead? How is there a dead man in your room? How did he even get up here? And who is he?"

"I don't know. I don't know. I don't know." Dr. Patterson flopped down onto the sofa. "This is horrible."

"You checked his . . . pulse, right? I mean, he's not just passed out in a drunken stupor?"

Dr. Patterson sat up. "I'm a doctor; of course I checked for a pulse. He doesn't have one. He's dead. You felt his arm. Rigor mortis is setting in. He's dead." She sat back and leaned her head back on the sofa.

As a medical doctor, this wasn't Dr. Patterson's first time seeing a dead body either. However, she wasn't handling it much better than I was.

Breathe.

"Okay, we need to call the police."

"No." She sat up again.

"We have to call the police. There's a dead man in your room. I mean . . . we can't just leave him here."

"Why not?"

She must be joking.

I looked at her face. She wasn't joking.

"Dr. Patterson, we—"

"Look, we're in a hotel suite with a dead body at five in the morning. I think we can drop the formalities and get on a first-name basis, don't you?"

I paused a beat and then burst out laughing. I don't know if it was shock or stress, but whatever the reason I couldn't stop laughing.

Laughter is contagious, and it wasn't long before we were both sitting on the sofa laughing hysterically. Just when one of us would stop the other would start back and then we were both laughing again.

Camilia was the first to stop. "All right, we're both probably suffering from shock and I don't want to slap you, so pull yourself together."

The idea of getting slapped had a very sobering effect on me and I forced myself to stop. "You know we have to call the police, right?"

She hesitated a beat but eventually nodded. "Why does this have to happen to me? Why now? Why did I come here?"

Because your only son is getting married and you wanted to meet and intimidate his fiancée with your conservative doctorness? Nope. Can't say that out loud.

"I should have stayed at home where I belong. Why didn't I just stay in the room that I was assigned?"

I snapped my finger. "That's it. Did you tell anyone that we switched rooms?"

She shook her head.

"Then we'll just switch back. You'll go back to your original room and I'll move back here. Then we'll call the police."

"But what about the others? Josephine, Irma, Dorothy, and Ruby Mae? They know we switched. Won't they . . ."

"Wild horses wouldn't drag it out of them. If we needed to bury this body in the parking lot, they would help dig the hole. Don't worry about them. Let's get you packed."

Camilia packed quickly and I tried to avoid looking at the corpse in the middle of the living room. However, when you try to avoid looking at something that's immediately where your eye goes. My eyes kept darting back to the corpse on the floor.

"Do you think we need to wipe down the room?" Camilia asked.

I stared. "Why?"

"You know," She leaned close and whispered, "To remove fingerprints."

"No. It's my room. You're my guest. It would be even more suspicious if there were no fingerprints in the room. Besides, that would be destroying evidence, and the police take a dim view of that."

"Oh yes. Right. Of course."

We took the elevator down to the other room.

"Samantha, you look dazed. I know this is shocking, but I meant it when I told you that I have no idea who that man is . . . was," she said.

"I believe you, but he looks familiar. I know I've seen him somewhere before. I just can't remember."

"This casino is very crowded. Maybe he worked here. Although I have no idea why he came to that suite to die."

"It's a nice suite." I shrugged. "There are three others on that floor, I think. Maybe he went to the wrong one."

"But how did he get in?" Camilia asked. "I would never leave the door open."

I clamped my mouth closed.

"What?"

"Nothing. It's just that when I left last night, you'd had several drinks, and maybe you had a few more afterward. And there's certainly nothing wrong with that. You're an adult. But maybe you don't remember leaving the party with the gentleman or even inviting him to your room."

"Samantha, I did *not* invite that man to my room," she huffed.

"I'm sorry. I didn't mean to insult you. I was just . . ."

She took a deep breath. "Trying to help. I know. I'm sorry. It's just that I've been very uptight lately. I'm up for a promotion and I've been working a lot. I can't remember the last time I went out and just had fun." She shook her head. "I guess I just wanted to have fun, and this seemed like a nice quiet out-of-the-way place to do it. No one knows me here."

"I'm sorry, but we'll figure it out. Don't worry."

I packed all of my belongings away. Because there was no dead body in my room and no chance of destroying evidence, I wiped the bathroom down and tidied up as I packed. When I was done we swapped keys.

I hurried up to the suite and unpacked. I picked up the phone to call the police but changed my mind. Instead, I took out my phone and took a picture of the corpse. Then I took the elevator back downstairs. This time I went to Nana Jo's room and knocked. It took a few knocks before she eventually unlocked the door.

"Are you here for the funeral?"

"Funeral? What funeral?" I asked.

"Mine. I'm dying." Nana Jo leaned against the wall holding her head. "I'm pretty sure my head's been used as a cymbal by a marching band, and I no longer have taste buds." She scraped at her tongue.

"Nana Jo, don't be so dramatic."

"Samantha Marie Washington, if you love me, please stop shouting and go away and let me die in peace."

I helped Nana Jo to the bed, picked up the phone, and asked for room service.

"I'll never eat again as long as I live. The idea of food—" Nana Jo ran for the bathroom.

I asked for something for a hangover. After Nana Jo finished purging I heard the shower. By the time she came out room service had delivered a glass of something that looked like tar. The server said, "The bartender swears this will have you feeling better in record time."

Nana Jo stared at the glass as though it were a snake, but eventually she took it, pinched her nose, and tossed it back like she was doing shots.

I thought she was going to hurl again, but despite making bizarre faces, she held it down. "Ugh. That was the most awful thing I've ever ingested." She belched and then lay on the bed.

"I guess that means you still have your taste buds."

Nana Jo was not amused. She belched again and scowled at me.

"Are you well enough to listen? I have a problem."

Nana Jo waved her hand as if she were a queen encouraging a peon to get on with it.

"Were you with Dr. Patterson . . . ah, Camilia all of last night?"

"Not all night. We partied hard with the stripper and then Dorothy challenged some guys to a drinking contest. Geez! In my day men could drink more than those lightweights." She paused. "I seem to recall Irma dancing on a table, and Dorothy was singing."

"What about Camilia?"

"No idea." She rolled over and looked at me. "Why?"

"Because sometime in between the stripper, the table dancing, and the karaoke, a man ended up dead in her suite."

Chapter 14

"Sam, it's too early and I'm too hungover for jokes."

"Not joking."

She examined my face for cracks that would indicate I was lying. She didn't find any. "You're serious?"

I nodded.

"Who is he?"

"I have no idea, but he looks familiar." I pulled out my cell phone and swiped until I came to the picture I'd taken of the dead man. I held up the phone.

Nana Jo stared. "That looks like that male sexist jerk from the book reading."

I turned the phone around and took another look. "You're right."

"The little misogynistic toad finally got what's coming to him. He probably insulted the wrong woman."

"Nana Jo! A man is dead."

"True. That's not good, but he's already dead so I'm sure it was a woman who did him in." Nana Jo looked at me. "Was it Camilia?"

"She said no. Said she's never seen him before."

"You believe her?" Nana Jo asked.

"Of course I believe her."

I wasn't very convincing based on the look Nana Jo gave me.

"I mean, I'm sure she didn't kill him. She wouldn't kill him. She wouldn't kill anyone. She's a doctor. They have to take an oath to help people, right?"

"Hmm. Not sure, are you?"

"Why would she? I mean, this is crazy. Why come to North Harbor and commit a murder?"

"Sam, for what it's worth, I agree with you. I don't think she would kill someone. But we don't know anything about her. We only have her word for it that she didn't know the little sexist toad. For all we know maybe she's been having a passionate affair with the man and he followed her here. They got into a fight and she stabbed him. Shot him. How was he killed?"

"No idea." I took a few minutes and shared what little information I knew with her. I also told her about switching back our rooms.

"I'm not saying she did it. I'm just saying we don't know for sure that she didn't do it. We don't know her. We don't know the dead guy. We don't know how he got up to the suite. We don't know anything." Nana Jo forced herself to stand.

"What do we do?"

"Have you called the police?"

I shook my head. "Not yet."

"You'd better get busy. I'm going to finish getting dressed and put on my makeup while you make a few calls."

"Calls? As in plural? Who am I supposed to call?"

"You need to call the police and notify them that there's a dead man in your suite. I'm guessing you should probably call the manager of the hotel. He or she will likely want to know why the police are here. And regardless of whether or not you believe Camilia guilty of murder, you should call Jenna."

I looked puzzled.

"She's going to need a good lawyer. Now, make your calls so we can get busy."

"Get busy doing what?"

"Figuring out who the dead guy is and who killed him."

Chapter 15

I started to dial Detective Brad Pitt of the North Harbor Police Department when something struck me. "Hey, the casino is on tribal land. Do you think Detective Pitt will have jurisdiction here?"

Nana Jo stopped applying her makeup and stepped out of the bathroom to stare at me. "That's a good question. Technically, it's not the United States. Remember what Jenna said when John Cloverton was killed?"

"Not really. Do you?"

"Honestly, no. There was a lot of mumbo jumbo about whether a crime happened on tribal land or not and, if so, was the person a United States citizen or a Native American. Start with Jenna. She'll know who you should call."

My sister isn't a morning person. Even though it was almost six and technically she had to be at work in two hours, she wasn't much more pleasant than when I'd called at two. I got her standard early morning greeting. "Is someone dead?"

"Actually, yeah. That's why I'm calling."

It took her a moment. "What?"

"Someone's dead. Nana Jo said—"

"Sam, this had better not be some sick joke."

"Just because I write murder mysteries doesn't mean I don't take death seriously. I would never joke about—"

"Stop talking and tell me who's dead."

I was so tempted to ask what she wanted me to do. Stop talking? Or tell her who was dead? However, I wasn't sure our siblingship could handle it. Besides, I needed her help. "Look, I don't know who he is. He was some guy who heckled me at the book reading the other day."

"Oscar Pembrook." Nana Jo stuck her head out of the bathroom.

"What?" I asked.

"My brain fog is starting to lift. I just remembered the Toad's name," Nana Jo said.

"What toad?" Jenna asked.

"The heckler guy. The dead man. Nana Jo remembered his name is Oscar Pembrook. Was. His name was Oscar Pembrook," I said.

"Now isn't the time for grammar lessons," Jenna said. "What happened?"

Dr. Patt—Camilia found him in my suite this morning."

"What was he doing in your suite?"

"No idea."

"Have you called the police?"

"Not yet. That'll be my second call, or maybe my third. Who has jurisdiction? The resort is part of the Pontolomas's land. Nana Jo remembered you telling us that the federal government was responsible and we weren't—"

"Crap." Jenna mumbled a few other words but nothing noteworthy. "This is a mess."

"Yep. That's why we called you. Well, one of the reasons."

"Look, call the police. No, call the hotel manager. Or better yet, didn't you say that the guy who gave you the free weekend passes gave Nana Jo his card?"

"Yeah, he did. I ran into him yesterday. His name's Kai Strongbow."

"He's a tribal leader. He should know who to call. But . . . darn it. The federal government will likely be slow. I don't suppose the dead guy was Native American, was he?"

"I don't think so."

"Of course not. That would be too easy. If he were Native American, then the tribal police could handle it. Okay, call Stinky Pitt and get him to come. Tell him you need to talk to him about something. Then call the tribal leader. I'll be there in about an hour."

"Jenna, thanks, I—"

The phone disconnected.

Nana Jo came out of the bathroom. "What did she say?"

I filled her in.

"Okay, I've sent text messages to the girls and told them to meet us in the dining room for breakfast."

"Breakfast? I thought you were so hungover you didn't want to think about food?"

Nana Jo shrugged. "I don't know what that sludge was they sent up, but it's amazing. I feel almost as good as new." She belched. "Almost. Anyway, I ordered one for each of them." She held up her cell.

"Maybe I should send one to Camilia."

"Already done. You call Stinky Pitt and tell him we'd like to treat him to breakfast. That'll get his attention."

"I can't just go downstairs and have breakfast with a dead man in my room. I mean, what if the maid comes in to clean and she sees him?"

"Put the DO NOT DISTURB sign on your door."

"Nana Jo. It's not right. Just because the dead man . . . I

mean, Oscar Pembrook, was a male chauvinist and I didn't like him doesn't mean that I should let him lay on the floor in my suite while I eat breakfast."

"Suit yourself. Call Stinky Pitt and take him up to the suite. Then meet us down in the dining room." Nana Jo grabbed her purse and headed downstairs.

I called. "Detective Pitt, this is Samantha Washington."

"Yeah, whaddya want?"

The English teacher in me cringed, but I swallowed my objections to his abuse of the English language. "I was wondering if you could meet me at the Four Feathers Resort and Casino. I was given a free weekend for myself and friends and I—"

"Free? I hear that place is really swanky."

"Yes, it's very nice. I was just hoping you would come and—"

"You want me to come?"

"Yes, that's why I'm calling. I have something I need to talk to you about. It's very important and I—"

"The plumbing's jacked up at my place and the toilets don't flush. Everything's backed up. Smells like a sewer in here. You got an extra free room?"

"I suppose so, but that's not exactly—"

"Look, if you got a free room, I can be there in twenty minutes."

"Okay, I'll meet you in the lobby." I hung up and stared at the phone. *That did not go at all the way I imagined.*

Twenty minutes later Nana Jo and I were waiting in the lobby for Detective Pitt to arrive. The hotel had redeemed another free room and I had the key in my hand.

"Good Lord, would you look at that?" Nana Jo inclined her head toward the entry doors.

Detective Bradley Pitt walked through the doors of the lobby. He was so over the top, it was almost like looking at a caricature. Detective Pitt and I were roughly the same height, five feet four. He was overweight, although I think he tried to contain it by wearing clothes that were two sizes too small. I can only imagine he thought as long as he could get into the smaller size, it was the right size. He was wrong. His outfits may have been quite stylish in the 1970s and may have fit too. Unfortunately, that wasn't true in the twenty-first century. Today's ensemble consisted of bright orange-and-green-checked polyester pants that just hit the tops of his ankles. His green polyester shirt was too tight and the buttons strained to contain the belly that extended over the top of his white belt. The white belt matched his white patent leather shoes. Like many men who were losing their hair, Detective Pitt parted his remaining hairs on the side and combed them over to cover his bald spot. As the balding area expanded, the part moved closer to his ear. The spectacle that was Detective Pitt needed to be seen to be believed.

"I'm glad you were able to make it, Stinky . . . I mean, Detective Pitt," Nana Jo said.

Nana Jo had been Detective Pitt's teacher in second grade and remembered the kids teasing him by calling him Stinky Pitt. Usually, we only called him by the unfortunate nickname behind his back. Although sometimes he could be a real jerk and we used it to bring his often overinflated ego back down to earth. We tried never to use the nickname in front of his peers on the North Harbor Police Force.

Detective Pitt frowned but must have remembered that he was getting a free weekend at a resort and forced his lips upward instead. "Yeah, it worked out with my plumbing problems."

I saw Nana Jo open her mouth to comment and jabbed her in the ribs. The last thing I needed was thoughts about Detective Pitt's plumbing problems in my head.

"I have something I need to discuss . . . actually, I need to show you. So, I thought we could go upstairs." I didn't wait for a response and walked toward the elevator, confident that Detective Pitt would follow.

He did.

Once we were inside the elevator and alone, I handed him his room key and inserted my key to get to my suite.

"This says I'm on the second floor. Why aren't we stopping?"

"Your room is on the second floor, but mine is on the fourth. You need a special key to be able to get up to four," I said pointedly.

"Well, la-di-da. Is that what you want to show me? Your penthouse suite? You wanna rub my nose in it?"

I ignored his mocking. "When I woke up this morning I found a dead body in my room. That's what I wanted to show you."

The elevator doors opened.

"A dead body? Who is it? Can't you spend one weekend without stumbling across a body?"

This is one of the times when Detective Pitt deserves to be called Stinky.

I unlocked the door and held it open.

"Maybe if you'd stop talking, you can find the answers to those questions." Nana Jo walked past Stinky Pitt and entered the room.

Detective Pitt sighed and entered.

For a few moments we all stood in the living room and gaped. The room looked the same as it had before I left except for the fact that there was no dead body lying on the floor. He was gone.

Chapter 16

Detective Pitt turned to me. "Where's the dead guy?"

"I have no idea. He was here earlier," I said.

Detective Pitt snorted. "In my experience corpses don't get up and walk away."

I stared at the floor and then looked at Nana Jo.

"What's happened? I don't understand. He was here. I saw him."

"Do you still have the picture?" Nana Jo said.

I pulled out my phone and scrolled until I found the picture and showed it to Detective Pitt.

He glanced at my phone for several moments and then handed it back. "Look, I'm sure you *thought* he was dead, but obviously you were wrong. Or he'd still be here. Dead guys don't just up and leave. So, what probably happened was you were here partying and some guy passed out on your floor. Maybe you didn't check his pulse and so you *assumed* he was dead. You go scurrying to your grandmother and you get me to come out here."

I started to interrupt, but he held up a hand.

"I'm not saying you did anything wrong. I mean, *amateurs*

make mistakes. You thought he was dead. You called the police. Fortunately for you, I needed a place to stay for the weekend, so I was willing to come. If I were working, or if you got another policeman who wasn't as accommodating as me, you could be charged."

"Charged? With what?" Nana Jo asked.

"Wasting police time can result in a fine or imprisonment for up to six months," Detective Pitt said.

"Why is it that whenever we meet, you're always threatening to arrest a member of my family?" Jenna said.

I'd been so shocked, I hadn't heard the elevator or the door open. I'd left the spare key to my room at the desk for Jenna.

Detective Pitt scowled. "Counselor. Don't tell me you're a part of this farce too."

"Detective Pitt, I'm not going to justify your comments by responding to them. Instead, I'm simply going to remind you that my sister and my grandmother have helped you solve murders countless times in the past. Even a murder where you were involved." She paused.

A red flush rose up the detective's neck. He looked as though he would choke.

I almost felt sorry for him. Almost. Jenna was a powerful defense attorney who knew how to go for the jugular. Her ability had gained her the nickname of the Pit Bull.

"So, it would behoove you to listen and be a bit more open-minded," Jenna said.

Detective Pitt sputtered, "What am I supposed to do without a body? No body, no murder."

Jenna turned from Detective Pitt to me.

"He was here. I have no idea what happened."

"I'm going to my room. If you find the body . . . call me." Detective Pitt marched out the door.

Now that Detective Pitt was gone, Jenna turned her granite gaze to me. "Sam, if this is some sick joke, I'm going to be the next to walk out. I can't believe I'm saying this, but you better have a dead body."

"He was here." I showed her the phone.

"Who is he?"

"Oscar Pembrook, I told you—"

"I know his name. I'm asking, who he was?" Jenna said.

I shrugged.

"It's a long story. The girls are waiting in the dining room. Come down and get breakfast and we can get started figuring out who killed that guy."

"First, let's make sure that Detective Pitt isn't right and that he isn't walking around here somewhere. Did either of you ask for him at the front desk?"

Nana Jo and I stared at each other for a few moments.

"Of course we didn't ask for him at the front desk. He's dead!" Nana Jo said. Then she turned and walked out. "I'll meet you two downstairs."

Jenna looked as though she wanted to eat me alive. Despite the fact that I had at least twenty pounds on my older sister, I knew she was wiry and could probably take me down in less than a minute. So I resorted to the technique that had saved me from her wrath from childhood. I ran.

Downstairs in the dining room Ruby Mae had secured a large booth back in a quiet corner, away from the masses. Jenna was the last to arrive, and the booth was so large there was still room for at least one more person. When Detective Pitt sauntered in I nearly choked.

"Great. We're all here. Let's place our orders and then we can discuss this unfortunate situation." Nana Jo waved a hand, and a nice girl who called Ruby Mae Grammy took our orders while another man dressed in a chef's apron brought out two platters of pastries and two large carafes of coffee.

Frank's ring music started up on my phone, "At Last" by Etta James, and his picture flashed up on the screen. I immediately sent the call to voicemail.

"Interesting choice for your fiancé's ring music," Camilia said.

"It's an inside joke." I sipped my water and prayed the heat that I felt rising into my face would go away quickly.

"I think you should change it to 'Save a Horse (Ride a—)' "

"Irma!" we yelled.

Irma swallowed the thought and coughed.

"Wow. All of this is free?" Detective Pitt asked.

I nodded.

"Almost worth listening to your crazy—"

"Detective Pitt," Nana Jo said.

The detective took a sip of his coffee. When he looked up he caught sight of Camilia. He gasped and stared.

"Who do we have here?" Dr. Camilia Patterson asked.

"I'm sorry, Dr. Patterson, this is Detective Bradley Pitt of the North Harbor Police. Detective Pitt has been kind enough to help us with several difficult situations in the past, and allowed us to assist in an informal capacity with some of his investigations."

"Detective Pitt, this is Frank's mother, Dr. Camilia Patterson," I said.

Camilia extended her hand and flashed a smile. "Please call me Camilia."

Detective Pitt was frozen and stared at the hand for several beats until I prodded him out of his stupor with a small poke to the ribs. He put down his cup and shook Camilia's hand. "Pleased to meet you. Call me Brad."

Call me Brad?

"Alright, now that the introductions are over, let's get this party started. Sam, do you want to tell everyone what happened?" Nana Jo pulled out her tablet and started to take notes.

I relayed the revised edition of what happened. The only variance to the truth was the fact that I claimed to have found the body instead of Camilia. Instead of her calling me, I called her. Everyone except Detective Pitt knew the truth. Other than a slight flush from Camilia and an accusatory glance from Jenna, no one else muttered one word.

"Now, Sam asked Detective Pitt here for the obvious reason that he is a policeman. However, we asked Jenna here because there's a question of jurisdiction. Jenna, perhaps you could explain?"

My sister wasn't a coffee drinker. She was a tea snob and took a sip from a cup of English breakfast tea before she started. "As we learned when we were dealing with the murder of John Cloverton, American Indians are United States citizens and therefore subject to federal, tribal, and state laws. However, for major crimes committed on federal Indian reservations, federal laws apply."

Camilia raised a tentative hand. "Excuse me, but who is . . . was John Cloverton?"

Detective Pitt blushed.

"He was a member of the Pontolomas Tribal Council and was running for mayor but was murdered. The question came up about which laws he was subject to." Nana Jo omitted any connection between John Cloverton and Detective Pitt. She also didn't mention that Detective Pitt was accused of the murder. A point that wasn't lost on the detective, if the flush that was now engulfing his ears was considered.

The servers brought our food, and for the next few minutes we ate in silence. Then Nana Jo asked Jenna to continue.

Frank's ring music started up on my phone and I sent it to voicemail again.

"The key difference between this murder and Cloverton was that Cloverton was a Native American but his murder wasn't committed on tribal land. I think in the case of this man . . ." Jenna turned to me.

"Oscar Pembrook," I supplied the name.

"He wasn't a member of the Pontolomas?" Jenna asked.

"I don't know, but I don't think so." I looked at Nana Jo.

"I doubt it. Based on the way Mr. Strongbow talked to him, I'd say no."

"We can't leave anything to chance. We should probably find out for sure. I'll talk to Kai Strongbow."

"Oh, darn. I was hoping I could talk to him. He sounds cute," Irma said.

"Josephine pointed him out to me yesterday and he's handsome. I wouldn't mind talking to him myself." Dorothy took a sip of coffee.

"Maybe that would be better. You could tell him you want to do a story about all of the good projects that the Pontolomas are doing for their community. You're still writing articles for Jacob's magazine, right?"

Jacob Friedman was Dorothy's great-nephew. He owned a regional magazine. Dorothy graduated from Northwestern University with a degree in journalism. She hadn't written anything in decades, but Jacob gave her press credentials that she used to get access to a best-selling author at a book festival. Dorothy stretched her journalistic muscles, and working on that article had reignited her passion for writing.

"Just remember, your goal is to get information on Pembrook, not getting a date with Strongbow," Nana Jo said.

"Fortunately, I'm great at multitasking," Dorothy joked.

"Ruby Mae, could you ask some of your relatives who work here what they know about Pembrook?" I asked.

Ruby Mae nodded. "I'm already on it. As soon as Josephine told me we had a murder to investigate, I made arrangements to talk to them. In fact, I'll be meeting my goddaughter as soon as we're done here."

"Perfect." Nana Jo typed that into her tablet.

"Jenna, maybe you could investigate the legal side and find out the jurisdiction. When you say *federal* is that the FBI?" I asked.

"Yes. The FBI works with the tribal police," Jenna said.

"Detective Pitt, could you make friends with the tribal police? Maybe, just find out if they found a body?" I asked.

Detective Pitt looked as though he wanted to say no.

Camilia flashed a big smile and said, "Maybe I could go with you. I'm a doctor, so maybe you could say you were showing me around and I wondered if they had a forensic laboratory or something like that?" She looked from Detective Pitt to me.

I stared at Camilia. *Was she flirting with Stinky Pitt?*

"Earth to Sam," Nana Jo said.

"Yes, of course. I'm sorry. I was just . . . Yes. That would be great." I turned to Detective Pitt. "That is, if you wouldn't mind taking Camilia around with you?"

Detective Pitt grinned. "Love to help."

"Great." Nana Jo wrote on her tablet.

"What about me?" Irma asked.

"Irma, you're so good at getting people to share information with you. I was hoping you could talk to one of the men who work at the hotel and find out how Oscar Pembrook got here. Was he a hotel guest? If so, how did he get up to the top floor?" I said.

"I already know that," Irma said.

We all turned to stare.

"What? How?"

"Josephine showed us the picture you sent her on your phone. I recognized him." Irma said.

"You did? Who was he?" I asked.

"Oscar Pembrook was an accountant. His firm won the right to audit the books for the Four Feathers. I have an accountant friend who told me all about him." Based on the way Irma preened, it was clear the friend was male.

"Wow. That was fast," I said.

"I've heard that before," Irma said.

"I didn't mean . . . I just meant that you were on the ball . . . I mean—"

"You should stop talking now. You're just making it worse," Jenna said.

"I mean, last night you were . . . drun . . . intoxi . . . when could you possibly?"

I should have listened to Jenna and stopped talking.

"After the party, I went to the bar and that's when I met Richard. We hit it off immediately. He's such a snazzy dresser. You can just look at his clothes and know that he spent a fortune on them. Nothing gauche. Just every detail attended to."

"Richard?" I said.

"Richard Pembrook. Oscar was his cousin."

"Did your friend know anything else about him?" Nana Jo asked.

"We didn't spend much time talking, if you know what I mean." Irma laughed. "But he did say that Oscar's wife would be at the top of the police's list of suspects."

"Why?" Nana Jo asked.

"He said Oscar had been catting around on her and she'd had enough, but she signed some prenuptial agreement so she wouldn't get a dime if she divorced him," Irma said.

I turned to my sister. "I don't suppose there's a way to find out anything about that prenuptial agreement and whether or not Oscar Pembrook had a will?"

"The will is probably filed with the court, but the prenup wouldn't be. The lawyer who wrote it would have a copy in his files. Both couples should have a copy in their possession. That's about it, but I'll see if I can find out who the attorney was. Maybe I'll get lucky. I can check."

"Great." I turned to Irma. "You've been really helpful. I don't suppose you found out anything else?" I asked.

"Like I said, we didn't talk much. It was early and we were both exhausted." Irma giggled.

Dorothy rolled her eyes. Nana Jo looked like she was about two seconds from tossing her tablet at her.

"He did mention something about a man named Max Manning. I think Pembrook beat his firm out for the Four Feathers accounting job and he was furious. We're going to see each other later, and I will do whatever I have to do to get information out of him."

"Do you want me to see what I can find out about this Manning person?" Nana Jo asked.

I nodded. "That would be great."

"What will you be doing?" Nana Jo asked.

"I'm going to have a massage," I said.

Chapter 17

The table was silent, and everyone stared at me until I explained that I recognized the robe Oscar Pembrook was wearing as one of the ultraexpensive ones that were only used by the spa. With any luck maybe someone would remember him and could provide a little information. It wasn't much, but it was a starting point. I had a lot of thinking to do and my mind was divided.

Frank called again and I sent it to voicemail.

We finished breakfast and went our separate ways. Everyone except Nana Jo and Jenna. They stayed at the table and stared at me.

"What?" I asked.

"You're going to get a massage?" Jenna asked.

"Didn't you have one yesterday?" Nana Jo stared at me.

"And why aren't you taking Frank's calls?" Jenna asked. "Did you two have a fight?"

"No. Of course not. We didn't have a fight. I was busy, that's all. I'll call him back . . . later."

"Hmm." Jenna squinted at me and sipped her tea.

"What's bothering you?" Nana Jo asked.

"Nothing. What makes you think anything is bothering me? It's been a stressful few months. I've been promoting my first book, planning a wedding, getting acquainted with my soon-to-be mother-in-law, and now I've got to figure out who murdered some strange man."

They both stared at me. As a former teacher, I understood the power of silence. Most people couldn't stand silence and needed to fill it with something, but I was determined to wait them out. The silence felt like an hour. A glance at my phone told me it was ninety seconds.

"All couples have fights. If you two had a fight, you should talk to him, not avoid him," Nana Jo said.

"We didn't have a fight. I just . . . I don't know. I need to focus on figuring out who killed Oscar Pembrook."

"You don't have to find the murderer. As far as the police are concerned, there hasn't even been a murder. There's no dead body," Nana Jo said.

"Especially if finding the killer is going to come between you and Frank," Jenna added. "You could just walk away."

"But I saw him. He was dead. I mean, he *is* dead. Just because his body's disappeared doesn't mean he isn't dead. What happens when they find his body?"

Almost in unison Nana Jo and Jenna shrugged.

"When they find his body the North Harbor Police, the tribal police, or the FBI will do the job they get paid to do. They will hunt down his murderer." Jenna sipped her tea. "You don't have to solve every problem or every murder you run across."

"You don't think I should get involved?" I asked.

"Not if it's stressing you out," Jenna said.

"Or coming between you and your fiancé Now, what's wrong?" Nana Jo reached out a hand and squeezed mine.

"How did Oscar Pembrook get up to the fourth floor?

And how did he get in Camilia's suite?" I looked from Jenna to Nana Jo.

"Good questions. You should ask Camilia," Jenna said.

"I did. She said she doesn't know. She swears that she'd never seen him before and didn't invite him upstairs." I took a few minutes and shared that she was up for a prestigious promotion and if word got out that she was involved in a murder, it could ruin her career.

"If her career is ruined, that's not your fault," Jenna said.

"But I feel responsible. She was only here at the Four Feathers because I invited her. Plus, that suite was supposed to be my room. If I'd kept the room, she wouldn't have been involved at all," I explained.

"Still not your fault," Jenna said.

"Wait, do you think the guy was up there somehow because he was looking for you?" Nana Jo asked.

I shrugged. "I have no idea. I can't understand why he would even know that I was here. I certainly can't imagine why he would bother to come to my room, naked, wearing only a bathrobe."

"He must have come for either you or Camilia," Jenna said.

"What does Frank think?" Nana Jo asked.

"I haven't told him."

"Why not? It's his mother. He should know," Nana Jo said.

"I know, but I'm just not sure it's my place to tell him. I mean, I'm hoping that Camilia tells him. She's his mother. She's the one who found the body."

"So, you're going to avoid his calls and hope that Camilia tells him?" Nana Jo shook her head.

"I don't know. I haven't figured it out yet. I'm a horrible liar and I don't want to lie to Frank. So I'm trying to figure out what I should do."

"You need to figure it out soon. It's not good to start your marriage by withholding information from your husband," Jenna said.

"I won't lie to him. And I don't like the idea of keeping secrets from Frank, but . . . this isn't my secret to tell."

"Frank isn't going to take kindly to finding out about this from someone else. North Harbor's a small town and news like this is going to spread," Nana Jo said.

"You're right. I'm going to talk to Camilia. If she wants to tell him, great. If she doesn't, then I'll tell him." I took a deep breath. It felt good to make a decision, even if that decision might ruin the relationship that I was building with Camilia. We weren't exactly BFFs, but at least we were on a first-name basis.

We talked for a few minutes longer, but I still wasn't sure what I should do. Jenna had to be in court and left. Nana Jo also left.

It was still early and the spa wasn't open yet. Nana Jo always said that writing helped me figure things out subconsciously, so I found a quiet corner, pulled out my notepad, and took a mental trip back in time.

"Beatrice, I love this tennis dress." Lady Clara spun around and struck a pose with her tennis racket over her shoulder. "Don't you, Jean?"

"Yes, it's very easy to move around and the fabric is wonderful," Lady Groverton said.

"Thank you. Excuse me," Beatrice mumbled and then hurried out of the room.

"I love the designs, but I think the skirts should be

a bit shorter." Beryl pulled up the button of her skirt to expose more of her leg. "What do you think, Dilly?"

"Hmm. Yes, I'm all in favor of more leg." Dilly laughed.

Jean Groverton flushed. She grabbed her plate and took a seat at the end of the table.

Lady Clara put down her tennis racket, picked up her plate, and started to fill it.

Peter Covington leaned closer to Clara and whispered, "Doesn't look like your matchmaking is working out quite the way you planned."

Lady Clara poked him in the ribs and took her seat.

Lord William sat at the table with his head behind his newspaper. He shook the newspaper and mumbled, "Country's going to hell in a handbasket."

"What was that, dear?" Lady Elizabeth asked.

"Third robbery in three months. Lord Montague got hit this time. Someone is breaking into estates and making off with not only the silver and the family jewels, but this . . . blackguard boldly stole the paintings off the wall." Lord William thumped the paper.

"Poor Lavinia. She must be beside herself," Lady Elizabeth said. "I need to send her a card."

Lord William turned to Peter. "I want to know what the police are doing about this. Folks aren't safe in their own homes. Protection. That's what the police get paid for."

"Uncle William, those robberies aren't Peter's fault," Lady Clara said.

"She's right, William." Lady Elizabeth poured tea.

"I didn't say they were. Certainly not his fault. I just want to know what's being done." Lord William turned to Detective Inspector Covington. "Sorry, I didn't mean any offense. I just meant—"

Peter held up a hand. "No offense taken. No need to apologize." He took a deep breath. "I assure you, we're just as frustrated as you are."

"Do you have any idea who's behind it?" Lady Elizabeth asked.

"Probably some gang of depraved hoodlums. That's what," Lord William said.

Lord Dilworth dropped his fork. "Sorry. I'm all thumbs this morning."

Thompkins had been standing nearby and quickly hurried to pick up the utensil and provide a replacement.

"Ha!" Max Chesterton laughed. "Have the police noticed any patterns?"

"You mean like a derelict who's been hanging about at all of the locations?" Lady Mildred asked.

"No. No. Nothing of that type." Max Chesterton grinned. "I was thinking more along the lines of an insider."

Lord Dilworth choked on his coffee.

Lady Groverton patted him on the back, but he waved her away.

"Something caught in your throat, Dilworth?" Max Chesterton grinned.

"You can all rest assured that the police are doing everything possible to locate the thieves. We will use every tool in our arsenal to catch and prosecute the criminals," Peter said. "However, I'm not at liberty to disclose any specifics."

"Right. Right. Well . . ."

Beatrice burst back into the room. Her cheeks were red and her eyes shot flames. She marched over to Max Chesterton and pointed. "You. You stole my designs."

For a few moments the room was completely silent.

"Beatrice!" Mrs. Smythe said.

Mrs. Covington gasped.

Detective Peter Covington stood and moved around to his cousin. "Bea, what are you talking about?"

"Him! He stole my designs." Beatrice pointed.

Lady Clara came up behind her. "Aren't those your designs in your hand, dear?"

Max Chesterton stared at Beatrice with a snide smile on his face but said nothing.

Beatrice held up the pages. "Yes. These are mine! He stole them, or tried to steal them. I want him arrested. I want to press charges."

Lady Clara frowned and turned to Peter. "But you have your designs. So he couldn't have stolen them."

"He did steal them. I went to my room to get the drawings and they weren't where I left them. I knew someone had to have taken them and I knew who." She glared at Chesterton, who ignored her.

"Okay, but where did you get them?" Detective Peter Covington asked.

"In his room." She pointed and spit fire like a dragon.

"You searched his room?" Detective Peter Covington asked.

"Yes, and I was right. I found them in his suitcase. He stole them." Beatrice glared.

Lady Elizabeth stood up. "Perhaps you all might find it easier to sort this out in private. Why don't you use the study?"

Beatrice turned and marched out of the room.

Detective Inspector Covington waited while Max Chesterton stood and sauntered out as though he didn't have a care in the world.

At the door Detective Inspector Covington turned to Lady Elizabeth. "As the mistress of the house, I would appreciate it if you would join us."

"Of course." Lady Elizabeth walked out of the dining room.

Lady Mildred burst into tears.

Torn between her mother and her fiancé, Lady Clara sat and provided what comfort she could to her mother.

In the wood-paneled study, Max Chesterton chose the most comfortable chair, which normally would have been occupied by Lord William. He sat back, crossed his leg over his knee, and gazed at Beatrice and Detective Inspector Covington as though he knew a secret joke.

"Beatrice you've leveled some very strong accusations against Mr. Chesterton—"

"They're all true," Beatrice cut off her cousin.

"I was going to say, we have yet to hear from Mr. Chesterton." He turned to glance at the man, who looked as though he hadn't a care in the world. "Do you have anything to say for yourself?"

"No. I don't." He laughed.

"Mr. Chesterton, I don't think you understand. You're being accused of theft. Are you denying that you took the drawings?" Detective Inspector Covington asked.

"I can hardly be accused of theft when Miss Smythe has the drawings in her possession. Now, can I?" he asked.

Shocked, Lady Elizabeth asked, "You don't deny taking them?"

"It's rather a complicated situation." He smiled. "You see, I wanted to see the designs, and because Miss Smythe wasn't inclined to show them to me, I made other arrangements," he said.

"You stole them," Beatrice said.

Max Chesterton shook his head. "I did not."

"You deny taking the drawings?" Detective Inspector Covington asked.

"I do," Max Chesterton said.

"How can you deny taking them when I found them in your room?" Beatrice said.

"I wanted to see the drawings, but you wouldn't show them to me. So, I made arrangements to see them."

"You stole them," Beatrice said.

"I assure you that the person who gave me the drawings did not steal them."

"You're both a liar and a thief. I did not give permission for you to see them. I would never have given you permission," Beatrice said.

Detective Inspector Covington squinted. "Who acquired the drawings for you?"

"The other B in B&B Fashions. Beryl." Max Chesterton smiled broadly.

"Beryl!" Beatrice screamed. "She wouldn't. She couldn't. She would never do that. She knows how I feel."

"I assure you that she would. She could. And she did." Max Chesterton laughed. "Go ahead and ask her if you don't believe me." He paused and gazed at Beatrice. "Ah . . . I think you know that I'm telling the truth."

Beatrice fumed.

"May I ask why you wanted to see the designs so badly that you were willing to go to such lengths to do so?" Lady Elizabeth asked.

"Beatrice is an excellent designer. I've told her so, many times. She understands women and women's fashions. Plus, she has an eye for color and cut that is fresh and flattering. These designs can put British fashions back in the spotlight and could challenge the top French designers. The designs are good, but B&B lacks the funding, the business sense, and the connections to move into the top tier of the industry. I intend to buy B&B Fashions and merge them with the House of Chesterton and once again sit atop the fashion pinnacle."

"Never. I will never sell my designs to you," Beatrice said.

Max Chesterton smiled. "I have already made a deal with your sister. She was more than willing to consider my offer. You'll design for the House of Chesterton or you will not design at all."

"I'll kill you before I allow you to steal my designs. I'll kill you." Beatrice burst into tears and ran from the room.

Chapter 18

"Samantha!"

I glanced up into the eyes of my fiancé.

"Frank, what are you doing here?"

"Good to see you too," Frank said.

I stood up and kissed him. "I'm sorry. It is good to see you. I was just surprised. I was writing and thousands of miles away."

Frank stared into my eyes. "Is that all?"

I wasn't able to maintain the eye contact and looked away.

"Something's wrong. What is it? Is it my mom? Is she giving you a hard time? Because I can have a talk with her. She's—"

"It's not your mom . . . not really." I took a deep breath and made a decision. "Let's go upstairs."

I took Frank by the hand to the elevator. When we got to the suite I opened the door.

He walked in and looked around. "Wow. This is impressive." He walked over to the window and looked out onto the nature preserve. "Was this for all of you? Or just you?"

"Just me. But I didn't sleep here last night."

He turned to stare, and his brow furrowed.

"I switched rooms with your mom."

The lines relaxed and he released the breath he'd been holding. "Okay, so my mom stayed here."

"You'd better have a seat."

He sat, and I told him everything, from the stripper to the early morning call from his mom and the dead body. I pulled out my phone and showed him the picture.

"I don't like this. I don't like you staying here. Why was he here? How did he get in here?"

I shook my head. "No idea."

"And Mom doesn't know?"

"She says she doesn't."

He frowned. "You don't believe her?"

"It's not that. I don't think she would lie about it. Not deliberately anyway, but . . . she'd been drinking and maybe . . ."

"You think she was drunk and just doesn't remember inviting a strange man to her room?"

"I don't know. I barely know her. I just don't see how he could have gotten in otherwise. You have to have a special key to even get the elevator to stop on this floor."

He rubbed the back of his neck. "There are ways around the key situation. He could have stolen her key. There are other suites on this floor. Maybe he's in one of those rooms. Or maybe he stole the key from housekeeping."

"But why? Why come in here? And where is the body now?"

"Good questions. You're sure he was dead?"

"I didn't check for a pulse, but he was cold and stiff and your mom said she checked."

"Okay, what else?"

"Nothing. That's it."

"Why were you avoiding me?"

"I didn't want to be the one to tell you all this. I wanted

your mom to tell you. It was her story. Not mine. I didn't want to lie, and I knew that if I talked to you, I'd tell. So . . ."

"So you didn't want to talk to me."

I nodded.

Frank pulled me close. He tilted up my chin so I was looking him in the eyes. "I love you. I always will. No matter what." He took a deep breath. "At the risk of sounding like the world's biggest hypocrite, I don't want us to have secrets. Sam, the things that I did before we met. The things that I did in the military and for the government, those aren't my secrets. There's national security involved and it could be dangerous."

"I understand."

"There are bad, ugly, horrible things that happen in the world every day. I wish I could forget it, but I don't want to keep secrets from you either."

"Frank, it's okay. I know there are things you did that you are sworn to secrecy about. I don't want or need to know. But if you need to talk about it . . . about anything, I'm here."

He hugged me. "Alright, we agree. No secrets unless it involves national security."

I laughed. "Agreed. Now, you should talk to your mother. I'm going to the spa."

"It sounds like even though there isn't a body, you're investigating this murder."

"We have to. Eventually, the body is bound to show up, and when it does Stinky Pitt is going to come here . . . and speaking of Stinky Pitt . . . there's something else I should tell you."

"Don't tell me he wants to arrest my mom for murder," Frank joked. "He's tried to arrest you, your grandmother, your stepfather, and Dawson for murder. Now he's going for my family?"

"Not exactly." I paused and looked for the right words.

None came. "I think Stinky . . . um, Detective Pitt is smitten." I waited for my words to sink in. "And I think your mom might actually—"

"Don't. Please do not tell me that my mom likes Stinky Pitt." He paused. "My mom? Dr. Camilia Patterson? Uptight. Conservative. A woman who refuses to leave the house unless her purse and shoes match? A woman who won't go to workout at the gym unless her underwear and socks match?"

I raised a brow and shrugged. "It seemed that way to me. They were sort of making goo-goo eyes at each other at breakfast, and she volunteered to go with him to talk to the tribal police."

Frank stared for several long moments. Then I noticed his lips twitch. Before long he couldn't contain the twitch and his lips were in a full upward curl. Then he burst out laughing. "Now that I want to see."

"You aren't upset?"

"Why would I be? She's an adult and free to date whoever she wants. I love the idea of my mom dating. She works too much, and as far as I know her only hobby is meddling in my life. It would be good for her to get away from the hospital and all of the social obligations that she does because they're expected for someone in her position to do."

"But?"

"But I can't believe that Dr. Camilia Patterson would ever be caught dead wearing polyester and I've never seen Stinky Pitt wearing anything else." Frank laughed.

"I know. They do seem like complete opposites. Your mom is pâté, caviar, and champagne and Stinky Pitt is . . ."

"Liverwurst, brats, and beer?" Frank chuckled. "You know, I'm sure my mom must have had a hot dog at some point in her life, but if she has, I've never seen it."

"Didn't you have cookouts when you were a kid?"

"Sure, when I went to my friends' houses. We had hamburgers and hot dogs like normal people. My mom didn't believe in eating processed meat. The one barbecue we had, she had the cook prepare filet mignon, grilled salmon, lobster tail, roasted corn, prosciutto-wrapped asparagus, and grilled strawberry shortcake."

"Fancy-schmancy. Although that grilled strawberry shortcake sounds delish."

Frank grinned. "Actually, it was all very tasty and the grilled strawberry shortcake was awesome. I'll have to make it for you some time. I played around until I figured out how to re-create it."

"And I bet you didn't just re-create it. You took it to the next level."

He grinned.

Cooking was Frank's love language and I loved that about him. I also loved that I got to enjoy the results.

He glanced at his watch. "So, I need to find my mom and have a conversation with her and then make my way back to the restaurant before the lunch crowd comes. What's my assignment?"

I didn't know much about what Frank did in the military, but he had connections that were able to get information that no one else could. At least, not without a court order.

"Do you think you could find out about Oscar Pembrook's finances?" I shared the information we'd learned from Irma. "Money is a good motive for murder."

Frank promised to get onto it. Then he kissed me. "Are you sure you want to stay here? I'm sure they would move you down to another room. I don't like the idea of you being here alone if there's a killer with a key to this room."

"Nana Jo is moving into the other bedroom."

"I pity the fool who would try to break in here with your grandmother and her peacemaker," Frank joked.

"Damn straight."

My back was to the door, so I didn't see Nana Jo enter until she spoke.

Nana Jo wheeled her suitcase into the room. "Do I need to go back downstairs? I haven't turned in my key yet."

"No. I'm leaving." Frank kissed me and headed for the door. "I don't suppose you know where I might find my mother?"

"Last time I saw her, she was twirling her hair and giggling like a schoolgirl while Stinky Pitt tried to suck in his gut and strutted through the casino like a pasty-faced polyester demigod."

Frank left in search of his mother and Nana Jo put her bags away. While I tried to avoid looking at the spot where Oscar Pembrook had lain.

"Let's go visit that spa," Nana Jo said.

Chapter 19

Nina was busy when we arrived, but she was finishing up with her client and would be available shortly. I took a seat while Nana Jo stayed at the counter chatting with the receptionist.

One of the best things about sleuthing with Nana Jo and her friends was that people talked to them. Ruby Mae could sit down anywhere and within ten minutes someone would sit down next to her and start talking. She said she had one of those faces that people wanted to talk to. Dorothy had been a journalist and not only knew how to get people to talk but, like Irma, she was a flirt. Men loved talking to both Irma and Dorothy. The girls also had an extensive network of family and friends that they could tap into for information when needed. Today Nana Jo was working the girls at the counter. It wasn't long before she had the two girls laughing and talking.

"Have you seen a little toad-faced man named Oscar Pembrook?" Nana Jo asked.

Both giggled. "OMG. He does look like a toad, doesn't he?"

One of the girls glanced over her shoulder and then leaned

forward and whispered something to Nana Jo. I couldn't hear the conversation, but based on my grandmother's facial expressions and body language, it must have been quite juicy. After a few minutes a tall, thin, well-preserved woman came from the back.

Nana Jo stepped aside so she wasn't blocking the way. One of the girls cashed out the woman while the other made eye contact with Nana Jo. When the woman was done Nina came out, and Nana Jo and I both followed her to the back.

When we were in the same small room that I'd occupied yesterday, Nina turned and asked, "Now, what can I do for you both?"

"Was that Mrs. Pembrook who just left?" Nana Jo asked.

Nina glanced from me to Nana Jo and then nodded. "Yes."

"This is going to sound really strange, but we're trying to find out if her husband, Oscar Pembrook, had a massage yesterday," I said.

Nina folded her arms across her chest. "I'm not supposed to talk about our guests."

"You won't get in trouble for talking to us. We promise no one will ever know where the information came from," Nana Jo said.

"We believe something's happened to him and we're hoping you could help us." I reached out and touched her arm.

"Something happened like what?" Nina asked.

"Sam, let me see your phone," Nana Jo said.

I unlocked the screen and passed it to her.

Nana Jo swiped until she found the picture and then showed it to Nina.

Nina stared and then stumbled. She put her hand over her mouth and her eyes widened. "Is he . . . dead?"

"Looks that way, but we don't know for sure, and we

can't find his body. So, maybe he was just unconscious and in need of help," Nana Jo lied.

"He's wearing one of those robes that you only have here in the spa, so we were hoping that maybe if you knew something about him, it might help us find him," I said.

"We just want to help," Nana Jo said.

Nina thought for several moments, then sat down. "He was here yesterday, but . . . I don't know if I should say anything because . . ."

"Because he wasn't alone. I get it, dear." Nana Jo patted her shoulder.

"We saw Mrs. Pembrook leaving. Were they maybe having a couples massage?" I asked.

A flush rose up Nina's face, which surprised me. The couples massage was advertised in the list of services that the spa provided. Based on my one contact with Oscar Pembrook, I could easily see him being completely inappropriate in front of the masseuse.

"It's okay to tell us. Did Oscar do something he shouldn't have?" I asked.

"No. That's not it," Nina said. "I don't know that I should . . . he specifically said he'd see that I was fired if I breathed one word to anyone."

Dear God, what had he done?

"We assure you that you will not get fired," Nana Jo said. "Did he get fresh with you?"

"Oh no. I mean, he pinched my butt, but I'm used to that. I just made sure the hot oil I used on him was extra-hot."

"Good for you."

"They didn't . . . get amorous in front of you?" I asked.

Her flush deepened, and I knew I'd hit the nail on the head.

"Good Lord, that must have left you with nightmares.

You poor thing. We'll never tell. I guess they couldn't wait until they were alone. Some couples are—"

"They did get . . . what you said. Amorous. But that's not the problem. I just stepped out. The problem is . . . the woman."

"Mrs. Pembrook?" I asked.

"That's the problem. The woman wasn't Mrs. Pembrook." Nina looked from Nana Jo to me and then back to Nana Jo. "The woman he was with was Mrs. Manning."

Chapter 20

"That low-down dirty toad-faced, two-timing slug." Nana Jo and I walked down the gravel path behind the spa.

"Who is Mrs. Manning?" I asked.

"Irma mentioned the name this morning. Afterward I Googled *Pembrook* and *Manning* and found out that Maxwell Manning is the head of Manning and Manning accounting firm. He and Pembrook used to be in business together. The firm was called Pembrook and Manning, but then Pembrook did some dirty dealing that got Manning booted out."

"Of his own firm?"

Nana Jo nodded. "I haven't had a chance to find out how he did it yet. But the two split up and Manning went into business with a cousin or someone and started Manning and Manning. The two firms have been in fierce competition ever since. Up until recently Manning and Manning had the Four Feathers account. A few days ago Pembrook outbid his old partner and got the account."

"Ahh. That explains why he didn't want to cross Kai Strongbow," I said. "Was it a lucrative account?"

"You bet your bippy it was. The Four Feathers casino alone

makes nearly a billion dollars every year. I don't know how accountants get paid, but I'll bet it was enough to afford expensive bathrobes," Nana Jo said. "I need to do some more research. I've got a call in to my friend the research librarian. He should have some information by the end of the day."

Nana Jo and I walked the same paths that I walked yesterday. Hard to believe it was less than twenty-four hours since I'd walked through here and run into Kai Strongbow. No such luck today. Instead, Nana Jo and I observed bunnies, deer, and pheasants. When we got to the footbridge that I'd taken yesterday. I was engrossed in thought until Nana Jo grabbed my wrist.

"Is that what I think it is?" Nana Jo pointed.

I followed her finger. Lying on the rocks was a figure in a white robe. It was face down in the water, but I didn't need to see the face to know that we'd found Oscar Pembrook's body. Again.

Chapter 21

This time we didn't take a chance of the body disappearing. Nana Jo stayed to keep an eye on Oscar Pembrook while I went for help.

I knew from experience that there were cameras everywhere throughout the casino. With any luck one of them would have picked up footage of the person who dumped Pembrook's body in the stream. From traveling to the casino with Nana Jo and the girls I also knew that all of the workers had radios and the ability to call for help. I rushed over to the first person I found wearing a Four Feathers uniform and told them there was an accident outside and someone was injured. *No need to mention a dead body yet.*

Within seconds six security guards swarmed the area.

I quickly explained that my grandmother was outside waiting for them while I came in for help. Then I led the small army of security guards outside to the footbridge.

This time Oscar Pembrook hadn't moved. He was still lying face down in the stream.

A couple of the security personnel looked as though they would lose their breakfast, while a few who were more seasoned took the lead in taking care of the body. The others were directed to close down the footpath.

I phoned Stinky Pitt and alerted him to the fact that Oscar Pembrook's body had washed up . . . literally . . . in the stream. He grumbled a bit but said he and Camilia were on their way.

It sure didn't take him long to get on a first-name basis with Dr. Patterson.

Moments later I heard a commotion as the security guards tried to restrain Stinky Pitt from accessing the path.

"Listen here, you rent-a-cop. I'm the real deal, and either you let me through or you'll find yourself behind bars, and I mean the iron ones," Detective Pitt said.

I hurried over to the gentleman who seemed to be the head of the tribal police and suggested that unless Oscar Pembrook was a member of the Pontolomas, perhaps it would be a good idea to cooperate with the local police until the federal government could be called. I wasn't sure if any of that was accurate or not, but I counted on the desire to pass the buck. If this wasn't a tribal murder, the sooner they could get this mess tossed over the fence to someone else, the better. I was right. He cocked his head and gave a quick nod, and Detective Pitt and Camilia were let through the barrier.

"John Little Bear, chief of police." The men shook hands.

"Detective Brad Pitt with the North Harbor Police Department."

"What brings you here so quickly, Detective Pitt?" Chief Little Bear squinted and gave Detective Pitt a long stare.

"I got a call from Mrs. Washington there and—"

"Chief Little Bear, maybe we can continue this conversation some place more private."

I didn't notice Kai Strongbow until he spoke. I wasn't sure where he came from, but there must be passages that only the staff used all over the facility. That would explain how they were able to decorate quickly on special occasions, and move various props throughout the facility without disturbing the casino guests.

Kai Strongbow and Chief Little Bear exchanged a meaningful glance and then the chief gave a slight nod.

"Would you all please follow me?" Kai Strongbow walked toward the hotel.

The Four Feathers staff parted at his approach like when Moses parted the Red Sea. One of the security guards rushed to hold the door open.

Dorothy must have gotten her great-nephew's agreement for an article because she was sitting in Mr. Strongbow's office when we arrived.

The office we were taken to was simple in that the walls were stone and the floor was wood and covered by a large tribal-inspired rug. There was a conference table with ten chairs. The only thing on the walls was a tapestry with a design I had learned is the emblem of the Pontolomas and four eagle feathers.

We sat, careful to leave the head seat for Kai Strongbow.

"Now, perhaps you can tell me what exactly is going on." Kai Strongbow directed his gaze directly at me, and I felt like a kid called to the principal's office in school.

I took a deep breath and spilled my guts. I told Mr. Strongbow everything, except the fact that Camilia had been the one to find the body, not me. Lies were too hard to keep straight and I had never been good at maintaining them for much more than a few minutes. When I was done there was a crackling sound in the room.

"You should have called us immediately. My team—"

Kai Strongbow held up a hand and stopped Chief Little Bear's reprimand instantly. "Mrs. Washington, I appreciate your honesty and I must once again apologize for the experience you have had while on our property." He bowed his head slightly.

"Thank you."

"Oscar Pembrook was not a citizen of the Pontolomas. Therefore, his death is a matter for the federal authorities." He glanced from Detective Pitt to Chief Little Bear.

Neither man looked pleased. Detective Pitt had a red flame that burned under the surface of his skin and his eyes bulged. He looked ready to explode. Chief Little Bear's eyes hardened to steel orbs. Yet he merely nodded.

"I'm sure you all realize that a scandal like this could negatively impact not only our businesses but also our good name in the community. The Pontolomas are engaged in a number of sensitive transactions with the state and we would prefer that this matter be handled as quietly and expeditiously as possible. We have come a long way from the negative stereotypes of Indigenous people as nothing but bloodthirsty savages, but we are also mindful of the fact that we still have a long way to go. If word were to get around that a white man was murdered here on Native soil, there would be some who would resent the efforts that have been made to compensate Indigenous people for past wrongs. They might use this unfortunate event as an excuse to further limit the gains made by our people and will hinder our ability to move forward with our plans."

"Some people are idiots," Nana Jo said.

"Just because a white man died here doesn't mean that a citizen of the Pontolomas is responsible," I said.

"Exactly," Dorothy said. "Perhaps the power of the press can help."

Kai Strongbow grinned. "Thank you." He turned his gaze to Chief Little Bear. "Our tribal police are expertly trained; however, murder isn't something they deal with regularly. Mostly within our community we are accustomed to dealing with theft, drunk and disorderly teens, vandalism, and domestic disputes."

"The tribal police are just as capable of handling a murder investigation as anyone else," Chief Little Bear said.

"The NHPD has to deal with hundreds of murders every year," Detective Pitt's said proudly.

I caught a quick flash of amusement from Kai Strongbow at Detective Pitts boast.

"The tribal council would like this matter resolved quickly and the North Harbor Police has more experience in this area." He turned to Detective Pitt. "Of course, not being familiar with the property could prove a disadvantage."

"We're accustomed to disadvantages too. Why, we have to deal with lying, cheating, vicious criminals every day." Detective Pitt shoved his foot further into his mouth.

"I was wondering if we could perhaps work together to come to a solution." Strongbow looked from Chief Little Bear to Detective Pitt. Then he turned his gaze toward me. "Mrs. Washington, I believe you are an extremely talented writer who has, on occasion, helped your local police."

Detective Pitt grunted and mumbled something that sounded like *meddling busybodies*, but we all pretended we didn't hear him.

"On occasion my friends and I have been able to provide a bit of insight to the police," I said. "At times many people are more inclined to talk to us, normal people . . . civilians, than the police."

"I wonder if I could prevail upon you to help in this matter," Strongbow said.

"The North Harbor Police is perfectly capable of solving a murder without bringing in civilians. We—"

"Detective Pitt, I have no doubt that you are experienced and capable, but this is tribal land. Therefore this murder investigation falls to federal law enforcement rather than local," Strongbow said.

"Talk about a diplomat. He shut Stinky Pitt up fast. He's good," Nana Jo whispered.

"I was suggesting that if we all worked together, perhaps we could have everything tied up by the time the feds arrived." Strongbow glanced around.

"I think that would be a great idea," Nana Jo said. "Sam is modest, but she's an expert. The girls and I can ask questions without drawing attention to the fact that there's an investigation underway like it would if the police were to interrogate suspects."

"Exactly what I was thinking." Strongbow smiled at Nana Jo.

"Mr. Strongbow, do you know how Mr. Pembrook died? I mean, was he murdered?" I asked.

"That is a very good question." Mr. Strongbow turned to Chief Little Bear.

"There are no obvious indications that tell us that Mr. Pembrook didn't die from natural causes." Chief Little Bear frowned.

"But?" Strongbow asked.

"I don't have as much experience dealing with murders as my colleague, but in my experience corpses don't get up and move. So, if Mrs. Washington is telling the truth—and I have no reason to believe that she isn't—someone moved the body out of the suite and into the creek. If this death was due to natural causes, why move the body?"

"Exactly. I think when we know the answer to that we will know who killed Oscar Pembrook and why," Kai Strongbow said.

Chapter 22

"Okay, what's the plan?" Nana Jo asked.

Kai Strongbow smiled. "We can't keep this quiet for long. But it's a weekend. We have three days before we must call the federal authorities. In that time I hope that you all will work together, and when the authorities arrive we will be able to hand them not only the body of Oscar Pembrook but his murderer."

"But we need forensics. Do you even have people capable of doing that?" Detective Pitt asked.

Camilia raised a hand. "Mr. Strongbow, I'm a medical doctor and I'd be more than happy to assist with an autopsy. I've done several over my career and I could work with your doctor."

"Great." Kai Strongbow nodded. "Thank you.

"Detective Pitt, perhaps you could work with Chief Little Bear to take care of the forensic details, including ensuring that the chain of custody for any evidence discovered is handled appropriately." Kai Strongbow received a curt nod from Detective Pitt and then turned his attention to me. "Mrs. Washington, I understand that your sister is a lawyer."

"Boy, he has a great network if he knows that," Nana Jo whispered.

"Perhaps she would accept a free stay this weekend and lend her knowledge and expertise to the investigation?"

"Thank you. She's in court now, but she was planning to come back later. You've been so generous that I'm sure she could stay in the suite with me," I said.

Strongbow gave a discreet cough. "I believe we may need to move you and your grandmother to another suite so that the police can check for evidence."

How did he know that Nana Jo had moved into the suite with me? That just happened a few hours ago.

As if she were reading my mind, Nana Jo whispered, "Eyes everywhere."

"Thank you, but we don't need anything fancy. A regular room will be fine."

Nana Jo poked me in the ribs. "Don't be ungrateful. We appreciate your generosity and would be happy to move into another suite."

Kai Strongbow smiled. "Excellent. Then perhaps we could meet again tomorrow? I don't want to interfere in your investigation, but if there is anything that I or the Tribal Council can do to help, we are more than happy to do so."

Mr. Strongbow stood, and that was the signal that this meeting was over. So we all stood and left.

Nana Jo stopped Chief Little Bear in the hallway. "Hey, who is he?"

Chief Little Bear frowned and stared at Nana Jo as though she was daft.

"You don't have to look at me as if I've gone batty. I know he's a member of the Tribal Council, but he's more than that. Isn't he?" Nana Jo asked.

"Kai Strongbow is the leader of the Tribal Council, a

high-ranking *Mide,* and a descendant of the great chief Wabaunsee."

"What's a Mide?" I asked.

"The Midewiwin, or Grand Medicine Society, is a religious society. A Mide is a spiritual adviser and healer," Chief Little Bear explained.

"That would mean that Kai Strongbow is a medicine man or shaman?" Nana Jo asked.

"I wouldn't use either of those terms to describe Kai Strongbow. Not to his face anyway." He smiled. "They are anglicized words used to categorize a diverse culture and people and don't tap into the heart and spirit of the Mide."

"I didn't mean any offense," Nana Jo said.

"I know. That's why I'm explaining. Kai Strongbow is an important and much-revered leader." Chief Little Bear nodded and then escorted Camilia and Detective Pitt away.

"I'm going back to talk to Kai Strongbow. He promised me a tour." Dorothy winked and then hurried back into the office.

Nana Jo and I stood in the hallway.

"We should grab our things from the room I—"

"Mrs. Washington and Mrs. Thomas." One of the hotel staff hurried over to us. "I'm glad I found you. We've packed all of your things and moved you to another suite on the same floor. The views will be equally stunning, but I am so sorry for your inconvenience." She handed over two envelopes with card keys.

"You guys are certainly fast. We just found out about the switch less than five minutes ago," Nana Jo said.

"We pride ourselves on being prompt." She leaned close and whispered, "But when Mr. Strongbow speaks we listen."

Mission accomplished, the bubbly worker smiled and returned to the front counter.

Nana Jo got a text. “It’s Irma.” She paused and read the message. “Well, well. According to Irma’s source, Maxwell Manning is in the bar near the high-limit room.” She closed her phone. “I’m going to see what Mr. Manning has to say.”

Nana Jo hurried off toward the high-limit room, leaving me alone in the hallway. I headed toward the elevator.

When the elevator arrived I entered and inserted my key, then pushed the top button. Before the doors closed, a young thin blond woman wearing sunglasses slipped inside.

“What floor?” I asked.

“The top.” She sniffed.

When the doors closed she leaned on the back wall and started to sob uncontrollably.

“Are you okay? Is there anything I can do?” I asked.

“Not unless you can bring back the dead.” She slid down the elevator wall onto the floor.

Chapter 23

On the top floor I stepped out and held the doors, but the crier refused to leave. Instead, she placed her head down on the floor and sobbed louder.

The doors buzzed from being held open too long, but I couldn't just leave her lying on the floor of the elevator crying and go about my life. So I got back into the elevator and let the doors close.

We rode back down to the lobby. The doors opened. An older gentleman took one look at the woman on the floor sobbing and turned away. "I'll take another one."

"Let's try this again." I reinserted my card key and pushed the top floor. Then I turned back to my prostrate passenger. "Look, you can't sit here all day and we can't just keep riding this elevator."

"Why not? Nothing matters anymore. Oscar's dead. My life is over," she said.

My gut was right. I had a feeling this woman must be the woman Oscar Pembrook had shared a couples massage with. Time to test my theory. "Mrs. Manning?"

She abruptly stopped crying and sat up. She squinted at me. "Do I know you?"

"Not yet, but I think it's time we got acquainted."

The elevator stopped at the top floor, and this time, I pushed the STOP button. "Come on." I hoisted her to her feet. When I had propelled her out of the elevator I pushed the STOP button again and let the doors close.

"Which one is yours?" I asked.

She pointed at a room across the hall from my old suite. *Maybe that's what happened. Maybe Oscar Pembrook somehow got disoriented and went to the wrong room? Possibly, but it still didn't explain how he got inside.*

"Where's your key?" I asked.

Mrs. Manning reached into her pocket, pulled out the credit card–sized key, and handed it to me.

I inserted the key and pushed the door open. Inside, I flipped on the lights and then helped Mrs. Manning into her suite.

The room was spacious and much the same as my suite had been. Once I had pushed, shoved, and half carried her into the room, I sat her on the sofa and flopped down beside her. From my seat I could see the door was still closing very very slowly. When it was almost closed the door hit the metal privacy latch.

The latch was secured near the top of the door frame and had a flap you could swing in place. Once the door was closed no one would be able to enter the room unless the flap was swung back and out of the way. However, we must have repositioned the flap when we entered so that it prevented the door from closing fully. *That must have been how Oscar Pembrook got in Camilia's suite. If she entered without paying careful attention and hadn't checked to make sure the door locked behind her, it would be possible for someone to enter the room.*

"One mystery solved. Now I just need to know who moved the body and why."

Chapter 24

"What?"

"Sorry, I was talking to myself." I stared at Mrs. Manning. "My name is Samantha Washington, but you can call me Sam." I extended a hand and waited.

Mrs. Manning stared at my hand as though she'd never seen one before and had no idea what she was supposed to do.

I took a deep breath. "I know you're Mrs. Maxwell Manning, but let's start with your first name."

"Felicity."

"Great. Felicity, I'm going to make you a cup of tea. You've had a shock, and I believe you're supposed to drink tea with lots of sugar for shock. At least that's what the people in British mysteries always do." I went over to the kitchen and got a mug from the cabinet. I found a tea bag, filled the single-cup coffee maker with water, and pushed BREW. Within moments the machine sprang to life. It simmered. Sizzled. Sputtered. And streamed hot water into the cup. While I waited for the machine to finish I searched my brain for a good way to find out what she was doing here with Oscar Pembrook.

When the coffee maker finally finished I emptied two packets of sugar into the cup, stirred it with a spoon, and took it to a no-longer-sobbing-but-still-simpering Felicity Manning. If super sweet tea was good for shock, maybe bluntness would be too.

"Felicity, I need you to take a sip of this and then tell me how long you and Oscar Pembrook have been having an affair."

Chapter 25

Felicity sputtered and spat out her tea. What didn't come out of her mouth and down the front of her shirt must have gone down the wrong pipe and gotten stuck in her throat. She coughed.

I patted her on the back.

When she finally stopped coughing she said, "How did you know? We were so careful."

"Really? You came to a resort at the same time as both of your spouses."

Her eyes expanded to the size of silver dollars. "Max knows?"

"I don't know, but if I found out, it couldn't have been hard for him to find out."

Felicity lay back down on the sofa and sobbed. "This is awful."

"It's not good. Now, why don't you tell me what happened? Maybe I can help."

Felicity stopped sobbing for a few moments and sat up. "Who are you?"

"Samantha Washington." I thought I had given her my

name already, but maybe she'd forgotten in her emotional state.

"Are you with the police?" she asked.

"No. Yes. I mean, sort of." I sighed. "It's complicated."

She stared.

"I'm sort of consulting with the police unofficially."

"You look familiar. Aren't you that author who owns a bookstore?"

My lips moved up into a smile before I could stop them. This was the first time someone put my being an author in front of the fact that I owned a bookstore. "Yes. I am."

"Oscar didn't like your book very much."

My lips moved back to neutral and I worked hard not to roll my eyes. "Yes, well, cozy mysteries aren't everyone's cup of tea. That's the beauty of mysteries. There's something for everyone."

"I don't read much."

"You and Oscar must have had a lot of other things in common."

"We did. We both hated the snow and cold weather in Michigan. We used to talk about packing our bags, getting on a plane, and traveling somewhere warm with blue skies, pink sandy beaches, and crystal clear water." She looked dreamily out into this future retreat. "In fact we—" She reddened but clamped her mouth shut.

"Is that what you two were planning?"

Her eyes widened again. "How . . ."

"I saw the brochures for Vanuatu on the counter in the kitchen."

"Oscar said it would be perfect. It has beautiful beaches with scuba diving and they speak English and French and . . ."

"And it doesn't have an extradition treaty with the United States?"

She dropped her gaze. "He said Max and Alexandra wouldn't be able to make us come back."

"Couldn't you just get a divorce if you wanted to get away from your spouses?" I asked.

"I asked the same thing. He said I wouldn't get the money if I did. Oscar said I was entitled to the money and I shouldn't have signed the prenuptial agreement."

"What money?"

"I don't really know. Oscar never really said. He didn't think I should tax my brain too much. He told me to leave all that stuff to him." Felicity shrugged.

I'll bet he did.

Felicity and I talked a bit longer. She didn't realize her husband was actually in the hotel until I told her. Then she panicked.

"You know the police are going to find out that you two were together. That you two were sharing a room and were . . . close."

"What am I going to do? Max is going to be furious when he finds out. He has a horrible temper and he hates Oscar. If he finds out that I was having an affair with him, he's going to lose it. He might . . ."

"Kill you?"

Chapter 26

It took a while to calm Felicity down to the point where she wasn't going to immediately pack and sneak out of the hotel. She was physically and mentally exhausted and agreed that a nap would be a good idea. She promised to stay put and I promised to check in on her later.

I went down the hall to my new suite and tested my theory with the safety latch and found that it worked just as I had surmised. I made sure that the door was thoroughly closed and went inside. My brain was running in a hundred different directions at the same time. I needed to take a few moments to calm down. I pulled out my laptop.

Max Chesterton stared at the door after Beatrice made her dramatic exit with a snide smile on his face. "I wouldn't have imagined that much passion was behind that calm milk toast expression."

"Mr. Chesterton, your behavior in this matter is

unacceptable. I think it would be best if you left." Lady Elizabeth sat straight and rigid in her chair. With her head held high and her chin up it was easy to see the resemblance between the mistress of the house and her royal ancestors.

Max Chesterton was a businessman and mindful that Lady Elizabeth was a favorite cousin of the monarch. It would not be in his best interests to be on the wrong side of the royal family. He bowed low. "Deepest apologies, your ladyship. I certainly would not dream of bringing dishonor to your home in any way whatsoever. Please, forgive me."

The lines across Lady Elizabeth's forehead relaxed and her back wasn't quite as rigid. "Shall I ask Thompkins to drive you to the train station?"

"If your ladyship would permit, my driver is having a minor repair made to my vehicle. Some type of pump needed to be replaced. The repairs should be completed by teatime. If you would permit me to wait until he can fetch me, I will make a quiet departure," Max Chesterton pleaded.

Lady Elizabeth and Detective Inspector Covington exchanged glances. The detective shrugged and Lady Elizabeth continued, "Of course. That should be fine."

"You're most gracious. I am truly sorry." Max Chesterton bowed and then walked out of the room.

There was a long pause.

"I'm terribly sorry for that," Detective Inspector Covington said.

"Why? None of it was your fault."

"My cousins . . . Beryl and Beatrice may be twins, but they couldn't be more different. Beryl is outgoing and talkative, but Beatrice is shy and introverted.

Beryl tortured Beatrice when they were kids, but when an outsider tried to intervene, they closed ranks."

"That's often the case with sisters."

"When they went into business together I hoped maybe they'd worked through their problems. Beatrice does the designs. She's pretty good too. But she's too shy to talk to business owners, buyers, anyone."

"Ah, I see. That's where Beryl comes in."

He nodded. "Exactly. Beryl is the face of the company and Beatrice does all of the designs."

"Do you believe Max was telling the truth? Surely Beryl wouldn't have tried to sell the business without her sister's permission. Especially knowing how Beatrice felt about Max Chesterton?"

"I wouldn't be so sure."

"If she did, I probably owe Max Chesterton an apology." Lady Elizabeth sighed. "I confess that I don't like the man. Maybe I was too harsh."

"You weren't."

Lady Elizabeth smiled. "Thank you, but you're hardly an impartial observer."

"That's the problem. I'm not impartial. A good copper is supposed to be. If things get complicated, I'll need to step aside."

"Complicated how? You don't think we'll have any further trouble, do you?"

"I have a feeling that we haven't heard the last of Max Chesterton."

"I 'eard 'er ladyship tossed the duffer out on 'is ear." Mrs. McDuffie pursed her lips as though she'd just tasted something sour.

Mrs. McDuffie was a stout middle-aged woman with a freckled complexion and fluffy red hair. She'd been the Marsh family housekeeper for many years and, despite her somewhat coarse language, she had a soft heart.

Thompkins sat in the cozy servants' hall as rigid at the large oak table drinking tea as he did when standing before the Marsh family.

The butler was opposed to gossip, but over the years he had relaxed enough to acknowledge that a good butler must also keep abreast of things going on around him. Lady Elizabeth and the other members of the Marsh family had been called upon to solve some difficult situations. Some of them even involved murder. Not something that happened often in the finer houses, but perhaps it was a sign of the challenging times in which they now found themselves. With the nation on the brink of war everyone would be called upon to be more vigilant in keeping the nation safe. Thompkins was proud that he and the other servants were able to step in and help by contributing information. Servants were often invisible to many of the people they served. They saw and heard things that had helped bring justice.

"I believe that Sir Chesterton's driver is expected any minute. As soon as he arrives, I'll have Frank help take the gentleman's luggage to his car."

"Pshaw! You call that a gentleman?" Mrs. McDuffie sipped her tea.

"It's a different time we live in now," Thompkins said.

""Ay, you're right there." Mrs. McDuffie nodded.

The back door slammed and Gladys rushed into the kitchen.

"Gladys, what did I tell you about slamming that door?"

Gladys was a young maid who was usually fresh-faced and shy. However, today she was flushed and shaking. “He’s dead.”

“Who’s dead? What are you going on about?” Mrs. McDuffie asked.

“That gentleman what was asked to leave.” Gladys gasped. “I was taking down the laundry and there he was. Face down in the grass.” Glady’s knees collapsed and she staggered onto a bench.

“Gladys, sit down and drink a cup of tea.” Thompkins rose and hurried outside.

Within moments the butler returned. The only indication that he was upset was a tinge of red that covered his ears.

“Is it true?” Mrs. McDuffie asked.

Thompkins nodded. “It’s true. I ran into Frank McTavish and he’s keeping an eye on the body until I can notify Scotland Yard.” Thompkins headed toward the stairs.

“That’s just bad manners,” Mrs. McDuffie said. “Coming to someone else’s ’ome to die. You would have thought he woulda waited until he got ’ome to die.”

“I don’t suppose he could help it.” Gladys looked at the housekeeper. “He was murdered.

Chapter 27

My cell phone brought me back to the twenty-first century. I glanced at the screen but didn't recognize the number.

It's probably spam.

The ringing continued.

I should ignore it.

But once I was back in the United States it was hard to reset my brain to go back in time and back across the pond. "Hello."

"Sam, this is Camilia. Can we talk?"

"Of course." I saved my mother-in-law's number to my Contacts and made a mental note to get a picture so that I would recognize her calls in the future.

"Is there someplace where we can get a good cup of tea?"

"The hotel offers afternoon tea in the pub. It's just off the library. Why don't you meet me in the lobby in ten minutes?"

She agreed and we disconnected.

I took a few minutes to freshen up and reapplied my makeup before heading downstairs. Frank loved me and would overlook it if my shirt was stained or my hair was mussed. Camilia and I may be on a first-name basis now, but I wasn't willing to believe that she'd overlook anything. Women rarely did.

I was the first to arrive in the lobby. According to the maître d', tea was available in the pub or in the library. I opted for the library and secured seating for us in a quiet corner.

The library was a large room with floor-to-ceiling bookshelves, a massive stone fireplace, and lots of overstuffed chairs that were perfect for relaxing with a book or looking out the windows that brought in tons of sunlight and overlooked the terrace. Each cozy seating area included a small round table that was just large enough for a teapot, two cups, and a tiered plate of sandwiches, scones, and pastries.

Camilia arrived a few minutes later and joined me at a secluded table situated near the window and close to the fireplace, which was lit and crackling, giving off a wonderful ambience.

"Isn't this lovely?" Camilia glanced around the room and then let her gaze linger out the window.

A waitress from the small pub/bar area brought us a pot of Earl Grey, plates, and goodies. We made small talk and filled our cups and then our plates with the sandwiches and treats.

It wasn't quite the same as when I had tea at Harrods with Nana Jo and the girls, but it was nice. After a few moments Camilia leaned forward.

"Sam, I owe you an apology."

"For what?"

"For . . . being a jealous spiteful old woman who realized too late in life that she has placed her career and her own wishes above that of her only child. Now it's too late and he's moved on. I was rude to you and you didn't deserve that. I hope that you will forgive me."

"No apology needed and I don't think you have any reason to be jealous of me. Frank loves you. You're his mom. I don't want to come between you two in any way."

"I know. Francis and I had a long talk today."

"Oh . . . I hope you understand, I—"

She held up a hand. "I should never have asked you to switch rooms. I should have taken full ownership of my actions. None of what happened was your fault."

What had Frank said? Yikes!

"Camilia, I don't know what Frank said, but I never—"

"I know, dear. I don't apologize often. I'm afraid I'm pretty rusty, so please let me get this off my chest." She took a deep breath. "Francis . . . Frank asked me what happened between you and me that would make you avoid his calls. As I was explaining to him, I realized that I'd put you in an awful situation. He loves you, and I can tell that you love him very much." She reached over and squeezed my hand.

"I do love Frank."

She nodded. "Francis . . . Frank is an adult. He doesn't need me to approve or disapprove of his choices. But, for the record, I believe he's made a wise choice."

Wow! Did she just call him Frank?

"Just as I don't need him to approve of my choices."

Hmm. Is she talking about Stinky Pitt?

"Anyway, I wanted you to know that I plan to tell Brad everything."

"You and *Brad* seem to be hitting it off pretty well." I grinned.

Camilia tried to keep her lips from curling, but they wouldn't cooperate. After a moment she gave up the struggle and embraced the smile. When she did her eyes lit up. "It's crazy, but there's just something about him."

Polyester?

"It's weird because we are complete opposites. I mean, his wardrobe is atrocious and today, when I was in the police lab and he came over, I had to prevent myself from taking my scissors and surgically removing that god-awful comb-over."

We both burst into laughter.

"But I think he has a kind heart. He's dedicated his life to serving and protecting the community. Sometimes men may exaggerate the truth when trying to impress someone, but did he really save your life by taking a bullet meant for you?"

"That's true. He has the scar to prove it."

"Clothes and hair can be changed. Character and courage cannot." She sipped her tea. "I'm not saying we're headed down the aisle, but . . . I would like to get to know him better."

"That's wonderful." This time I squeezed her hand.

We sipped tea and ate. Eventually, Camilia glanced at her watch.

"I want to take a shower and change. Brad and I are going to skip the meeting and go out to dinner together. We need time to get to know each other." She blushed. "Anyway, I told him that I would tell you what we've found out."

For the next fifteen minutes she filled me in. I took notes on my phone so I wouldn't forget. When we were done she hurried off for her date. She had a pep in her step much like a high school schoolgirl getting ready for prom.

I sat at the table after she left and thought through everything I'd learned. Almost as interesting as the details she'd learned about Oscar Pembrook was thinking about Dr. Camilia Patterson's cashmere and pearls on a date with Stinky Pitt's polyester.

Chapter 28

"Sam!"

Jenna waved her hand in front of my face.

"Sorry. I was writing."

My sister sat in the chair that Camilia had vacated. The same waitress who had served us earlier hurried over and removed the dirty dishes. She replenished the tiered foods, brought clean plates and cutlery.

"Would you like more Earl Grey?" she asked.

Jenna frowned. "Do you have Royal English Breakfast?"

The server nodded and went to fulfill my sister's wish.

Jenna frowned at the snacks. "Is there anything on here that I can eat?"

My sister was a picky eater. She didn't like eggs or cheese. That meant the cream cheese and cucumber sandwiches and the egg salad were a pass. She didn't like raisins, so that ruled out the scones on the middle tier. She frowned at the top tier of pastries, which included a pecan pie tartlet, assorted cookies, and a strawberry shortcake.

"Try the strawberry shortcake, shortbread cookies, and lemon tarts," I suggested.

She loaded her plate and took a bite.

The server returned with the tea.

"I've been in court all day. I didn't get lunch, so I'm starving." Jenna sipped her tea and ate.

We chatted about nothing until she finished. Then she told me that as soon as the twins finished at the bookstore, they were going to come to the casino.

"Is everything okay at the bookstore?" I asked.

Jenna waved her hand. "Fine. The bookstore's fine. It's Friday night and they are twenty-one. They've both been working hard and wanted to come and enjoy themselves."

I shared the latest news with Jenna: that Oscar Pembrook's body had turned up as well as the special request we'd gotten from Kai Strongbow.

"Great." She rolled her eyes.

"Did you bring a bag?" I asked.

"Nana Jo told me to get my heinie over here or she would put me over her knee and spank me. So, yes, I have my bag. I left it in the suite."

Despite Nana Jo's age, we both knew she was capable of doing exactly as she threatened. Hence my sister's presence.

Both of our phones rang, mine with a Motown ringtone that was specific for Nana Jo. "The Imperial March," or "Darth Vader's Theme" from *Star Wars*, was Jenna's ringtone for our grandmother.

"Speak of the devil." Jenna glanced at her phone. "Wants us to meet her in the lobby," she read.

"Yep."

I signed my name and room number on the check and we collected our belongings and prepared to leave.

Zaq and Christopher entered the hotel as we got to the lobby. They both hugged me.

"Hey, Aunt Sammy," Zaq said.

"And your store is fine." Christopher kissed me and gave me a hug. "Although we did make a few changes."

I pulled away and stared up into my nephew's eyes. At over six feet tall, they were both almost a foot taller than their mom and me.

Christopher grinned. "Nothing bad. Zaq changed all of your passwords and installed cameras all over the store and I completely redid your website and author bio on social media. It's all good."

I raised a brow and he chuckled. "Just kidding. We didn't do anything other than what we told you earlier."

"Thank you both." I kissed each of my nephews.

"You're welcome," they said.

"I've got to run up to the room. I'll be back down shortly." I got into the elevator and took it up to the top floor. I grabbed a jacket and hurried back to the elevator.

The elevator went down one flight and Dorothy and Nana Jo entered.

"Wait until you hear what we learned," Nana Jo said.

The elevator doors closed, and we went down one more flight. The doors opened and we were hit by an overwhelming musk.

I blinked several times to clear my eyes. When I opened them, standing in the elevator was what appeared to be Elvis with a dead animal on his head.

I screamed.

Dorothy grabbed Elvis by the arm and twisted.

When he screamed and bent over Nana Jo flung the animal to the ground. Then she reached inside her purse, pulled out her peacemaker, and fired two shots.

Chapter 29

"Are you crazy?"

Flattened against the back of the elevator, I had tried unsuccessfully to hoist myself up and away from the creepy animal by climbing the elevator's sleek walls. I froze when I recognized the voice. "Detective Pitt?"

"Get this lunatic off me or so help me God I'll arrest all three of you."

Dorothy released the hold she had on Detective Pitt and he stood up.

Nana Jo stared at the creature she'd just shot.

"Assault with a deadly weapon. Carrying a concealed weapon." Detective Pitt glowered. "You're going to jail."

My eyes stung and I blinked to clear them.

A voice from the heavens asked, "Is everything okay?"

I glanced around. It took several moments for my eyesight to clear enough for me to realize that the voice was coming from one of the interior cameras at the top of the elevator.

"Yes. We're fine," I said.

"Good Lord, what is that creature?" Nana Jo pointed to the furry black beast lying on the elevator floor.

I kicked it with my foot. When it rolled over that's when I saw that it wasn't a dead rat or any other mammal. It was a plastic mask with fur attached.

"What on earth?" I asked.

Detective Pitt leaned down and picked it up. He shook it out and then held it up. "You shot my toupee."

"Toupee?" we said.

"Yes. And I expect to get every dime of my money back." He poked a finger through the hole. "Three payments of sixty-nine dollars. I never even got to wear it. Tonight was going to be my first chance." He hesitated. "I have a date." He blushed.

Nana Jo leaned back against the elevator wall. "Sweet Mother of God. I thought you were being attacked by that thing. And you must have bathed in cologne."

"I dropped the bottle. I must have gotten more cologne on than I planned." Detective Pitt sniffed. "Too much?"

"My eyes are burning. Maybe if I hadn't had tears in my eyes, I might have recognized that . . ." Nana Jo waved at the toupee.

"Why are you dressed like Elvis?" Dorothy asked.

"Elvis?" Detective Pitt glanced down at his flared polyester pants and tight polyester shirt with a puzzled expression.

The elevator started to move and we descended to the bottom. When the doors opened Chief Little Bear was the first person I saw.

"What happened in here?" he asked.

Several feet behind Chief Little Bear a crowd was gathered.

Jenna, Christopher, and Zaq wiggled their way to the front of the crowd and the elevator. Jenna took one look and immediately went into action. "Would you please give us a minute?" she asked.

Chief Little Bear nodded and then turned and dispersed the crowd.

I quickly filled Jenna in.

"What is that god-awful smell?" Jenna asked.

I shot a glance toward Detective Pitt.

Jenna sighed. "Detective Pitt, I'm terribly sorry for the damage to your . . . um . . . yeah. To make up for your inconvenience we—"

"Three payments of sixty-nine dollars. I want my money back. And this other loony tune ripped my shirt." He held up his arm, which indicated that the button had been ripped from the cuff of his shirt.

"What size do you wear?" Jenna asked.

Detective Pitt sucked in his gut. "Thirty-six waist and a forty long in pants. I take a medium shirt."

Jenna turned to Christopher. "Please go to the gift shop and pick out a new outfit for Detective Pitt." Because I was standing next to her, I heard her whisper to get a forty waist and thirty-eight short pants and extra-large shirt.

Christopher nodded and headed off.

"After this . . . unfortunate incident, you will probably want to take another shower. Please permit my son, Zaq, to assist you." She then whispered to Zaq, who raised a brow and glanced at his mom but said nothing. Instead, he smiled and struck up a conversation with the detective.

Surprisingly, Detective Pitt allowed himself to be escorted back up to his room in a different elevator.

Chief of Police Little Bear returned. He knelt and picked up a bullet casing from the ground. He stood up and opened his hand, showing the bullets. "Weapons are not permitted on Native soil."

Nana Jo had already returned her peacemaker to her purse. If Chief of Police Little Bear searched her, he would find that she was carrying a concealed weapon.

Jenna went into action. It was then that I got to see a different side to my sister. Instead of her normal pit bull persona, she was a kind friendly easy-to-get-along-with golden retriever. She reminded him that as a United States citizen on Native land she still had rights, and it wasn't worth the trouble to get other federal groups involved, was it?

"I'm sure you know that Oscar Pembrook was shot." He gazed at the casings. "But this isn't the same caliber of bullet or I might be forced to not only confiscate the weapon but hold the person who was wielding it." He stared hard at Nana Jo.

"Oscar Pembrook was shot?" I asked.

He nodded. "Looks that way."

"What's the problem?" Jenna asked.

He shrugged. "Something just doesn't feel right. I'll know more when I get the autopsy report. For now, I suggest that anyone carrying weapons would want to keep them locked away in the safe in their room. If there was another incident, I would be forced to take action." He looked pointedly at Nana Jo again, then tipped his hat and walked away.

When we were alone Jenna glared at Nana Jo.

"If you'd seen that thing on his head, you might have shot it too," Nana Jo said.

Jenna shot a glance at the camera inside the elevator. "Upstairs."

We all got back in the elevator and took it up to our suite. None of us spoke again until we were safely in our room.

"Look, you're going to need to lock that gun away, or give it to the twins to take home when they leave. Those are your two choices," Jenna said.

Nana Jo took a deep breath and then went over to the room safe. She took her gun out of her purse and locked it away. When she finished she turned to Jenna. "Happy?"

"No. I would have preferred it if my grandmother hadn't tried to shoot a toupee. What were you thinking?"

"Did you see it? There's no way I thought that thing was a wig." Nana Jo walked over to the bar and poured herself a drink.

"Pour me one too," Dorothy said. "Josephine's right."

After a few minutes and a couple of drinks we were finally able to laugh at the situation.

I turned to Jenna. "What did you tell Zaq?"

Her cell phone dinged, indicating that she'd just gotten a text message. She pulled it out and stared, and then turned it around to show us the picture. "I told him that if he got close enough, he was to take some scissors and cut that comb-over."

We stared at the picture. It took a few minutes before I recognized the man smiling into the camera was Detective Pitt. For the first time since I'd met him there was no polyester in sight. Instead, he was wearing a pair of tan cotton slacks that fit and reached his ankles, a white button-down cotton shirt, and a navy blazer. Most importantly, the long hairs that once spread across his dome were nowhere in sight.

A second ding showed a picture of Zaq holding up a thin ponytail.

"Wow," Nana Jo said.

"He cleaned up nicely," Dorothy said. "I hope he took a long bath. That musk oil nearly made me gag."

I stared at the photo. "They deserve a raise. They're miracle workers. I've never seen Detective Pitt look so . . ."

"Normal?" Jenna asked.

"Yes, and Camilia will be so happy." I smiled. For a brief moment an idea flashed across my mind.

"What?" Nana Jo asked. "You've got that look."

"What look?" I asked.

"That I'm-J.-B.-Fletcher-and-the-light-bulb-just-went-on look. Have you figured it out?" Nana Jo asked.

I searched my brain for the bolt that had flashed across it just moments before, but whatever had been there was gone now. I shook my head. "I haven't figured it out, but something about that elevator . . ."

"Let it go. It'll come back to you," Dorothy said.

"Let's get back to work before our medical doctor and police detective decide to run off to Vegas and get hitched," Nana Jo joked.

"Before one of the prime suspects makes a run for the border," I said.

"Or before I have to figure out how to keep my grandmother from getting arrested and sent to federal prison," Jenna said.

"Actually, Nana Jo might not be the only family member you need to keep out of jail," I said.

Jenna sighed and poured herself a drink. "Our next family reunion is going to be in the Michigan state penitentiary." She tossed back her drink.

Chapter 30

Jenna wanted information, but I fended her off until we got everyone together.

Normally when we go to the casino we eat at one of the buffets. It's fast and the food is good. Tonight we had reservations at the VIP members' buffet. The VIP Lounge was a smaller room only available to Four Feathers members who used their member card when they played the various games and had obtained the "copper level." Thanks to a concerted effort on our part, we managed to get to that status by all using the same cards. For three months we all played using Dorothy's card. For three months we all played using Nana Jo's card. In the last three months everyone played using my card. We'd managed to hit the golden or rather copper status on all three cards and now could dine in the private dining area. Each copper level member could bring one guest. On the weekends the buffet lines were long, but thanks to Ruby Mae's family we had no trouble getting seated whenever we wanted in the main dining room. However, Friday night in the VIP buffet was all-you-can-eat-crab night. We tended to eat in the VIP Room whenever we found ourselves at the casino on Friday nights.

We indulged in a massive amount of crab dipped in warm butter and then sat and relaxed with coffee and orange tea.

Nana Jo pulled her iPad out of her purse. "Alright, let's get this party started. I think we all have information to share, so let's get down to it."

Even though everyone knew that Oscar Pembrook's body had been found, Nana Jo did a quick recap.

"Now, who wants to go first?" Nana Jo asked.

I raised my hand. "I was able to confirm what Irma shared earlier. Oscar Pembrook was having an affair with the wife of Pembrook's former partner, Felicity Manning. In fact, Felicity is here in a suite just across the hall from my old suite. And I think I figured out how Pembrook got into the room." I quickly explained about the security latch.

There were a few questions, but everyone acknowledged that they'd run into that same thing from time to time while staying in hotels.

"Not only was Felicity Manning having an affair with Oscar Pembrook but she also was under the impression that they were going to sneak off to Vanuatu together," I added.

"Vanuatu? Where is that?" Dorothy asked.

"I've never heard of it."

Nana Jo looked it up. "It's in the South Pacific."

"Let me guess. There's no extradition treaty with the U.S.?" Jenna asked.

"You got it."

"Now, what has Oscar Pembrook been up to that made him need to escape to an island with no extradition treaty?" Dorothy asked.

"I think I can answer that," Nana Jo said. "Maxwell Manning and Oscar Pembrook were friends. But, according to Alexandra Pembrook, Oscar Pembrook was embezzling money."

"From his own company?" I asked.

Nana Jo nodded. "It wasn't his first time either. Apparently, the first time was when he was in business with Max Manning. Alexandra claims Oscar embezzled money and had it transferred into one of his partner's bank accounts. He was ousted from the company by the board of directors, but Max Manning always proclaimed his innocence."

"How does she know it was Oscar Pembrook who did the embezzling?" Jenna asked.

"According to Alexandra, Pembrook told her. He admitted he set up Manning," Nana Jo said.

"Oscar was a lying son of a b—"

"Irma!"

Irma broke into a coughing fit that was probably the result of decades of chain smoking before she kicked the habit and having to swallow too many swear words.

"Did Manning know that Oscar framed him?" I asked.

"Alexandra says he did. She said he'd been searching for proof for years and he just got the proof. She said he was madder than a wet hen," Nana Jo said with a thick Southern drawl.

"Did she really say that?" Jenna asked.

"Sure did. She's from Georgia." Nana Jo shrugged. "She looks like a contestant in a beauty pageant. She talks like Elly May Clampett from *The Beverly Hillbillies*, but she's sharp as a whip."

"Did she know that her husband was having an affair with Felicity Manning?" Ruby Mae asked.

"She had to," Jenna said. "Why else would she be here at the same time that her husband was here with his girlfriend?"

"Right." Nana Jo nodded. "She knew. She said she was trying to get proof of the affair. She or her lawyer found some loophole in the prenup that would enable her to get something out of the years she toiled being married to that male chauvinist."

"Having seen Oscar Pembrook in action I'm sure she deserved combat pay for mental anguish, but what on earth compelled her to marry him in the first place?" I asked.

"She swears he was as sweet as cherry pie when she first met the old leech." Nana Jo rolled her eyes.

"What changed?" I asked.

Nana Jo shrugged.

"That gives both her and Max Manning a reason to kill Oscar Pembrook," I said. "We need to find out where they were when Pembrook was killed."

"Do we know the time of death?" Nana asked.

"Camilia thinks he must have died between two and three this morning," I said. "Pembrook was shot, but she doesn't believe that's the cause of death."

"What!"

"She's running tests, but she thinks Oscar Pembrook may have been poisoned."

Chapter 31

"Poisoned?"

"How?"

"What type?"

Questions were hurled at the speed of sound and came in all directions.

"Slow down and give her a chance to breathe." Nana Jo glared around the table, and the barrage stopped.

"Honestly, I don't know. Camilia said the facilities weren't what she is accustomed to and some tests are just going to take time. They will probably need to send some of the lab work out to the state crime lab. She just feels that there wasn't enough blood for the bullet to have killed him." I pulled up my notes and reviewed them to be sure I'd gotten everything.

"That makes everything harder. We're not looking for someone with a gun. Now we're looking for a poisoner," Dorothy said. "Don't they say poison is a woman's weapon?"

"Maybe, but it might be a weapon of convenience. Anyone could have slipped the poison to him. I think we need to focus on the facts and not follow gender stereotypes. I'll talk to Camilia again tomorrow." I glanced around the table. There were no objections.

"I'd like to go next." Ruby Mae finished casting yarn onto her knitting needle. She counted the stitches and then continued. "I talked to several people today. My godson, my granddaughter, and my great-nephew. They were all familiar with Oscar Pembrook. According to them, no one liked him very much. He came often, with the woman you described as Felicity Manning. Jordan, my great-nephew, has been trying to quit smoking, but he admitted that he fell off the wagon." She pursed her lips and shook her head. "Anyway, he was outside sneaking a cigarette."

"Why'd he have to sneak?" Dorothy asked.

"They're only supposed to smoke in designated areas. Before COVID they could smoke anywhere, but now they can't."

"It's a shame. I smoked for forty years. Now you're treated like a leper if you smoke." Irma shook her head and burst out coughing.

"He was hiding outside behind this planter. He said there are so many cameras all over this place, but there's one corner where the camera's broken. He went there to sneak a cigarette, and he heard two men arguing. He peeked around the corner and got a look at them." She glanced up from her knitting. "Wanna guess who it was?"

"Oscar Pembrook and Max Manning?" Nana Jo said.

"Bingo! Manning was furious because Pembrook got the Four Feathers accounting contract. He swore he'd get Pembrook if it was the last thing he ever did." Ruby Mae looked up from her knitting.

"I've spent a lot of time with Kai Strongbow." Dorothy blushed. "I don't believe he had anything to do with Oscar Pembrook's murder. That just isn't his style."

"What do you mean?" I asked.

"I've tried a lot of cases in my time and one thing I've learned is that anyone can kill if they become desperate enough," Jenna said.

"True, but it's the way he was killed. If Kai Strongbow wanted to kill Oscar Pembrook, I think he'd just do it. I can't see him poisoning him and then shooting him and moving the body." Dorothy shook her head. "However, I did ask him about being a Mide."

"What's that?" Jenna asked.

We took a few minutes to fill her in on what we'd learned from Chief of Police Little Bear.

"We'd refer to him as a medicine man or healer. He showed me around a garden he tends with all of his special plants. Some of them are poisonous. He has the skill to poison, but I just don't see him doing it. Plus, I haven't figured out what his motivation would be," Dorothy said.

"You seem to be a bit smitten," Nana Jo said.

"He's a good-looking man, but I know my job. Don't worry about me." Dorothy looked down at the table.

Nana Jo reached across and patted her hand. "We know. We know."

Irma raised her hand. "I'd better go next because I need to leave soon. I'm meeting Richard for cocktails in the bar." She grinned.

Everyone nodded their approval.

"Richard knew about Felicity. He also suspected that Oscar used some underhanded tricks to get the Four Feathers contract," Irma said. "Even though they're cousins, Richard was a poor cousin, while Oscar was rich. And Oscar never let him forget it. He treated Richard like some type of indentured servant. If he needed someone fired, he'd send Richard to do it. He'd call him at all hours of the day or night. *Pick up my car from the dealership. Go bring my lunch. Pick up my insulin from the pharmacy.*"

"Why didn't he leave?" Ruby Mae asked. "Why put up with it?"

"Richard is just one of those saints who always sees the good in people. *Poor Oscar. He just needs a friend. Oscar isn't so bad. We were close when we were children. I just can't abandon him now.* The man has the patience of Job. I would have poisoned his Cheerios, but Richard just kept looking out for him." Irma pulled out her compact and checked her lipstick. "Anyway, Richard said Oscar Pembrook was *not* planning on running away with Felicity Manning."

"How does he know?" I asked. "She's got the brochures up in her suite."

"Because Richard bought the plane ticket. Oscar Pembrook made him print his ticket and bring it to him. That's why Richard was here," Irma said.

"Ticket?" I asked.

"Exactly. One ticket. Not two." Irma held up one finger. "If Felicity Manning found out that Oscar Pembrook was planning to dump her and leave her here, she had a grade-A motive for wanting the old buzzard dead."

Chapter 32

That was a lot of information to take in. I needed to digest everything because right now my head was swimming around in melted butter and crab legs. We agreed to take the evening off and would regroup for breakfast tomorrow morning.

Jenna wasn't into gambling, but a well-known jazz pianist was playing in one of the bars and she was meeting a friend to go listen.

Dorothy headed for the high-limit room to try her luck while Nana Jo headed for the blackjack table. Irma had a date with Richard. Ruby Mae had promised a first cousin, who was passing through on her way from Alabama to Detroit to attend a funeral, that she'd meet her by the massive fireplace near the entrance to talk and catch up on old times.

I went in search of a quiet place to think.

I found it in the area between the casino and the hotel. I found a comfortable chair and sat. I tried to sort through all of the information. Pretty much anyone who knew Oscar Pembrook had a reason to want to kill him. But just because they wanted to kill him didn't mean that they did.

Maxwell Manning hated Oscar Pembrook and was overheard threatening him. Plus, Manning knew that Oscar Pembrook had framed him for embezzlement, which had cost him his shares in the company. He'd had to start over. Now, Oscar Pembrook was having an affair with his wife. That seemed like a motive for murder. And Max Manning was here at the hotel.

Felicity Manning had risked everything for Oscar Pembrook. She seemed to genuinely care about him. Although I couldn't for the life of me imagine why. If she found out that Pembrook didn't plan on taking her with him when he left for Vanuatu, after she'd gambled everything for a life with him, how far would she go?

Alexandra Pembrook knew her husband was having an affair. If he left her, she got nothing. But did she stand to inherit now? Maybe Jenna could find out. Still, I knew if Frank cheated, I might be tempted to kill him. But would I poison him?

Kai Strongbow had the knowledge to poison Oscar Pembrook, but I agreed with Dorothy: Poison didn't seem like his style. I could easily see Strongbow strangling Oscar Pembrook or shooting him. I couldn't see him poisoning him and leaving his body in my suite. Still, I couldn't just discount him as a suspect because I liked him.

An idea was floating around my mind like a feather floating in the wind. I tried to catch it, but whenever I reached out the wind would take it higher. I needed a distraction. I pulled out my notebook and prepared to slip back in time to the twentieth century.

"Dead? He can't be." Lady Mildred stared blankly at the man who would soon be her son-in-law.

"It's true, Mother." Clara paced.

Lady Elizabeth sat quietly in a corner.

"Was it his heart?" Lady Mildred asked.

"Did he have a bad heart?" Detective Inspector Covington asked.

"I don't know. I assumed . . . gentlemen often do, it seems." Lady Mildred twisted a handkerchief.

D.I. Covington looked to his fiancé for guidance. Lady Clara gave him a slight nod.

"No, it wasn't a heart attack. Max Chesterton was shot," D.I. Covington responded.

"Shot?" Lady Mildred gasped. "A shooting accident. How horrible."

D.I. Covington and Lady Clara turned to Lady Elizabeth.

"No, dear. I'm afraid it wasn't a shooting accident," Lady Elizabeth said. "There was no shooting today."

"Then how?" Lady Mildred asked.

"We're still in the early stages of our investigation, but we have every reason to believe that Max Chesterton's death was no accident."

"Not an accident?" Lady Mildred stared wide-eyed at the detective.

"Yes, it was not an accident," Lady Elizabeth emphasized.

"You don't mean . . . you can't be saying . . ." Her hands fluttered and she dropped her handkerchief.

Lady Clara clasped her mother's hands. "Mother, Max Chesterton was shot. Someone deliberately shot him."

Lady Mildred swooned.

Lady Elizabeth rang the bell. Within moments Thompkins appeared.

"Would you please bring smelling salts and a cup of hot tea with plenty of sugar? Lady Mildred has had an awful shock."

Thompkins bowed and hurried out to carry out his orders.

Lady Clara helped to lay her mother onto the sofa. When Thompkins returned they administered the smelling salts.

"This can't be. This is a nightmare." Lady Mildred tossed. "How could you let this happen?" She gazed at D.I. Covington.

"Mother!" Lady Clara said. "This is not Peter's fault. He is here to celebrate our engagement. He didn't invite Max Chesterton here in the first place, so if anyone is to blame, it's—"

"Clara, no." Peter shook his head.

"Clara's right," Lady Elizabeth said. "This certainly isn't Peter's fault. But I can assure you that we will get to the bottom of this. Now, you've had a terrible shock. Drink this tea and then you should probably go upstairs and lie down."

Lady Mildred did as she was told. When she finished her tea Lady Clara helped her mother upstairs, leaving Lady Elizabeth and Detective Inspector Covington alone.

D.I. Covington paced. "She's right. A murder right under my nose. This is a right old mess."

"Now, you stop that. How were you to know that someone would kill him? And how were you supposed to stop it?"

Peter Covington stopped pacing, turned, and stared at Lady Elizabeth. "I could have arrested my cousin Beatrice after she threatened to kill him."

"You can't seriously believe Beatrice murdered Max Chesterton?" Lady Elizabeth said.

"I don't know what to believe. All I know is that he's dead and, as far as I know, she's the only one who had a motive. She didn't play tennis with everyone else. Which gives her the opportunity to have killed him."

"What about the means?"

D.I. Covington paced for a few moments. When he stopped he turned a tortured expression to Lady Elizabeth. "Remember a few years ago, when the press went wild reporting about the bodies under the bridge in Lancaster?"

Lady Elizabeth nodded. "I remember. Weren't they also called the Jigsaw Murders?"

D.I. Covington nodded. "It was a horrible case. A physician, Buck Ruxton, brutally murdered his common-law wife and a maid." He shook his head. "He went to great lengths to prevent the bodies from being identified."

"It was a terrifying case," Lady Elizabeth said.

"My aunt was worried about Beatrice and Beryl's safety. She had two pistols that had belonged to my uncle. She gave them to the twins and asked me to teach them to shoot."

"Oh my. That means Beatrice has a gun," Lady Elizabeth said.

Peter Covington nodded. "Yes, and she knows how to use it."

Chapter 33

My phone vibrated. A call from Frank pulled me out of the 1930s and back to the present.

"Good evening, beautiful."

I smiled. "Good evening, handsome."

We spent a few moments flirting, but I know Fridays are a busy time for the restaurant and we needed to get to the point.

"I talked to my mom."

"I know. She apologized. You didn't need to do that."

"Yes, I did. If for no other reason than I needed her to stop calling me Francis."

"But Frank, she's your mom and—"

"And you're going to be my wife. She needs to respect that. I love my mom. I always will, but either she accepts and respects my choice or . . . she will find that she's missing out on the wonderful future we're going to have together."

"Frank, you make it sound like we're going to exclude your mom from our lives and that's not going to happen. You know that, right?"

"I know that, but she doesn't."

"Frank!"

He chuckled. "It didn't take much convincing. I think you'd already started winning her over."

"Really?" I asked.

"Really. Plus, it gave me a chance to let her know that I will support her decision to date and maybe marry whoever she chooses, and trust me, the thought of my mom with the king of polyester was tough." He laughed.

I sent a text to Jenna, asking her to send the picture she'd gotten from the twins. While I waited for her response, I shared the incident from the elevator. Frank laughed so hard at Nana Jo shooting Detective Pitt's toupee that I thought he would choke.

"I would pay good money to have seen that," Frank said.

"That incident opened the door for change." I shared how Jenna got the twins to help with a makeover. The picture came and I forwarded it.

"He let them cut the comb-over?"

"Yep. No polyester and no comb-over. He did it all to impress your mom."

Frank whistled. "He doesn't even look like the same person."

"He seriously looked like a bad Elvis impersonator. Plus, that cheap toupee looked like someone took one of those plastic Halloween masks and glued fur to it. I've never seen anything like it."

"Maybe I can see the camera footage. That would be hilarious."

A light bulb went on in my brain. "That's it. The camera footage."

"Right. Casinos have cameras everywhere. I'll bet if you ask nicely that Chief of Police Little Bear will make you a copy."

"That's what I was trying to remember."

From the background I could hear that Frank was getting pulled away to resolve an issue at the restaurant. "Before I forget, I talked to a friend of mine and had him run a check on Oscar Pembrook. Looks like I wasn't the only one investigating him."

"What do you mean?"

"The IRS is also investigating him. Apparently, he's been spending a lot more money than he's been reporting to the IRS."

"That explains why he was looking to move to Vanuatu."

"Seriously? How'd you hear that?"

"From his girlfriend." I quickly filled Frank in on everything we'd learned.

The background requests for Frank's assistance were getting louder and more urgent. "I've got to go. Is there anything else you need me to look into?"

"Nothing specific, but I'll reach out if I think of something."

We took a minute to make sure that we said the important things to each other before disconnecting. That last minute always left me flushed and breathing hard. I put my hands on my cheeks and could feel that the heat in my core was also in my face.

I made a note to investigate the cameras. I also jotted down what I'd learned from Frank regarding the IRS investigation.

The IRS caught Al Capone for failing to file tax returns. I wonder what Oscar Pembrook was up to that put him in their crosshairs.

Chapter 34

The biggest problem with staying at a casino resort was that I lost all sense of time. It was always light, bright, and busy. I glanced at my watch and couldn't remember the last time I'd stepped outside. *It was probably when Nana Jo and I found Oscar Pembrook floating in the creek bed. Holy cow. Did all of that happen today?*

I yawned. I was exhausted. I watched people moving between the casino and the hotel and noted that several guests had small dogs. "I wonder if I could have brought Snickers and Oreo?"

I packed up my things and went to the front desk to ask.

"We allow small dogs under thirty pounds."

"Both of my dogs together don't weigh twenty pounds."

I didn't stop to think. I didn't go up to my room. I didn't discuss or debate the merits of my actions. I simply walked out to my car and drove home.

I need to check on the bookstore anyway. At least that's what I told myself. My nephews were great at running the bookstore, even though they weren't big mystery readers themselves. Still, it wouldn't hurt to check things out.

Writing and driving were two of my best stress relievers. Before I started writing, whenever I needed to think I would hop on the interstate. It wasn't a long drive from the Four Feathers to my bookstore, but I did get a chance to think.

Did Felicity Manning know that Oscar Pembrook wasn't planning to take her with him? Did Max Manning know that his wife was having an affair with his nemesis, Oscar Pembrook? Did Alexandra Pembrook really not care that her husband was having an affair?

There was something else. Something flittered across my brain, but when I tried to reach out and grab it, it disappeared.

I pulled into the garage and heard the poodles barking. They were upstairs in Dawson's apartment. Within minutes the door opened and two brown fluffballs ran down the stairs. They barked and jumped and panted with excitement.

"You act like you haven't seen me in years. It's only been about twenty-four hours." I scratched their bellies. "Do you need to go potty outside?"

I opened the door and let the poodles out to take care of their business.

Dawson came downstairs. "I thought you weren't coming back for two more days."

"I'm not. This is all a figment of your imagination." I sniffed.

"Okaaay."

I explained that I was bringing the poodles to the resort with me.

"Um . . . they have a grooming appointment tomorrow," Dawson said.

I stopped in my tracks. "I don't remember making a grooming appointment and the groomer usually sends me a reminder." I pulled out my phone to see if I missed it.

"You didn't make it. I did."

I glanced at him. "Okay. Did something happen?"

Oreo rushed into the garage and I got a whiff of something not so pleasant. I scrunched my nose. "Did he get skunked?"

"I let them out last night and he took off after something. I gave him a bath. Several baths. But there's still an odor."

My stinky poodle wagged his tail and gazed at me with love in his eyes.

"Oreo, you can't go chasing after skunks."

His tail wagged so much that his entire rear moved. He was full of joy and I couldn't be angry with him for long.

"You're still my good stinky poodle boy," I cooed. "You're a fierce poodle, but you can't go after skunks.

Snickers sat and gave me her he's-dumb-as-a-box-of-rocks look.

"Unfortunately, you poodles don't get to come to the casino. You're going to get a bath."

Oreo wagged his tail.

I stood up. "You're going to need money for the grooming."

"I got it. It was my fault. I should have flipped the lights on before I let them out. That would have scared the skunk, and then Oreo wouldn't have gotten sprayed."

"Nonsense." I pulled up an app and sent the money to Dawson to cover the grooming plus extra for a tip.

We spent a few minutes getting caught up. Because I was home I went inside to check out the changes the twins made.

There were two new displays featuring authors that I read and enjoyed. Kay Charles had a new book in her Marti Mikkelson paranormal cozy series. And Tracy Clark's latest Harriet Foster police procedural was featured. Christopher had an eye for marketing. I hoped that both books would get a sales boost.

He'd rearranged the display of *Murder at Wickfield Lodge*, my debut mystery. He'd also downloaded a picture of the second book in the series, *Death During a Hunting Party*, and was offering a giveaway for preorders. Anyone who preordered the book and showed proof would receive a bookmark, a signed bookplate for their book, and a 10 percent discount at Market Street Mysteries. It was a good marketing campaign. I just needed to order more bookmarks. A few months ago I didn't even know what a bookplate was. I suppose "bookplate" sounds a lot more exciting than a label with the author's signature. Still, it was a great idea. I never knew that preordering books was important until my publicist explained that preorders were viewed as a predictor of a book's success by retailers. As a bookstore owner, I utilized various systems like Edelweiss to check for the next hot ticket that every reader wanted to buy, but as an author I didn't see the connection. Thankfully, my marketing-minded nephew was better at connecting the dots than me.

I walked around the bookstore, but there wasn't much for me to do. Between the twins and Dawson, everything looked to be fine. A reference book that I had ordered about World War II had come in, so I tucked it into my bag, locked up, and left. I gave the poodles a few extra cuddles and then let them upstairs with Dawson and left.

Driving back to the Four Feathers, I allowed my mind to drift and went on autopilot.

We needed to get information on the prenuptial agreement that Oscar Pembrook had with his wife. Would she inherit now that he was dead? Was that how those worked? Did Felicity Manning have a prenup? If she'd left her husband for Oscar Pembrook, would she forfeit everything for love? Hmm. I pressed a button and called Frank.

"Good evening, beautiful. What can I do for you?"

There was a loud background noise that told me Frank was still busy, so I skipped our normal flirting time and cut straight to the chase. "Can you check on Maxwell Manning's finances? I'm curious if Felicity's interest in Oscar Pembrook mightn't have been more the result of a desire to . . . shall we call it *upgrade* or *level up* than out of pure love for Oscar Pembrook."

"Ouch. Is she that mercenary?"

"I don't know, but Oscar Pembrook wasn't a very nice man. I just can't see a young attractive woman like Felicity deliberately choosing him. He wasn't handsome. He wasn't even kind. He was . . . a toad. She could do better."

"Got it. I'll see what I can find out."

I appreciated Frank and took a minute to explain how thankful I was for him and a couple of ways that I might show him my gratitude. He gasped and I couldn't help smiling. My flirting skills were improving.

We disconnected and I was still smiling as I turned off the interstate and drove down the long dark winding road that led to the Four Feathers.

A glint of light hit my rearview mirror.

The lights were coming quickly. Suddenly the driver turned off their headlights and rammed into the back of my car.

I gripped the steering wheel tightly. My first instinct was to turn on my flashers and pull over. However, another glance in the rearview mirror showed that the car that hit me was revving its engine.

Tires squealed as the car rammed into the back again.

That's when reality hit me. This wasn't some drunk driver who had accidentally hit my vehicle. This was a deliberate attempt to run me off the road.

Instead of pulling over I put the pedal to the metal and gunned my car.

The road leading up to the Four Feathers wound around curves and nature preserves. Deer, wild turkeys, and a host of other nighttime creatures were road hazards that required caution. However, I took the curves at high speed.

My heart thumped so loud as the blood rushed through my ears that I could barely hear anything other than the sound of my heart beating and the tires squealing through the turns.

I took an almost ninety-degree turn on two wheels and nearly went plowing through a swamp when the lights of the casino came into view.

The two-lane road split and the left hand led to the casino, while the right lane led toward the parking garage.

I took the left lane and skidded to a stop in front of the entrance within feet of a terrified valet parking attendant.

I jumped out of the car and got a glance at the other vehicle as it rushed down the right lane past the parking garage entrance and around the back of the building.

Chapter 35

I collapsed on the ground and sat shaking until Jenna, Nana Jo, Detective Pitt, and the tribal police arrived.

My car was drivable, although I was in no shape to do it. One of the valets took my keys and promised to park my car. Inside the casino a member of the tribal police took my statement. I couldn't tell him much. The vehicle was white. I was never great with car models. The only thing I knew for sure was that it was a large SUV. I could see from his face that wasn't much help. There were probably lots of white SUVs. Still, he promised to file a report with the North Harbor Police and send me a link.

Kai Strongbow helped me to a seat in front of the massive fireplace in the hotel, which was quiet. He then had one of the servers bring me a glass of brandy. I wasn't much of a drinker, but I felt in need of something to steady my nerves.

My hand shook as I drank, but the amber liquid burned my throat and sent a rush of heat through my body. Within moments I wasn't shaking nearly as much.

"What happened?" Nana Jo asked.

"I don't know. I have no idea who it was or why they deliberately rammed me."

"Could it have been an accident?" Jenna asked.

I shook my head. "No way."

Kai Strongbow frowned. "Mrs. Washington, I want you to forget about this incident with Oscar Pembrook. I think we need to leave this to the professionals."

"You think this is connected to Oscar Pembrook's murder?" I asked.

"Don't you?" he asked.

I didn't need to think about it. There was no other reason why someone would try to run me off the road.

"I'm sorry for placing you in this position. While you're on tribal land, you will have security nearby to make sure that no other attempts are made." The tone of his voice and the steel in his eyes indicated this was not a question but a statement of fact. I was to have a security guard whether I wanted one or not.

"I appreciate that, but I assure you that I will be keeping a close eye on my granddaughter, and if anyone so much as looks cross-eyed at her, I'm going to turn them from a rooster to a feather duster," Nana Jo said.

The corners of his lips twitched and his eyes softened, but he merely nodded.

We didn't talk again until we were upstairs and safely in our suite.

"I don't like this." Jenna paced.

"Me either." Nana Jo went to the safe and removed her peacemaker.

"I'm not thrilled about it either," I said. "But it must mean something."

"What?" Jenna asked.

"It must mean that we're getting close to Oscar Pembrook's killer. But . . ."

"But?" Nana Jo asked.

"But I have no idea who that is."

Chapter 36

One glance through the peephole showed that a tribal policeman was standing guard outside the door to my suite. Without a single word Nana Jo opened the door, took one of the dining room chairs, and placed it in the hall for the officer.

I was exhausted. I successfully contained two yawns, but the third one escaped.

"You need to rest," Jenna said.

My phone rang, and Frank's ringtone and picture came up. "I don't think I'm going to get much sleep." I took the phone into the bedroom.

I considered not telling him about the accident, but I chose honesty over convenience. I knew he would want to come here immediately, and the last thing I needed was three security guards following me around.

It took over an hour to convince him that I was okay. I was sore and knew that tomorrow I'd be even more sore from the collision, but that was nothing a good soak and a nice long massage wouldn't cure. But with tribal police following me around and Nana Jo wielding her peacemaker like a gunslinger from the O.K. Corral, I was perfectly safe.

"Frank, seriously, I'm not allowed to go to the bathroom alone anymore. Jenna created a spreadsheet for my security buddy for the next two days. In addition to the tribal police I'm to have one of them with me at all times. Every hour of my day and night is accounted for. I love you and I love that you want to protect me, but there are no free slots in my bodyguard roster."

Frank didn't like it, but he acknowledged that there wasn't much more that could be done. "I would feel better if I were there."

"I know, but you need to get the renovations done at your house."

He swore. "You could come home?" he said.

"I could, and I'd be lying if I said I didn't think about it."

"But?" Frank asked.

"But I'm angry. I don't like the fact that someone tried to run me off the road."

"You could have died."

"I don't think they were trying to kill me. If they wanted to kill me, why not just pull up beside me and shoot me?"

Frank paused.

"We know the killer has a gun. They shot Oscar Pembrook. I think he or she just wanted to scare me."

"Did it work?" he asked.

"It did. I was scared. But it also made me angry. It made me more than angry. It made me mad. How dare they! How dare they attack me like that. They could have hurt me or someone else. Because of this . . . terrorist, I've got a policeman sitting outside my room. I can't go where I want to go or do what I want to do without a host of people trailing around behind me. I didn't do anything wrong, but now I'm the one who's restricted and afraid. Well, I won't have it. I won't live in fear. That's what terrorists do. They scare you so that you're afraid to go to marathons, concerts, or casinos. I refuse.

I refuse to limit myself in going where I want to go and doing what I want to do. If I do that, if I quit and go home, then the bad guys win. It's not fair. It's not right and I'm not going to do it."

Frank was silent. Then, "I understand, but I don't like it."

We discussed it a bit longer. Frank wasn't thrilled that I wasn't willing to quit, but I assured him that I would be cautious. He was going to come tomorrow for dinner and would assess the situation then.

"And what do you plan to do, Fred Flintstone? Club me over the head and drag me back to Bedrock?" I joked.

Frank chuckled at my reference to *The Flintstones*. "If I thought it would work, I'd do it, but I would have to take out a tribal policeman, your grandmother the aikido blackbelt, your sister the pit bull, and the rest of those crazy women from the retirement village before I could get to you."

We joked a bit longer but eventually moved our conversation to more personal matters before we said good night.

After our stimulating conversation I found sleep evasive. I tossed and turned and eventually gave up trying to rest. I got up and pulled out my laptop. Maybe writing would help me sort through the details.

Lady Elizabeth sat on the sofa with her knitting in a basket nearby. Lord William sat in a chair with his leg propped up. He'd overindulged the previous evening and triggered his gout. He wasn't at the point of excruciating pain yet and was hopeful if he made a course correction he could avoid the debilitating stage where he contemplated amputation.

Lady Clara paced in front of the window.

The door opened and Detective Inspector Covington entered the room. "It's official. They're sending Detective Jacobs to lead the investigation. I'm to take a back seat and assist the local constable until he arrives tomorrow."

"Why?" Lady Clara asked.

"I'm too close to the case and the suspects, according to Chief Inspector Buddington." D.I. Covington leaned against the wall.

Chief Inspector Buddington was a large man who also happened to be Lord James Browning, the Duke of Kingsfordshire's, godfather.

"That's exactly why you should be allowed to investigate. You know everyone," Lady Clara said. "Couldn't James put in a word and—"

D.I. Covington was shaking his head before the words were out of Lady Clara's mouth.

"That's just what I don't want. Everyone knows we're engaged. I'm already hearing murmurs that I'll get special treatment because my fiancée is a distant cousin of the king. If the chief inspector issues an order, that's it. I can't go around him and ask his godson for preferential treatment. No matter how much I dislike the order, I have to follow." He leaned close. "That means you too."

Lady Clara held up three fingers. "Girl Guides honor."

"Darned foolish waste of money if you ask me," Lord William said. "Already got a chap here on the spot. Knows all the parties. You'll get to the bottom of the sordid mess faster than some stranger sent from London. When it comes to murder being close to the suspects is important." Lord William frowned.

"That's just a polite way of saying they don't believe I can be objective." He rubbed the back of his neck. "Dash it. They may just be right."

Lady Clara walked over to her fiancé and hugged him. "I don't believe that. You've always been fair. I know you'll do the right thing. But have you ruled out the possibility that someone else could have done it?"

"The chances that Max Chesterton was murdered by a mysterious stranger passing through the village aren't going to fly."

Lady Elizabeth picked up her knitting and began to cast the yarn onto her needle. "Even if Max Chesterton had been murdered by a stranger passing through the village, no one would believe it."

"That's right. They'll just think I arrested the stranger to distract attention away from my family."

"It isn't fair. No one who knows you would believe that." Lady Clara stomped her foot.

Peter Covington smiled. "Darling, you're hardly unbiased."

"It's the truth. I don't care what anyone says." Lady Clara folded her arms across her chest.

There was a soft knock at the door. Thompkins entered and closed the door behind himself. He gave a soft discreet cough. "I beg your pardon, but this telegram just arrived for Lady Clara."

Lady Clara frowned, but after a moment she walked over and took the telegram.

The butler turned to leave but stopped when Lady Elizabeth said, "Thompkins, I think you'd better stay."

He bowed and stood straight and still near the wall.

Lady Clara unfolded the telegram and glanced.

"It's from James." She read the telegram. Her brow furrowed. After a few moments of intense concentration she moved to a table near the window, took a pen, and began to scribble on a notepad. After a few minutes Detective Inspector Covington leaned over her shoulder. "What on earth are you doing?"

Lady Clara took a few moments before responding. "It's a cipher."

"James sent you a cipher?" Lady Elizabeth asked.

"Yes." Lady Clara counted and continued to scribble on her notepad.

"What in the devil is a cipher?" Lord William filled his pipe, dropping tobacco onto the chair and his lap.

"It's a coded message," Lady Elizabeth said.

"Coded? Why would he send coded messages to Clara?" Lord William said around the stem of his pipe.

Lady Clara put down her pen and reviewed the message quickly. "It's one of the special skills that I've learned at Bletchley Park."

"What does it say?" Lady Elizabeth asked.

"MI5 has had Max Chesterton under observation," she read.

"I wondered about that . . ." Lady Elizabeth said.

"Observation? Spying? The government was spying on a British citizen?" Lord William blustered. "You expected it?"

"Yes, dear. England's on the verge of war with Germany and Max Chesterton showed a great deal of sympathy toward Hitler and the Nazis." She put down her knitting and looked up. "Let's face it. We can't be too careful."

"Lady Elizabeth's right. Under normal circumstances our rights as Englishmen would prevent such an invasion of privacy, but we aren't in normal circumstances."

Detective Inspector Peter Covington gazed out of the window.

Lady Clara took his hand and gave it a squeeze.

"What does James want us to know?" Lady Elizabeth asked after a few moments.

"He wants me and Peter to go through his things before anyone from the Yard can take them away."

"How in the dickens can he know that Peter was removed from the investigation already?" Lord William asked.

Lady Elizabeth smiled. "Go on, dear."

"He says Peter will know what to look for."

Detective Inspector Peter Covington nodded.

"I'm to look for coded messages," Lady Clara said.

"We'd better hurry." Peter and Lady Clara left.

"Why are you smiling?" Lord William asked.

"That will be a great distraction for both of them." Lady Elizabeth nodded. "Peter and Clara can work on ciphers and secret documents while we work on figuring out who murdered Max Chesterton."

Chapter 37

"Sam. Wake up." Nana Jo banged on my door.

I lifted my head from my laptop. It took a few minutes to reorient myself.

"If you don't open this door in thirty seconds, I'm kicking it down," Nana Jo threatened.

"I'm coming." I hurried to open the door. "What's wrong?"

"Frank's been calling you and you didn't respond, so he's on his way up here. So unless you want the National Guard, an elite military group causing World War III by invading the Pontoloma Nation, you need to text him."

I scurried to find my phone and realized that I'd accidentally put it on silent. There were seventeen messages from Frank. I didn't stop to read any of them. Instead, I called.

"I'm sorry. I'm sorry," I yelled before he could say anything.

"Do you know how worried I was?"

"I'm sorry."

"You promised to text every four hours."

"I know, but I accidentally turned my phone on silent mode and I fell asleep. I'm sorry."

Frank took several deep breaths.

"Do you forgive me?" I asked.

"I will, but you've just taken about five years off my life."

"I'm sorry."

Frank was almost to the exit of the Four Feathers, so he was going to come up to check things out for himself.

I hurried off the phone and hopped into the shower. I was still drying off when I heard Frank's voice in the living room.

I slipped a dress over my head, pulled my hair back into a ponytail, and whittled my makeup routine down to the bare necessities of mascara and lipstick.

When I came out Frank was standing by the coffee maker talking to Nana Jo.

"I'm sorry."

Frank scowled.

I rushed over and hugged him.

He held me tight and I felt his heart race.

After a few moments he whispered, "I was afraid you . . ."

"I know and I'm sorry." I felt horrible for causing him to worry.

Nana Jo cleared her throat. "Look, I hate to break up this lovefest, but we need to get busy figuring out who killed Oscar Pembrook and tried to run Sam off the road."

Frank growled, but he released me and stepped back. "What time is your meeting?"

"In twenty-five minutes. I need to put my face on, so you two make this quick because we need to get this moving."

Nana Jo went into her bedroom and closed the door.

"Any chance I can convince you to go back with me?" Frank asked.

I shook my head.

"I thought not." He sighed and pulled out his phone. "I got some of the information you wanted."

"That was fast."

He swiped his phone until he found what he was looking for. "Manning and Manning Accounting is Maxwell Manning's company, and they are on the verge of bankruptcy."

"Yikes. That can't be good for an accounting firm."

"Right."

"He must be a horrible accountant."

"He isn't. My sources say it isn't because of mismanagement."

"Then what?"

"Oscar Pembrook's been stealing his clients. He offers to do the same work for less than half what Manning charges."

"How can he do that? Were Manning and Manning's prices that exorbitant that he could afford to slash the price and still make a profit?" I asked.

"That's just it. Manning and Manning's prices weren't unreasonable. They were fair."

"But then how could Pembrook afford to undercut them?"

"That's the rub. He couldn't."

I paused and stared at Frank. "But that would mean that Pembrook would have a loss."

Frank nodded. "Exactly. Pembrook hated Manning so much that he was willing to take a loss on those accounts. He was blowing through his savings and had overextended his company to the brink of a financial collapse."

"But he would destroy his own company along with Manning's."

Frank nodded. "Pembrook would take all of Manning's clients and force him to file for bankruptcy. He'd been embezzling money for years and siphoning it off into an offshore bank account. Based on what you told me, Pembrook was planning to skip out with or without Manning's wife to Vanuatu and leave his executives holding the bag."

"What an evil man."

When I had all of the information that Frank had accumulated in just a few short hours, I walked him down to the lobby.

As soon as the door opened, the tribal policeman stationed outside my door stood. He nodded and followed us to the elevator. This wasn't the same policeman who had been on guard last night. This one looked to be in his late thirties. He had long black hair that was parted down the center and braided. His two braids reached nearly to his butt.

He accompanied Frank and me to the lobby and stood back while we said our goodbyes.

"Maybe this was a good idea. Coming here for myself, I feel better about your security," Frank said.

"Did Nana Jo backflip you?" I joked.

"I'm smarter than that. I alerted her that I was coming so I wouldn't get backflipped or shot," he said.

I stood back and stared. "How did you get up to the top floor? You didn't have a key."

"I have a very particular set of skills. Skills I have acquired over a very long career." Frank grinned as he recited a slightly different version of the speech that Liam Neeson made in the movie *Taken*, which I knew was one of his favorites.

I tried to get him to reveal his secrets, but Frank refused. After a few minutes his phone rang and he left, reminding me he'd be back later.

Me and my shadow went to the dining room. Ruby Mae, Irma, and Dorothy were already there. Camilia and Detective Pitt entered together. They were holding hands.

Detective Pitt pulled out a chair for Camilia and then sat next to her.

I sat on the opposite side of the table. I was tempted to drop my napkin so I'd have an excuse for looking to see if they were holding hands under the table, but I squashed my nosiness like a bug. They were adults and if they wanted to hold hands, that was none of my business.

He was wearing the same pants he'd worn last night but had on a different shirt. It was polyester but not as flashy, and he didn't look like a throwback to the 1970s.

"Good morning." Nana Jo rushed to her seat.

Jenna followed. She was upright, awake, and dressed, but her face indicated that until she had at least one cup of tea, approach with caution.

The waitress brought a mug with steaming hot water and a box of tea choices. Then she smiled and backed away. Smart woman.

We all took advantage of the breakfast buffet and quickly got down to business.

Although everyone had gotten a text message about the incident last night, we shared the information again.

There were expressions of concern, which I acknowledged, and then we got down to work.

"Who wants to go first?" Nana Jo asked.

I was surprised when Jenna raised her hand. "I got information on the prenuptial agreements. First, Felicity and Maxwell Manning. If they get divorced, she's to get fifty thousand dollars. That's it. No alimony. They don't have children, but if they did, she wouldn't get child support. She doesn't get the house. Nothing."

"That's odd," Dorothy said.

"It sure is. She must have been head over heels in love to have signed that," Ruby Mae said.

"Or dumb as a box of rocks," Irma said. "She could have gotten half of his assets."

"Not necessarily," Jenna hedged.

"How long have they been married?" I asked.

"Five years." Jenna smiled.

"Felicity Manning looked pretty young," I said.

Jenna nodded. "You got it."

Everyone looked from Jenna to me. Finally, Dorothy said, "Well, I don't got it. Can one of you fill me in?"

Jenna and I exchanged a glance. "I don't have any proof, but if I had to guess, I'd place Felicity Manning at twenty-one or twenty-two."

The light bulb went on in everyone's heads and there were some murmurs.

"Which means that if she was married to Maxwell Manning for five years, she was a minor and not old enough to have consented," Nana Jo summarized.

"Eww!"

"Why that dirty old lech!"

Jenna held up a hand. "I haven't seen their marriage license and she may have gotten her parents' consent to marry, but . . ."

"If she was a minor, would the prenup be legal?" I asked.

Jenna shook her head. "Contracts between minors aren't legally binding. So if she divorced him, she could easily challenge the prenup."

"Why the conniving little cookie." Nana Jo tapped her tablet.

"We don't know for sure that's what happened," Jenna said. "Like I said, if her parents gave permission for the marriage, they may have signed the prenup too. I haven't seen it. I just got the details from a friend I know who works with Manning's attorney."

Jenna took another sip of her tea. "Oscar Pembrook's prenup was also interesting because if Alexandra Pembrook divorced him, she got nothing. But a few months ago she took out a five-million-dollar life insurance policy on Pembrook."

"Wow!"

"Five million dollars?"

Detective Pitt whistled. "So, if she and Pembrook got divorced, she got nothing. Now that Pembrook's dead, she—"

"Has five million reasons to want him dead."

Chapter 38

"It's almost always the spouse," Detective Pitt said around a mouthful of eggs and bacon.

"Really? How fascinating." Camilia gazed into Detective Pitt's eyes as though he'd just revealed the location to the fountain of youth.

"Absolutely. You mark my words. It's the spouse. Nine times out of ten." Detective Pitt doubled down and went all in.

"Nothing like marriage to a misogynistic toad to drive a woman to murder," Nana Jo murmured.

"Exactly. Her husband was cheating. He was having an affair and planning to leave her. He leaves and she gets nothing. She kills him, she's five million dollars richer. You mark my words. It was the wife." Detective Pitt emphasized his words by flinging his fork and a small piece of egg fell on his shirt.

Camilia Patterson took her napkin and wiped off the egg.

Holy cow. She's a goner.

"Camilia, were you able to determine the time of death? That will help us know if Stinky . . . um, I mean Detective Pitt, is correct," Nana Jo said.

Camilia wiped her mouth. "The time of death is hard. We know it happened sometime between two, when I went up to the room, and five, when I found him. However, whoever moved him confused things by putting him in the stream. It got cold outside overnight and the creek water was cold. Both of those facts will play a role in time of death."

"We need to determine where Alexandra Pembrook was during that time frame." I turned to Nana Jo.

"I'll see what I can find out." Nana Jo made updates on her tablet.

"There are cameras everywhere in the casino." I turned to Detective Pitt. "I was hoping you could work with Chief of Police Little Bear to see where our suspects were."

"That'll take hours." Detective Pitt frowned. "I thought maybe Camilia and I could go swimming."

The thought of Detective Pitt in a pair of polyester swim trunks nearly made me gag.

"Swimming? We have a murder to solve. I'm not going to have some lunatic attacking my granddaughter while you go swimming," Nana Jo said.

Detective Pitt's face resembled a beet.

"Josephine's right. We have work to do." Camilia patted his arm. "You view the camera footage. I did a toxicology exam, but there's one more thing I want to check."

"Was there something you found?" I asked.

"We take pictures of the entire body during an autopsy and make note of anything unusual, no matter how small."

"Was there something unusual?" Dorothy asked.

"There was a small puncture wound right behind his left ear. I barely noticed it, but I want to run a couple more tests." Camilia frowned. "It may be nothing, but . . ."

I shared the information that Frank had found about the state of both Manning and Pembrook's companies.

Dorothy raised her hand. "Kai Strongbow said that they

may have found the gun that was used to shoot Pembrook." She turned to Camilia. "They were going to test the bullets from the gun with the one you took from the body."

"My great-grandson used to work at Manning and Manning Accounting. He's going to meet me here for lunch. I should have some information to share after that." Ruby Mae shot a quick glance at Detective Pitt. "Plus, I told Daryl about the attempt on Samantha's life, and even though the police don't have jurisdiction, he wanted to help. He's going to see what he can find out about Pembrook. He'll be here in about an hour."

Detective Pitt's face went from beet red to white as the color drained. "He's coming here?"

Ruby Mae nodded. "He sure is."

"You all are amazing. The way you all work together . . . it's just like one big happy family." Camilia smiled.

"We are a family, and families look out for one another." Nana Jo glanced around the table. "That's everyone except Sam."

"I'm going to have another conversation with Felicity Manning." I turned to Irma. "Do you think you could ask Richard what medications Oscar Pembrook took?"

"Sure thing. He's been running around trying to hold the business together now that Oscar's gone. Richard's a good accountant and he plans to make sure the Four Feathers audits get done, along with all of their other clients. We're going to dinner tonight. In the meantime I met a really cute banker in the bar. We're going to get better acquainted in just about an hour." Irma patted her beehive hair.

"You're supposed to be sleuthing, not getting acquainted with bankers," Nana Jo said.

"I'm very flexible." Irma flashed a smile at Nana Jo. "Plus, I can multitask. Clarence's bank just happens to be where Pembrook Accounting banks. I heard Richard talking to him last night. If I play my cards right, maybe I can find out something about the company's financial situation too."

"Good idea. We can always use collaboration for Frank's information. Plus, maybe we can learn something about Oscar Pembrook's personal accounts," I said.

Irma smiled.

Nana Jo rolled her eyes.

"Let's meet back here for lunch. We need to get this wrapped up quickly." Nana Jo closed her tablet.

Everyone got up and went on their way, but I stayed at the table. After a few moments Nana Jo came back and sat down next to me.

"What's bothering you?"

"Nothing much. I just feel a bit . . . restricted." I shot a glance toward the table behind me. "It's going to be hard to get anyone to talk freely to me, especially Felicity Manning, with a member of the tribal police following me like a Brink's security guard.

"Alright, what are you plotting?" Nana Jo asked.

"*Moi*? Plotting?" I batted my eyelashes innocently.

"Spill it."

I leaned close and whispered my idea.

Nana Jo frowned. "Sam, that's downright mean. You can't do that."

I frowned. "Really?"

"Yes, really. You are too kind of a human being to do that."

"Oh." I took a deep breath.

"I'll have to do it." She stood up.

"I can't ask you to do that."

"You didn't ask. I volunteered. Now, let's go upstairs. This plan requires some preparation."

Chapter 39

My plan for getting a few moments of freedom involved dousing food with Epsom salts and then offering it to my bodyguard. Writing murder mysteries, I've stumbled across a lot of useless facts. However, as I walked to the elevators, I saw my bodyguard in a new light. He smiled and waved at each person he saw. He held the door for women. He wasn't just an annoying spotlight signaling to everyone who passed by that I was a target. He was a human being. Not only that but he was a nice person. Darn it. Nana Jo was right. There was no way I could deliberately cause this poor man to be inconvenienced. Nor would I be able to permit Nana Jo to do it.

"Nana Jo, I can't do this." I stopped and turned to my grandmother.

"I know."

"No, I don't mean that. I mean I can't allow you to do it either."

"I know."

I stared. "What?"

"You're just frustrated and tired. I know my granddaughter. You're the same person who makes her fiancé drive mice out to the country rather than letting him kill them. There's no way you'd harm a human." She patted my arm.

"But how am I going to get Felicity to talk to me?"

"You're creative. I have faith. You'll figure out something."

We walked to the elevator. We were getting inside when my shadow got a call.

He took the call and then stopped and came to me. "I'm sorry, but I have an emergency. Someone will be here to take over for me in less than five minutes. Would you mind if I—"

"I don't mind in the least. I'll be fine." I smiled big and thanked God for a few moments of peace. I'm not sure how celebrities, politicians, or the royal family deal with having someone following them around everywhere they go. That would drive me bonkers.

The elevator arrived and my security waited until Nana Jo and I were safely inside before scurrying away.

"Quick, let's get you upstairs before the replacement arrives." Nana Jo inserted the card into the elevator.

"Hold the door."

I hunted for the right button while Nana Jo used brute force to hold the doors open. A tall thin woman ran inside, and Nana Jo stepped aside so the doors closed.

I was so focused on myself I didn't notice that the elevator wasn't empty

Just as the doors were closing, I heard a gasp from the corner. I turned and saw Felicity Manning.

"Felicity, I was just coming up to talk—"

"Murderer." Felicity lunged. Her nails were sharp claws.

Chapter 40

I was stunned and froze.

Fortunately, Nana Jo's reflexes were better than mine and she stepped in between Felicity and her intended victim, grabbing Felicity's wrists. With one twist Felicity screamed and then dropped to her knees.

Alexandra Pembrook glanced around Nana Jo's shoulder at the sobbing mass on the floor. She scowled. "Felicity. I should have known you'd find some way to make a scene."

The elevator reached the top floor and the doors opened. Waiting outside the doors was Chief of Police Little Bear and three other tribal policemen.

The chief assessed the situation and stepped forward. "I'll take it from here."

Nana Jo dropped Felicity's arm and stepped out of the elevator.

Two of the tribal police went into the elevator and hoisted Felicity to her feet.

Little Bear turned to me. "Are you injured?"

"No."

"Would you like to press charges?"

That was when a light bulb went on. He must have been watching the camera footage and assumed that Felicity was coming after me.

"She wasn't attacking me," I said.

"I was the little gold digger's intended victim and I *do* want to press charges." Alexandra Pembrook folded her arms across her chest and stared at Felicity.

"Chief Little Bear, would it be possible for us to talk? I'm sure if we could all just sit down together, we can get to the bottom of this unfortunate incident without anyone being arrested." I glanced at Alexandra Pembrook.

Nana Jo opened the suite and held the door open.

Chief Little Bear extended an arm and Alexandra Pembrook marched inside. It took two policemen to drag Felicity inside. I followed and Chief Little Bear entered last, closing the door behind him.

Felicity was deposited on the sofa, where she promptly pulled her knees up to her chest and fell down onto her side.

I sat down next to her. "Felicity, why did you call Alexandra Pembrook a murderer?"

"Because she killed Oscar," she cried.

"Liar! I did no such thing." Alexandra pointed. "And if you continue making accusations like that out in public, I'll sue you for libel."

Jenna came out of the bedroom. "Slander."

"What?" Alexandra asked.

"It's slander. Libel is when someone writes false things about you. Slander is defamation through oral or spoken communication."

"Okay, I'll sue you for slander," Alexandra said.

Felicity remembered where she'd placed her courage. She sat up and glared at Alexandra. "Go ahead. Sue me. It's not slander if it's true. You did murder Oscar. You nagged and nagged him until he had high blood pressure. High cholesterol. And diabetes."

"I'm not responsible for that. He ate and drank like a college frat boy. I was constantly reminding him to take his medication and check his blood sugar. If it wasn't for me and his cousin Richard, he would have keeled over years ago," Alexandra said.

"You tried to kill him. He told me. You deliberately put sugar in foods that didn't need it and fed him carbs. Then you misplaced his insulin pens. Do you deny that?" Felicity said.

"Yes. I deny it. I can barely boil water. The cook prepares all of the meals. Oscar refused to eat healthy foods. He ate what he wanted whenever he wanted. And I never touched his insulin pens. Richard took care of that. Not me."

"You sucked the life out of him with all of your demands. He had to work like a dog to keep you in your fancy house overlooking Lake Michigan and your fancy car. Designer shoes and trips to Paris. Always demanding more and more. Oscar couldn't take it anymore. That's why he was planning to leave you and go to Vanuatu. We were going together." She spat the words out.

If Felicity expected a response, it wasn't laughter. However, that was what Alexandra Pembrook did. She laughed.

"Sweet Mother of God. Is that what he told you?" Alexandra laughed. "I wondered what line Oscar fed you to get you to go out with him."

"It's the truth," Felicity said.

"Hardly." Alexandra held up a finger. "First, Oscar is the one who wanted the big house overlooking Lake Michigan. Not me. I hate that monstrosity. It's cold in the winter and a furnace in the summer. There's sand everywhere, and with all of the icy spray hitting the glass you can barely see down to the rocks."

Felicity revved up to speak, but was cut off when Alexandra continued. She held up another finger. "Secondly, the car, the shoes, and the trips to Paris to buy the latest fashions were all Oscar's idea. Not mine. I was the wife of a successful businessman and had to look the part or it was a negative reflection on him. Oscar had a status that had to be maintained. Only the most expensive house. The most expensive car. A white Rolls-Royce. Can you believe it? Who drives a Rolls-Royce sports car in Michigan? That car spends more time in the shop with the mechanic than it does with me." Alexandra paced. "I would have preferred something with four-wheel drive that could get me out of the driveway in the winter, but that wasn't good enough for the wife of the great Oscar Pembrook. And not only that but I had to look like the trophy wife he deserved. He was the one who demanded it. Can you believe that? If I missed a hair or nail appointment or, heaven forbid, failed to get my lip waxed once a week."

Felicity gawked.

"Why on earth did you put up with it? It's not like Oscar Pembrook was God's gift to womankind. The man looked like a white-haired troll with a frog neck." Nana Jo looked from Alexandra to Felicity. "And what on earth could you possibly have seen in that narcissistic dictator?"

Felicity huffed. "Oscar was . . . deep."

"Pshaw." Alexandra snorted. "Is that what they call it?"

Felicity colored. "He was smart. He knew how to manage businesses, and he was confident. He knew what he wanted and he went and got it."

"You little nitwit. Oscar was just using you and you were too naïve to see it," Alexandra said.

"What do you mean?" Felicity sniffed.

"What Oscar wanted was money and revenge, and he used you to get both of them."

Felicity stared open-mouthed, so I asked the question. "How?"

"Oscar hated Max Manning and he vowed he'd take him down if it was the last thing he ever did. So, he seduced Max's wife." She pointed at Felicity. "She knowingly or unknowingly gave him inside information about Manning and Manning's clients and Oscar stole them one by one until Manning and Manning was on the verge of collapse."

Felicity gasped. "That's not true."

"It's true all right. Maybe you should ask your husband." Alexandra stopped pacing and stared at Felicity. "Geez. You really are naïve, aren't you?"

That last jab must have struck a nerve. Felicity sat up straight and returned to her earlier mantra. "That doesn't change the fact that you killed him. Oscar told me he gave you a gun and that you were an excellent shot. You found out about us. You found out that he was leaving you and that we were going to Vanuatu. That's when you shot him."

All eyes turned to Alexandra.

She had stopped pacing and the blood drained from her face.

"What about it, Mrs. Pembrook?" Chief Little Bear asked.

"I didn't shoot Oscar," Alexandra said.

"Hand over the gun." Chief Little Bear extended his hand.

"I don't have it. It was stolen," Alexandra said.

One of the tribal police stepped forward and whispered to Chief Little Bear.

"Mrs. Pembrook, what kind of car do you drive?" Chief Little Bear asked.

"Car? My car's in the shop. I'm driving Oscar's car."

"What kind of car is that?"

"A white Lexus GX 550. Why?" Alexandra asked.

Felicity tugged at her ear and dropped her gaze.

Chief Little Bear shot a glance in my direction before turning back to Alexandra. "I have reason to believe that your car may have been involved in an accident. I'm going to need you to come with me to answer a few questions."

Alexandra didn't like it. She looked as though she wanted to refuse to go, but the realization that she wasn't in her own suite must have hit her. Technically, she wasn't even in her own country. Tribal lands were a different nation. With different rules. "I demand an attorney."

Chief of Police Little Bear looked to Jenna.

"I can't represent her. That could be a conflict of interest," Jenna said.

"Perhaps you could serve as a sort of mediator until Mrs. Pembrook can acquire legal counsel of her own?" Chief Little Bear asked.

"I can assist as amicus curiae or friend of the court until Mrs. Pembrook's lawyer arrives."

"What's that?" Mrs. Pembrook asked.

"It means I can assist as an impartial adviser, but nothing you tell me is confidential. So don't tell me anything you wouldn't want broadcast on the six o'clock news." Jenna walked toward the door.

Alexandra huffed and marched out of the suite with a tribal policeman on either side and Chief Little Bear bringing up the rear.

Chapter 41

Felicity was exhausted from her emotional encounter with Alexandra Pembrook. Nana Jo helped her to her room.

Alone, I paced inside the suite. The car that tried to run me off the road was a white SUV. I couldn't determine the make and model, but it could have been a Lexus. Plus, Felicity had said that Alexandra had a gun and knew how to use it. Could Detective Pitt have been right? Was it the spouse? I needed to think.

I pulled out my laptop. Focusing on something else was a good way for my little gray cells to focus.

"Don't threaten me, Chesterton. I'm warning you. If you make trouble for me, I'll make sure it's the last thing you ever do." Flossie wrung her hands as she stared at the floor.

"What did Mr. Chesterton say to that?" Mrs. McDuffie asked.

"He said, 'Or what? You'll go to the police?'" Flossie shivered. "Then he threw his head back and laughed. It was awful, I can tell you. I felt a cold chill run up and down my spine. Just like that Basil Rathbone flick *Son of Frankenstein.* It was just awful."

"Now, Flossie. You listen 'ere. Mr. Thompkins and I want the truth. Not some made-up story you dreamed up at the cinema. This is important," Mrs. McDuffie said.

"I don't tell falsehoods." Flossie stood straighter and stared at the housekeeper.

"Well, I'm not saying you do. You've always been truthful, but this is important," Mrs. McDuffie said kindly.

"Where were you when you overheard this conversation?" Thompkins asked.

Flossie's cheeks colored and her gaze, which had been steady moments earlier, dropped.

"Go on. I know you snuck out to go to the pictures with that George Tamper, the grocer's son," Mrs. McDuffie said.

"George said if I didn't go to the pictures with him, he might just take that Amy Barton because she wasn't chained down like a slave and could come and go as she pleases because she—" Flossie stopped abruptly and covered her mouth.

"Amy Barton's a sour-faced little piece of baggage who's no better than she ought to be," Mrs. McDuffie huffed.

"Go on, Flossie. Where were you?' Thompkins repeated.

"Well, like I said, I was coming back, but the doors were locked. It was after curfew, but the lock's broken on the door by the back study. If you—"

Thompkins unfurled his brow. "Go on."

"If you jiggle the knob, you can get in. So, I did that and went into the study. I was just about to leave when I heard someone coming. So, I moved behind the curtain and waited."

"You were hiding behind the curtain when Mr. Chesterton entered?" Thompkins asked.

"Yes, sir. I thought I was going to faint when the two of them come in the room like they did. My knees were shaking so much I had to hold them with my hands. I was so nervous, thinking it was Mrs. McDuffie that come in and . . . well, it wasn't," Flossie said.

Mrs. McDuffie snorted.

"And who was with Mr. Chesterton?" Thompkins asked.

For the first time Flossie hesitated. "I couldn't see, because of the curtain, but it sounded like a woman. I don't know for sure, but she sounded . . . posh. Like Lady Clara."

Mrs. McDuffie gasped. "You don't mean Lady Clara threatened that man?"

"Lawd no. It weren't her. I just mean the lady talked genteel, like Lady Clara. It wasn't no servant, that's for sure." Flossie tapped her cheek in an effort to remember.

Thompkins coughed. "There are quite a number of ladies here." He paused. "You have heard Lady Mildred speak."

Flossie shook her head. "Not her. The person who spoke with Mr. Chesterton wasn't whiny like her."

"Flossie," Mrs. McDuffie said.

"Sorry, but it weren't her."

"How about Mrs. Covington? Or her sister, Mrs. Smythe?" Thompkins asked.

"I don't think so. I don't think it was either of them." Flossie paused. "They don't talk as posh as Lady Clara. Besides, the person with Mr. Chesterton didn't sound old."

Flossie, still in her teens, viewed anyone over their mid-twenties as old. Thompkins tried again. "That leaves Miss Beryl and Miss Beatrice Smythe? Or Lady Groverton?"

Flossie hesitated. "Maybe. I haven't heard them speak much. But if I had to guess, I'd say it was that Lady Groverton."

"Now, Flossie. This is very important. You actually *heard* Lady Jean Groverton threaten Chesterton?" Thompkins asked.

"It sure sounded like a threat to me," Flossie said.

Mrs. McDuffie and Thompkins exchanged glances.

"What did Mr. Chesterton do after that?" Thompkins asked.

"That's the odd part." Flossie paused. "He laughed."

"Laughed?" Mrs. McDuffie asked. "What would make a man laugh after 'e's just been threatened?"

"Are you sure they weren't joking?" Thompkins asked.

"It sure didn't sound like a joke to me. And after Lady Groverton said what she said, and Mr. Chesterton laughed, then she said, 'I swear, if you make trouble for Lord Dilworth, I'll stab you through your cold black heart.'"

Chapter 42

A light bulb came on.

"That's what I was trying to remember." I sat up, grabbed my purse, and rushed out of the door and down the hall to the suite that Felicity Manning occupied. I knocked on the door and waited impatiently for her to answer.

Felicity finally opened the door.

"What did you mean when you accused Alexandra of murdering Oscar by withholding his insulin? Were you just blowing smoke? Or did Oscar really tell you that?"

Felicity narrowed her gaze. "Is this some kind of trap? Are you trying to get me in trouble so that woman can sue me for slander?"

"I'm trying to figure out how Oscar Pembrook died."

"He was shot. That's what they said. That policeman said Alexandra shot him."

"What are you talking about?" I asked.

"They found the gun she used in the back of her car. She shot Oscar and they arrested her."

"Are they sure?"

"Of course they're sure."

"I mean, are you sure it was Alexandra's car?" I asked.

Felicity tugged her ear and fidgeted. She was a terrible liar. "Of course it was."

"What type of car do you drive?" I asked.

"A red BMW. Why?" Felicity narrowed her gaze.

Darn it. I guess I was mistaken about Felicity's reaction about the car.

"I told you, she killed him. She was a horrible person. Oscar told me. She didn't understand him. She didn't love him. She was a mean spiteful hateful woman. That's why he started seeing me. He didn't like cheating. He wanted to be free. He needed to get away from her.

Sure. You keep telling yourself that.

"Oscar was a sensitive man. Alexandra was a mean hateful person and she killed him. I hope she fries in the electric chair." She turned to me. "Does Michigan use the electric chair?"

"Michigan banned capital punishment back in 1963."

"Bummer."

I took a good look at Felicity. She had changed since I'd last seen her. Now she was dressed in a short skirt and a low-cut blouse that emphasized her biggest attributes, and she had on makeup. "You must be feeling better."

She flushed. "Yeah, well, Oscar's dead and I need to think about my future."

"Your future?"

"My future. Max knows that I cheated. If he dumps me, I'm sunk. I don't have a lot of skills, so . . ." She shrugged.

"Felicity, you're a smart woman." I slipped a hand behind my back and crossed my fingers in a childish attempt to counter the lie. "You don't need a man to take care of you."

She turned and stared. "I have no education. No work experience . . . well, none that I can put on a résumé." She grinned. "And I have expensive taste. So I need to use what I have to get what I want while I'm still young." She pushed up her chest and pulled her blouse down so that more flesh was exposed. "Now, if you don't mind, I have to get busy."

I turned and left. In the hallway I watched as a hotel worker pushed a laundry cart down the hall. He stopped in front of one of the suites. He knocked on the door and waited a few minutes. When no one answered he inserted his pass key and entered.

Another light bulb went off in my head. *That's how Oscar Pembrook's body was moved.*

I pulled out my cell to text everyone to let them know that Alexandra had been arrested, so we were finally able to end our investigation and spend the remaining hours we had at the Four Feathers just enjoying ourselves. There were only four suites on this floor, so it wasn't a long hallway. Texting and walking was a skill I'd mastered, much like walking and chewing gum. I walked toward the elevator while fully focused on my phone. The doors opened and I nearly collided with a man.

"Excuse me," the man said.

"I'm sorry."

The man was tall and thin with a head of white hair. He was immaculately dressed, and without looking at the labels in the back of his clothes, I knew he'd spent a fortune on his outfit. He was older, but he looked familiar. When he smiled I realized who he resembled.

I stopped. "Excuse me, but are you Richard Pembrook by any chance?"

The man gave a tentative smile and stared with a puzzled look on his face. "Yes. Have we met?"

"Not yet, but my name's Samantha Washington." I extended my hand and we shook. "We have a mutual friend."

He waited.

"Irma."

A smile spread across his face and his eyes twinkled. "Irma. She's a wonderful woman. Such a loving, giving person."

I squashed Nana Jo's voice, which was playing in my head, plastered a benign smile on my face, and continued, "Yes, she is."

We stared awkwardly at each other for a few moments.

"Well, it was nice meeting you, Samantha." He turned to walk away.

I searched my brain for something to say that would give me time to question him. "Condolences."

Richard turned back to me.

"On the death of your cousin. Oscar Pembrook was your cousin, wasn't he?" I asked hurriedly.

"Yes. He was. Thank you."

"His sudden death must have been a terrible shock. Were you two close?" I asked.

"We had been close once. As children, we were more like brothers." He grinned at the memory. "Over the years we drifted apart." Richard Pembrook shrugged. "But his death was hardly sudden. I mean, Oscar made lifestyle choices that . . . well, I'm surprised Max didn't shoot him long before now."

"Max?"

"Yes, Maxwell Manning." Richard Pembrook shook his head. "Max had to know about Oscar and Felicity. Plus, Oscar did everything in his power to steal Max's clients. His goal was to ruin Maxwell Manning."

"I had heard there was some . . . strife between the two, but I didn't realize it went to that level. I mean, that's incredible." I feigned surprise and hoped that my voice didn't give away the fact that I knew much more about Maxwell Manning and Oscar Pembrook than I should. My mind raced. "But I thought it was Alexandra who shot Oscar."

"Alexandra? What gave you that idea? No way." He shook his head. "You just have to know Alexandra. She's smart, funny, beautiful, kind, and . . . well, she would never have harmed a hair on Oscar's head. Although God knows she certainly was provoked."

"Really?"

"Sure. Oscar wasn't the easiest person to live with. I know. I worked with him for years. He could be a real jerk when he wanted to."

Didn't I know it.

"No, it couldn't have been Alexandra who killed Oscar. If anyone shot him and dumped his body in the creek, it had to be Maxwell."

You didn't need to be clairvoyant to see Richard had a major-league crush on his cousin's wife. I hadn't been told that the information from Felicity was confidential.

"The police found a gun in her car, and I think they're running tests to determine if it was the same gun used to kill her husband."

Richard Pembrook gawked. "But the white Lexus belonged to Oscar, not Alexandra. Oscar deliberately got a white Lexus just like Max Manning's." Richard Pembrook paced for a few moments and then went down the stairs, mumbling something that sounded like, "They got the wrong car."

Chapter 43

I watched the door that Richard Pembrook had just gone through and considered following him to find out why he thought Alexandra Pembrook was innocent. Was it just because he was secretly in love with his cousin's wife? Or maybe it wasn't a secret? Could Richard and Alexandra have been having an affair? As a writer, I have a vivid imagination. But I couldn't imagine those two together no matter how much I stretched my imagination.

While I stood in the hallway and waffled between minding my own business and following Richard Pembrook, the elevator dinged and the doors opened. Nana Jo got out.

"What are you doing just standing there?" Nana Jo asked.

"I just met Richard Pembrook. He seemed distressed at the thought of Alexandra Pembrook getting arrested for her husband's murder. I was deciding if I should follow him or just let it go."

"If he's distressed, I'm sure the Four Feathers's staff will look after him. These folks are wonderful. Why don't you get another massage or go down and have tea? You've only got a few more hours left in this paradise. You might as well enjoy yourself." Nana Jo headed to the suite.

I stood a few moments longer but decided maybe she was right. Maybe this was one case that I didn't need to solve. The tribal police had already beat me to it. I got in the elevator and made my way back downstairs to the library area near the pub.

I sat at the same table that I'd occupied the day before and gazed out at the natural beauty. I let my mind wander. A deer stuck its head out from behind a bush and I held my breath as I watched. After a few moments the deer stopped grazing and froze. Based on the way its ears twitched, it must have heard a noise. In a flash the deer was gone.

A waitress brought my tea and a tiered tray of scones, pastries, and sandwiches and left me to enjoy my respite in peace.

This was a lovely spot and I could see myself coming here to enjoy a break even when I wasn't staying at the resort. Or maybe we should consider serving tea at the bookstore. My book launch party had featured a high tea. The bookstore was closed on Sundays, but I was considering offering a book event for other local authors. Maybe a cozy mystery tea party? I was sure between Dawson and Frank, I could take care of the food. Tea was easy. And since I'd joined the ranks of published authors in North Harbor, I'd learned that I wasn't alone. Maybe I could get a big name mystery author to come for a book reading and signing.

I thought through the possibilities while I munched on the treats and drank tea. Eventually, I pulled out my notepad and jotted down some of my ideas. My mind drifted back to Alexandra Pembrook. She didn't strike me as a killer. Although Nana Jo was right. Oscar Pembrook could have driven any woman to contemplate murder. Still, I just didn't see her shooting her husband and hauling his body down to the creek.

I'm missing something.

Something floated in the back of my mind, but whenever I got close to it, it flitted away.

My cell phone vibrated. I glanced down and recognized Camilia's number.

"Hello, Camilia."

"Sam, I just saw your message that the police have a suspect."

I shared what I'd learned from Felicity Manning.

"That's great. I can't tell you how thrilled I am to have this behind me. Now when I go back home tomorrow, I can leave with a clear conscious."

"Where are you?"

"I ran a few more tests and I really wanted to take another look at that puncture wound."

"Find anything interesting?" I asked, although I prayed she wouldn't share if she had. I wasn't eager to hear details of Oscar Pembrook's autopsy.

"If the police arrested Alexandra Pembrook for murdering her husband, she's the unluckiest murderess on the planet."

"What do you mean?"

"Oscar Pembrook would have died anyway. His liver was pickled. His arteries were blocked. And don't even get me started on his colon."

Please don't tell me about Oscar's colon.

"His blood sugar was so out of whack that I'm surprised he was able to walk."

"What do you mean?"

"Low blood sugar would have made him almost comatose. So if someone wanted to shoot him, he wouldn't have been able to put up much of a fight."

Camilia was finishing up and planned to go back to her room to get showered and changed. She and Brad were going out to dinner later.

We disconnected. Again, I reached out for the thought

that eluded me, but it disappeared as quickly as it appeared. I stopped trying to catch it and let my mind wander in a different direction. I let my mind float back to the British countryside in 1939.

"I don't care what she heard. There's no way you'll be able to convince me that Jean murdered Max Chesterton." Lady Clara folded her arms across her chest and scowled at the Marshes' butler.

Thompkins coughed.

"Clara, Thompkins was only repeating what Flossie heard," Lady Elizabeth said gently.

"Lady Elizabeth's right. Don't shoot the messenger," Detective Inspector Covington said.

Lady Clara unfolded and gave Thompkins an apologetic glance. "I'm sorry, Thompkins."

The butler gave a brief nod.

"Did Flossie say what happened after Lady Groverton threatened Max Chesterton?" Lady Elizabeth asked.

Thompkins coughed. "She said there was a noise from the hall. They ended their conversation and she returned to her room."

"I believe Flossie is a reliable person, but is she truthful?" Lady Elizabeth looked to the housekeeper.

Mrs. McDuffie straightened her back. "My girls are all truthful. I'm not saying they're perfect. Girls will be girls. She oughtn't to have been sneaking out to go to the pictures. But I'd stake my life and my reputation that she's telling the truth."

Lady Elizabeth nodded. "I thought so but wanted

to be certain. Lady Jean Groverton is the daughter of Lord Eustace Groverton."

"Eustace is a member of the House of Lords. Good man. I don't agree with all of his views, but he's a good man. Served in Egypt with his brother, Lawrence," Lord William spoke around the stem of his pipe.

"Lawrence was older than Eustace, wasn't he?" Lady Elizabeth asked.

"Hmm. Would have inherited if it hadn't been for the bloody war." Lord William flushed. "Sorry."

"Lord Eustace needs to take better care of himself. He drinks too much. He smokes too much. And he doesn't get nearly enough exercise. Poor Jean and her mum are worried to death," Lady Clara said.

"Weren't the Grovertons robbed recently too?" Lady Elizabeth asked. "I seem to recall Lady Whitting mentioning it in a letter."

"Jean mentioned it, but I don't know exactly what was taken," Lady Clara said.

Lady Elizabeth sat quietly. After a few moments she pulled out her knitting.

"This thief, when he's caught, needs to be made a public example. The press is portraying the fella as some type of Raffles or gentleman thief. Well, I tell you, there's nothing *gentlemanly* about a thief." Lord William waved his pipe for emphasis. Tobacco flew all around him.

"Wasn't the robbery discovered after the big dinner party they hosted to welcome Count Raczyński?" Lady Elizabeth asked.

"Raczyński?" Detective Inspector Covington asked. "The Polish ambassador?"

Lady Elizabeth nodded. "Yes. He was an incredibly nice man."

"Do I want to ask what the Polish ambassador to the United Kingdom was doing at the home of a British peer?" D.I. Covington asked.

"Probably best not to ask questions," Lady Clara said. "What made you think of him?"

Lady Elizabeth knitted silently. Her hands moved silently and automatically. Her mind was millions of miles away.

"Aunt Elizabeth!" Lady Clara waved a hand in front of her aunt's eyes.

"I'm sorry, dear." Lady Elizabeth smiled. "I suppose it's all the knitting I do, but I can't help but notice patterns."

"What type of patterns?" Detective Inspector Covington asked.

Lady Elizabeth turned to the housekeeper. "Mrs. McDuffie, would you bring me my dispatch case with correspondence?"

Mrs. McDuffie rose to retrieve the case.

"Earlier, when you were reading about the robbery at Lord Montague's, I recall we received an invitation to their house. I was thinking earlier that if the timing was different, we might have been there."

A slightly out of breath Mrs. McDuffie returned with the dispatch case and placed it on the table next to Lady Elizabeth.

Lady Elizabeth put aside her knitting, opened the case, and sorted through her correspondence. She pulled several papers aside. The others she returned to the case and closed the lid. When she was finished she turned to the butler. "Thompkins, do you think you could locate the newspapers immediately *after* the dates in these invitations?" She handed him the letters she had pulled from the pile.

Thompkins took the letters, bowed stiffly, and then hurried out of the room.

"It occurred to me that all of the robberies occurred after a dinner or hunting party," Lady Elizabeth said.

"I'm not sure how that helps us. The thief took advantage of the fact that there were a number of strangers present, and with everyone busy shooting, playing tennis, or dancing, that he would have a great chance to get his hands on the valuables while everyone's attention was diverted," Detective Inspector Covington said.

Thompkins returned silently and handed Lady Elizabeth four newspapers along with her correspondence. "I was able to locate all but one, which I believe has been disposed of in the fire."

"That's fine. We have plenty to go on here. Peter, would you take the newspapers?" Lady Elizabeth handed him the papers and then turned to Lady Clara. "Clara, would you read the dates for each party."

Lady Clara sorted the letters so they were in chronological order and then read the first date.

"That was Lord Whiteside's hunting party, wasn't it?" Lady Elizabeth asked her cousin.

Lady Clara nodded.

"Peter, can you tell us if there was a robbery at Lord Whiteside's?" Lady Elizabeth asked.

Detective Inspector Covington reviewed the paper until he found the article he was looking for. "He was robbed. The thief took a pair of gold cuff links, a silver picture frame, and an emerald necklace." He read on silently. "Only it seems the thief didn't get away with the goods. He must have dropped them during his escape because everything that was missing was recovered."

Lady Elizabeth nodded and picked up her knitting. "I suspect, if you check all of the dates for those invitations, you'll find that's when the robberies occurred."

Lady Clara and Detective Inspector Covington cross-checked two more dates and found that Lady Elizabeth was correct.

"So, the thief either 'ears about a posh event and takes advantage of the situation to steal?" Mrs. McDuffie said.

Thompkins coughed. "Or the thief is invited to the event?"

Lady Elizabeth smiles. "You're both right. I believe the thief is an invited guest who takes advantage of the situation."

"The blackguard!" Lord William yelled. "The dastardly fellow is worse than a worm. He knows his victims. They're his friends. He sits at their table, eats their food, drinks their wine, and then robs them blind. He should be flogged."

Lady Elizabeth nods. "Maybe our thief isn't such a scandalous crook after all."

"What do you mean?" Detective Inspector Covington asked.

"I think I know where you're going with this." Lady Clara gave her cousin a shrewd look. "Each of these invitations involved prominent figures. A shooting party where one of the invited guests is the ambassador of Poland. A dinner party where the Belgium prime minister will be attending."

"Exactly." Lady Elizabeth nodded. "That's why I believe rather than dealing with a Raffles, we're actually dealing with a Scarlet Pimpernel."

"*What?*" Lord William asked. "How did you leap to that conclusion?"

"Each event was probably hiding some political maneuvering. I suspect if you look at the guest lists, you'd see a lot of the same names."

"You mean like the Cliveden Set?" Lady Clara asked.

Lady Elizabeth nodded. "Lady Astor, Lord Montagu, and Lord Lothian were probably all invited guests."

"Is that why you declined?" Lady Clara asked.

"Lady Astor is a shrewd woman. She knows that Winston's predictions about Hitler and the Nazis were right. People are starting to see that he wasn't a warmonger like he was portrayed in the press but was actually a visionary. She also knows that King George is my cousin. She thinks if she can get William and me on her side, we might use our influence to convince them to accept her policy of appeasement rather than standing up and fighting for what's right."

Lady Clara leaned over and kissed Lady Elizabeth. "She obviously doesn't know you."

"But what is the point of the thefts?" Detective Inspector Covington asked. "Wouldn't the thief want to lay low and *not* draw attention to these political maneuvers?"

"I suspect that our 'thief' is leading a double life, just as Sir Percy Blakeney did in *The Scarlet Pimpernel.* Our aristocrat is pretending to merely be a gullible fop who is an advocate for appeasement. In reality, he's a hero working in England's favor from the inside, by drawing attention to these seemingly innocent gatherings by stealing small items." Lady Elizabeth smiled.

"Stealing?" Mrs. McDuffie pursed her lips. "It's so . . . common."

"I suspect that's why he's so bad at it. Within a week or two of each crime the items are found and returned." Lady Elizabeth turned to Detective Inspector Covington. "Is that a common occurrence with thieves, in your experience?"

Detective Inspector Covington rubbed his neck. "Not at all. Any thief that clumsy would have been caught immediately."

"But what does that have to do with Max Chesterton's murder?" Lord William asked.

"That's what we need to figure out," Lady Elizabeth said.

Chapter 44

"Sam!"

I had a moment of déjà vu as I looked up into my sister's eyes. "I'm sorry. I was—"

"Writing. I know." Jenna sat in the seat across from me and touched the teapot to see if it was warm. "What kind of tea is this?"

"Earl Grey."

She put the pot back on the table and got the attention of our waitress. Once she had put in her order for English breakfast tea and requested a refreshed tea tray, she took a shortbread cookie and leaned back in her seat.

"Did they arrest Alexandra Pembrook?"

"She's not under arrest. They're detaining her as a material witness. She's in her room waiting for someone from the OJS to come and question her."

"What's the OJS?"

"Office of Justice Services. She called her lawyer and he should be here soon." Jenna leaned back, stretched out her legs, and kicked off her shoes. "So I'm free."

I gazed out the window. The pattern was becoming clearer,

but there were still a few holes. I think I knew who was playing the fop in this tale, but I needed to be sure.

I collected my things and rose to leave.

"Where're you going?" Jenna asked.

"I need to talk to two men."

"Alone?" Jenna asked.

I stopped and thought for a second. "It's a casino. There are thousands of people here. I'm not alone."

Jenna grabbed her purse. "There's no way you're going to talk to two potential murderers alone. That's crazy."

"There are tons of people and cameras everywhere."

"The cameras didn't prevent someone from murdering Oscar Pembrook."

"I know how to be careful. It's not my first rodeo," I stole a line from Nana Jo.

Jenna gave me her you-poor-pitiful-thing look. "This may not be your first rodeo, but I'm a criminal defense lawyer. Between the two of us, I'd say I have more experience talking to killers. No matter how many mysteries you've solved."

I hated to admit it, but she had a point.

"Okay, fine, but it's not like I'm going to do anything stupid like accuse one of them of murder. I just want to ask them a couple of questions."

"Can this wait until I've had my tea?" Jenna asked.

"Fine."

When she was done, we walked out of the pub and toward the elevators.

"Fine, then I'll be there to make sure you have a witness."

"Is that the only reason?" Jenna wasn't the most actively involved in any of our previous mysteries. I was surprised by her willingness to tag along. There had to be another reason. "I mean, let's face it. You haven't questioned my sanity in the past."

"Don't fool yourself. I've often questioned your sanity."

I stuck out my tongue at her. Stopped walking and turned to face my sister. I folded my arms across my chest and waited.

Her lips twitched. "Given the incident with the car, I think it would be best for you not to go wandering off alone."

"The tribal police have a suspect and have pulled my security. I'm safe."

"Maybe, but if I let you go off talking to suspects alone and something happens, Nana Jo will put me over her lap and spank me."

"So you're more afraid of Nana Jo than potential murderers?" I grinned.

"Exactly. Now let's get this over with."

Chapter 45

We took the elevator back up to the fourth floor. There were only four suites. One was mine. Across the hall was my old suite, which was not being used. I knew which suite had been used by Felicity Manning and Oscar Pembrook.

I hesitated outside that door. Earlier, Felicity was on the hunt for her next meal ticket. I knocked anyway.

To my surprise, she opened the door. "What?"

"Who knew about you and Oscar?"

"No one. We were very careful."

"Yeah right." Jenna rolled her eyes.

"What's that supposed to mean?" Felicity asked. "It's not like we broadcasted to the world that we were having an affair."

"No, but you came to a resort within miles of your home," I said.

"Where your husband's firm was not only well-known but they were on-site for financial audits," Jenna said.

"A casino with cameras everywhere," I said.

"Surely you don't think it's a mere coincidence that both

your husband *and* Oscar Pembrook's wife just happened to be here at the same time?" Jenna said.

"Not to mention Richard Pembrook, Oscar's cousin."

Felicity stared open-mouthed from Jenna to me at each statement. Then she glanced up and down the hallway. "You'd better come inside." She went inside the room, leaving the door open for us to enter.

Jenna and I walked inside.

"Now, let's figure out who knew that you and Oscar would be here so we can figure out who killed him," I said.

Felicity walked over to the bar. She opened a beer and took a swig. Only when she put the beer on the counter did I see that her hand was shaking.

"Alexandra killed Oscar," Felicity said.

"Pshaw," Jenna snorted. "Alexandra Pembrook was too smart to commit such a messy murder."

"What do you mean?" Felicity asked.

"I don't believe Alexandra Pembrook would be stupid enough to bring a gun to shoot her husband and then leave the gun in her car. I mean seriously? Even Stinky Pitt knows that the spouse is the number one suspect in any murder."

"Stinky Pitt?" Felicity asked. "Who or what is that?"

"Never mind." Jenna waved away the question with her hand. "The point is, why not toss the gun into the woods? Or, better yet, into Lake Michigan? But her car? Ridiculous. A first-year law student could argue that out of court."

"But Chief of Police Little Bear, he said he was detaining her." Felicity took another swig.

"Of course he did. He couldn't let her go, but he knew she didn't kill him. If he thought she had killed her husband, he would have her locked up instead of letting her chill out in her hotel room." Jenna huffed.

I stared at my sister. I had only seen her in full-blown lawyer mode a couple of times. Her reputation as a pit bull was well-deserved.

"Now, who else knew about you and Oscar?" I asked.

"No one." This time when she took a swig of beer, her hand shake was much more pronounced and she spilled beer on the counter when she replaced the can.

"It's not like you two were discreet," I said.

"What do you mean? We were very discreet. I never told anyone about Oscar. He even bought a car exactly like Max's so if anyone saw me in a white Lexus, they would think I was with Max." She stuck out her chin.

Jenna and I exchanged looks.

That's why Felicity had a moment of panic when Alexandra mentioned she drove Oscar's white Lexus to the casino instead of her car.

"So Oscar drove a white Lexus?" I asked. "Is it here? Did he drive it to the casino?"

"Well . . . no." A red flush went up Felicity's neck.

"Spill it," Jenna said.

"Alright." She took a deep breath. "We were leaving, and Oscar thought it would be a good parting shot if he left his car at Max's house. That way Max would know. So . . ."

"So, Oscar Pembrook left his car parked at Maxwell Manning's house and you drove here?" I asked.

Felicity nodded.

"So, if your husband went home, he would have noticed the car," I said.

Felicity took another drink.

"What about Richard?" I asked.

She thought for a few minutes. "Well, yeah, Richard knew. Oscar was always calling him to run errands, but you can't honestly believe Richard would kill Oscar."

"Why not?" I asked. "From everything I've heard Oscar Pembrook treated him like a servant, not a partner."

"But Richard is so . . . I don't know. He's tame. Meek. Mild-mannered." She shrugged and then shook her head. "No way."

"Exactly. No one would believe that meek mild-mannered Richard would harm a fly. It was the perfect cover."

I turned and saw Richard Pembrook pointing a gun.

Chapter 46

"How did you get in here?" Felicity asked.

"The same way I got in before." Richard held up a key. "Oscar was always ordering me around. *Bring me my insulin. Pick up my dry cleaning. Get my oil changed, my car washed. Yadda. Yadda.*"

"But how did you get a room key?" I asked.

"You had to know Oscar, and after nearly fifty years I knew my cousin. He didn't want to be inconvenienced. He couldn't be bothered to actually get up and walk to the door. It was easier for him to get me a key. He'd tell me to let myself in and then leave the key on the table when I left."

"So when you picked up the airline ticket you let yourself in and shot him?" I asked.

"Not exactly. That's how the plan was supposed to work." Richard scratched his ear.

Jenna made a move forward, but Richard squawked.

"Don't make me shoot you, Counselor."

My mind raced. I didn't think he would shoot all three of us, but he might. I needed to keep him talking. "So what went wrong?"

"I knew from years ago that Max always kept a gun in his glove box. So I snatched it from the white Lexus and came upstairs."

"You didn't know that the gun was registered to Alexandra Pembrook?" Jenna asked.

"No. If I had, I would have gotten another weapon." Richard frowned.

"What happened next?" I asked.

"Ah, well, I let myself into the suite and there he was, naked as a jaybird and lying on the sofa." Richard grinned. "Oscar opened his eyes and started to fight."

"Where was Felicity during this struggle?" Jenna asked.

"I told you. I was downstairs in the bar," Felicity snapped.

"She was. I saw the cheap little gold digger hanging all over some male stripper." Richard sneered. "The fact that Oscar would humiliate a woman like Alexandra with the likes of her made me sick." He pointed the gun at Felicity.

"Why, you—"

Richard leveled the gun at Felicity, cutting off whatever biting retort she had planned.

"I shot him, but we struggled and he managed to get away."

"He didn't make it far, though, only across the hall?" I suggested.

"The door caught on the security latch. I'd left the gun in the other room, so I couldn't shoot him again. Then I remembered I'd picked up his insulin from the pharmacy. So I gave him a nice big dose." Richard chuckled. "That did the trick."

"Ugh. You monster," Felicity spat.

"How'd you get him out of the room?" Jenna asked.

"I was covered in blood from the struggle, so I couldn't walk downstairs like that. But I managed to get into the closet at the end of the hall. I found a uniform and changed into it."

"But then Camilia woke up and called me. We'd found Oscar's body," I said.

"I waited outside the door and heard your plans to switch rooms. So I knew I needed to act fast."

"You took one of the laundry hampers and rolled it down to the room and put Oscar inside," I said.

Richard nodded. "Very good. What else did you figure out?"

"You took his body downstairs and outside and dumped him into the creek," I said.

"When we were bidding on the audit work for the Four Feathers we spent a lot of time touring the facility. I knew where all of the cameras were located. I also knew that the laundry room had a door that led around by the creek." He chuckled. "Oscar joked that if the washers ever broke down, the women could always wash the linens in the creek and beat them with rocks."

"Male chauvinist pig," Jenna mumbled.

"So, dressed as a worker, you just got in your car and walked away?" I asked.

"Not until I disposed of the gun. I left it where it would be sure to be found." He frowned.

"You didn't realize they would think Alexandra was the one who used it," I said.

"I never would have done it if I thought they would accuse Alexandra. But we're going to take a little walk. We'll go downstairs and out the back."

"What are you planning to do to us?" Felicity asked.

"He's going to kill us," I said.

"Irma said you were smart. That's exactly right. I'll shoot you two." He moved his gun to indicate Jenna and me. "I'll write a letter where Felicity admits to killing Oscar. When you two confronted her, she killed you. Then, overcome with remorse, she kills herself."

"Not very original," Jenna muttered.

"True, but it'll do in a pinch. I may even have to do a bit of acting myself. You know, I played Macbeth in high school." He gazed back into his memory and grinned. After a moment he refocused on us. "I'll explain how I always knew Felicity was unstable. So I kept a close watch on her."

"No one will believe that," I said.

"You'd be amazed what people will believe. Now, move."

Chapter 47

Richard stepped aside so that Jenna, Felicity, and I could precede him out of the room. He put the gun in his pocket. He kept us close and put an arm around my shoulders. Felicity was in between me and Jenna. Bunched together, we made our way to the elevator.

"Don't make a sound or as God is my witness, I'll shoot. I don't have much to lose at this point."

The elevator dinged and the doors opened, and we stepped inside.

We turned around to face the front and the doors closed.

But it wasn't until the doors closed that I saw Nana Jo in the corner of the elevator.

"Nana Jo, he has a gun!" I shouted.

Richard pulled the hand holding the gun out of his pocket.

Nana Jo must have been expecting it because she had assumed her stance. She spun around and kicked the gun out of his hand. Then she crouched low and did a sweeping kick that took Richard by surprise and left him on the ground.

Jenna scrambled for Richard Pembrook's gun.

Felicity screamed and flattened herself against the back wall of the elevator.

I glanced down and saw Nana Jo's purse on the floor. I reached inside and pulled out her peacemaker.

When the elevator reached the bottom and the doors opened Chief of Police Little Bear and two other tribal police were waiting with weapons pointed, ready to fire.

Richard Pembrook was on the elevator floor with Nana Jo's knee in his back.

Chapter 48

"The federal authorities are on their way to collect Richard Pembrook," Kai Strongbow said.

"Where is he now?" I asked.

"Handcuffed and locked in a cell at the tribal police station," Chief Little Bear said from the corner of the room where he stood. "Which one of those guns belonged to Pembrook?"

Jenna passed over the gun she'd been clutching since we left the elevator.

"Thank you." Chief of Police Little Bear placed the gun on a nearby shelf and returned his attention to Kai Strongbow.

I discreetly slipped Nana Jo's peacemaker back into the purse that was lying on the table. However, I could tell by the twitch of the police chief's lips that my actions hadn't gone unnoticed.

Kai Strongbow sat at the head of the table and tented his hands. "Now, Mrs. Washington, could you tell us what really happened?"

I recapped what we had learned from Richard Pembrook. When I finished he paused for a few moments.

Ruby Mae looked up from her knitting. "That explains why my great-niece said that the laundry hampers were disappearing. Lawd, that man had that staff running all over the place looking for those hampers."

"What I don't understand is why," Dorothy said. "Why kill him?"

"And why now? His cousin had been treating him like dirt his entire life," Irma said.

"The worm turned," I said.

"Richard Pembrook finally got fed up with being his cousin's whipping boy," Nana Jo said.

"Richard was aware of everything his cousin had been doing to destroy Maxwell Manning. He knew the end was in sight. Getting the Four Feathers accounting contract away from Manning and Manning Accounting was the final straw. The company couldn't survive," I said.

"And Oscar Pembrook was about to leave the country with Manning's wife. If Richard was going to make a move, he'd have to do it now," Jenna said.

"His only error was getting mixed up about the cars. Oscar bought the same type of car as Max Manning. Richard thought he was leaving the gun in Manning's car when he was actually leaving it in Oscar Pembrook's, which drove suspicion toward Alexandra."

"But who tried to run you off the road?" Nana Jo asked. "That couldn't have been Alexandra Pembrook."

"Oh, I know this one." Irma raised a hand.

We all turned to stare.

"Richard misplaced the keys to Oscar's car," Irma said. "He had to get a spare set from Felicity, but she must have given him Oscar's keys instead of the set that went to Max's car."

"Remember when Felicity said Oscar left his car at her house?" Jenna said.

"I'll bet Richard got the cars confused. He must have taken Oscar's Lexus instead of Max's," Nana Jo said.

"That's right. He took his cousin's car and tried to run you off the road. Then he planted the gun in the glove box, thinking he was implicating Max Manning," Chief of Police Little Bear said.

"When he was really pointing the spotlight on Alexandra Pembrook," Nana Jo said.

"I have a question." I looked at Chief of Police Little Bear. "How did you know we were in need of help?"

"The cameras." Chief Little Bear grinned.

"If I never look at another piece of camera footage, it'll be just fine with me." Detective Pitt rubbed his eyes. "We've been looking at camera footage for hours."

"Poor baby. Is there anything I can do to help?" Camilia rubbed his back.

"I might be able to come up with something." A smile lit up Detective Pitt's face.

Nana Jo rolled her eyes.

We talked a bit longer, but then we all got up to leave.

Kai Strongbow extended his hand. "I want to thank you. Thanks to you, a killer will be brought to justice and an innocent woman's reputation will remain unscathed." He bowed his head.

"Thank you so much for this lovely experience. The hotel is wonderful and I had a great time . . . well, apart from the dead body and someone trying to kill me."

Kai Strongbow shook his head. "My sincere apologies."

We said our goodbyes and left Kai Strongbow and Chief of Police Little Bear to sort through all of the issues with the federal authorities.

"Well, I've still got a few more hours left, so I'm going fishing." Irma pushed her chest up and strutted off in the direction of the bar.

"I'm going to meet my great-niece for dinner, and to thank her for telling me about the laundry hampers. She'll be tickled pink to know that her clue turned out to be important." Ruby Mae smiled and walked away.

"I'm going to change, and then Kai is going to take me to a naming ceremony," Dorothy said.

"What's a naming ceremony?" I asked.

"Traditionally, the Pontolomas believed that when a child was born the Creator couldn't see their face. The tribe had a ceremony where the child was given a name and then the Creator would be able to see them,"

"What's involved in the ceremony?" Nana Jo asked.

"I'm not sure. I'll find out tonight. Kai is conducting the ceremony. It sounded a lot like a christening, except for the eagle feathers and smudging the godparents with sage." Dorothy shrugged. "I know there's a meal afterward and I'm looking forward to that." She walked away to get ready for her date, leaving Jenna, Nana Jo, and me.

"I'm going to have a massage and then go spend some time with my sons." Jenna started toward the elevator, then stopped and came back. "I have one question."

"Just one?" Nana Jo said.

"What's any of this have to do with the Scarlet Pimpernel?"

Chapter 49

I explained that Sir Percy Blakeney in *The Scarlet Pimpernel* pretended to be a weak, mild-mannered fop, only concerned with clothes and appearances. But it was only a cover to hide the fact that he was heroically rescuing aristocrats who were going to be sent to the guillotine during the French Revolution.

"Don't tell me you see Richard Pembrook as heroic?" Jenna asked.

"No, but Irma mentioned his clothes and how he dressed. Then everyone kept talking about how meek and mild he was, and how he put up with Oscar Pembrook's bullying, and I wondered why. Why put up with being treated like scum? Everyone else wanted to kill him and he wasn't even treating them as poorly as he treated his cousin. Heck, Nana Jo almost drop-kicked him like a football after only knowing him for about five minutes."

"Truth!" Nana Jo said.

"So why not Richard?" I shrugged. "I guess it made me wonder if he had some ulterior motive behind putting up with his cousin."

Jenna shook her head and went off muttering about the Scarlet Pimpernel.

"What time is your date with Frank?"

I glanced at the time. "I have a couple of hours. I think I'm going to go take a shower and put on something nice. What about you?"

"Freddie is coming to meet me and we're going to have some fun." Nana Jo winked at me and then hugged me. "I'm really proud of you."

I decided to go back to the pub and sit by the window.

"Back again? Tea?" My waitress smiled.

"It's so peaceful sitting here by the fireplace and looking out the window at nature from the safety of the hotel." I laughed.

Settled in with a fresh pot of tea, a new tiered plate full of goodies, and the warmth of the fireplace, I gazed outside and allowed the beauty and serenity of nature to calm my spirit and my mind. After several cups of tea and more cookies than I would ever willingly admit to eating, I pulled out my notebook and allowed my mind to drift backward in time and travel across the Atlantic Ocean to the British countryside.

The entire party gathered in the drawing room. Detective Leonard Waterstone hovered near the window.

Detective Waterstone was a short, squat, ruddy-faced man who wore a wrinkled trench coat over a cheap wrinkled suit. He worked hard to maintain an image that belied his intelligence. He spent years cultivating a persona that included the blank expression of a copper of limited capacity. At Scotland Yard he was known to be a shrewd detective of above-average intelligence.

Detective Inspector Covington was well aware of Waterstone's mental acuity. He also knew how effective his persona of incompetence could be. Time and again criminals underestimated his ability. That was when they slipped. And that was when Detective Waterstone tightened the rope and nabbed his killer. This wasn't his case. All he could do was stand back and watch.

"Murdered? That's horrible," Mrs. Covington said.

Lady Mildred blanched at the words and closed her eyes to shut out the horror of the words. "What is this nation coming to?" Lady Clara sat nearby with the smelling salts at the ready.

Lady Elizabeth sat on the sofa near the fire and knitted.

Lord William sat in his favorite chair and smoked his pipe.

Beatrice stood in a corner, her arms folded across her chest with a stony-faced expression. "I suppose you think I killed him?"

"Beatrice, hush. I'm sure the detective doesn't think any such thing." Ida Smythe rose and rushed to her daughter's side. "Obviously it must have been some deranged tramp wandering through the woods."

"Pshaw," Beryl snorted.

Lady Jean Groverton sat like a stone statue barely blinking.

"What a frightening time. When men are shot in their back like a common criminal." Beryl walked over to Lord Dilworth. "I just don't feel safe anywhere."

Detective Waterstone's gaze drifted around the room. One of these aristocrats was a cold-blooded murderer. He was mindful of the relationship that the Marsh family had to the King. One false step could mean the end of his career. He sharpened his gaze and stood straighter.

"Did anyone notice any vagabonds or tramps roaming around the grounds?" Detective Waterstone asked.

"Well, I hardly know. I mean, since the war it seems there are men everywhere," Lady Mildred said.

"Mother, please. Of course there were no tramps on the grounds," Lady Clara said.

Lord Dilworth gazed into the fireplace.

"Perhaps it would help if you could all tell me where you were this morning between nine and one?" Detective Waterston asked.

"Surely you can't believe that one of us . . ." Lady Mildred leaned back in her seat and closed her eyes. "Clara, I think I'm going to faint, dear."

Lady Clara fanned her mother and applied the smelling salts.

"I believe at the time you mentioned that I was having a conversation with the cook. There was a question about the pheasants," Lady Elizabeth said.

"Pheasants?" Detective Waterston asked.

"For dinner. The gamekeeper hadn't provided enough. So William took his rifle and secured several more. That's right, isn't it, dear?" Lady Elizabeth glanced at Lord William.

"Yes. Frank Mactavish and I went shooting. Bloody good bevy too," Lord William said.

"William!"

"Apologies for my language, dear," Lord William said.

"That accounts for Lady Elizabeth and Lord William, now—"

"I can't take any more of this. If you don't get on with it, I shall scream." Beatrice walked up to the detective. "Go ahead. Say it. You think I shot him." She turned to face the room. "You all think I shot him."

"Of course not."

"Nothing could be further from the truth."

"Bea always was high-strung." Beryl laughed. "Don't be so melodramatic."

"I'm not high-strung and I'm not being melodramatic. You all heard me threaten him. He stole my designs. He wanted to ruin my company. I wanted to kill him." Beatrice flopped down on the sofa in tears. "But I didn't. I only wish I had, but I didn't."

Lady Elizabeth placed a comforting arm around Beatrice. "Of course you didn't kill him, dear. It's obvious who murdered him."

All eyes turned to Lady Elizabeth.

Detective Waterstone gawked. "It might be obvious to you, but I'm just a dumb copper and I have to admit that I haven't quite figured this one out."

"Lord Dilworth, I think you'd better come clean and tell them what you've been up to. Don't you?" Lady Elizabeth said.

Lady Jean Groverton gasped.

Lord Dilworth turned away from the fire and gazed at Lady Elizabeth. "You know?"

"Yes, dear. And I think you've been very brave, but this is a murder investigation and it's time to tell the truth."

Lord Dilworth took a deep breath. "For months I've been hiding the fact that I've been spying."

"What?"

"England is on the brink of war, but there are those within our government who have attempted to broker a deal. Those who believe it's better to appease Germany rather than standing up for what's right."

"The Cliveden set?" Lady Clara asked.

"Oh, Dilly, you're not—"

"No. I'm not." Lord Dilworth rushed to Lady Jean Groverton's side. "I only pretended to go along with them so that I could find out what they were up to."

"Ah. That explains it." Lady Clara smiled.

"Explains what?" Lord William asked.

"Just the telegram I received." She glanced over at her fiancé. "Please, continue."

"If I had information to share, I would take something small. A bracelet, a silver picture frame, a pair of cuff links," Lord Dilworth hurriedly added. "I made sure that the items were returned. The thefts made it to the newspapers. Then I would receive an anonymous letter with instructions. I wrote down what I thought might be useful and left it somewhere. Sometimes, it was a hollowed-out hymnal in a church or behind a brick at the base of a statue."

"It sounds so clandestine and dangerous," Beryl said.

"Who sent the letters?" Detective Inspector Covington asked.

"I don't know. The only identifying mark was a symbol. A simple flower," Lord Dilworth said.

"Like the Scarlet Pimpernel?" Lady Elizabeth asked.

"Sounds silly now, but yes. That's exactly what I thought." Lord Dilworth ran a hand through his hair.

"I must have been delusional—imagining myself as some heroic adventurer."

"I don't understand what any of this has to do with Max Chesterton's murder," Detective Waterstone said.

"Max Chesterton was a Nazi sympathizer. I suspect he was one of the usuals at the house parties designed to broker a deal that would keep Britain out of a war with Germany by bowing down to Hitler and agreeing to the theory of appeasement." Lady Elizabeth glanced at Lord Dilworth. "Am I right?"

"You're right." Lord Dilworth nodded. "Chesterton figured out I was the one stealing. I don't think he figured out why, but I couldn't wait around to see."

"Is that why you killed him?" Detective Waterstone asked. "You wanted to protect your secret, so you shot him."

"No. Dilly didn't do it. I know he didn't do it." Jean sobbed.

"It wasn't Lord Dilworth who murdered Max Chesterton, was it? Beryl?" Lady Elizabeth looked up at Beryl Smythe.

"Me? Why on earth would I murder Max Chesterton? I barely knew the man," Beryl said.

"That's not true, though. You'd been meeting with Max secretly. That's how he convinced you to steal your sister's designs and sell him the business," Lady Elizabeth said.

"No. Beryl would never." Ida Smythe stared at her daughter. "Tell them, Beryl. Tell them you didn't do that."

Beryl threw her head back and laughed. "How'd you know?"

"You told us yourself," Lady Elizabeth said. "Detective Waterstone said Max Chesterton was murdered. He never mentioned how. You gave yourself away when you said, *He was shot in the back of the head like a common criminal.* I suspected it was you, but it wasn't until that moment that I knew for sure."

"Mind if I have a cigarette?" Beryl reached into her purse and pulled out a revolver. She pointed in the direction of Detective Waterstone.

Detective Inspector Covington moved forward.

Beryl reached over and grabbed Lady Clara. She pulled her in front of her like a human shield with her arm around her neck.

Both detectives stopped.

"Now, you all stay right there and Lady Clara won't be harmed." Beryl inched backward toward the door.

Lady Jean stood. "Clara, jujitsu."

With one hand, Lady Clara grabbed hold of Beryl's wrist. She grabbed her elbow with her other hand. She bent her knees and leaned sharply forward and, in one fluid motion, flipped Beryl over her head and to the ground.

Lady Jean quickly grabbed the gun.

Detective Waterstone rushed over and took charge of Beryl.

Lady Mildred swooned.

Detective Inspector Covington grabbed Lady Clara. He gazed in her eyes. "Darling, are you alright?"

"Of course."

He pulled her close and kissed her firmly. "What on earth did you do?"

"It's called jujitsu. We learned it at Bletchley Park as part of our self-defense course."

"Self-defense?" Peter asked.

From the back of Wickfield Lodge there was a lovely stone terrace with magnificent sweeping views of the rose garden, hedge maze, fountain, and the wooded copse below. It was evening and none of the grounds were visible by moonlight. But Peter Covington and Clara Trewellen-Harper weren't interested in the scenery. The couple walked hand in hand through the hedge maze to the center fountain. In front of the fountain was a bench.

Clara and Peter sat shoulder to shoulder on the bench. Alone in the dark they weren't the detective inspector and her ladyship. A man and a woman sat together in the cool of the night. A breeze caused Clara to shiver and Peter removed his jacket and put it around her shoulders.

"Cold?" he asked.

"Not anymore." Clara snuggled close.

After a few moments Peter said, "It's not too late."

"Too late for what?"

"To change your mind. To back out."

"Of course it is."

"No, Clara, I'm serious. You can say you made a mistake. Toss me over. I'll take it like a man. I won't cause a fuss." He gazed in her eyes. "You should run. No one would blame you. No decent girl in her right mind would want to marry someone with a cousin who will go on trial for murder."

"Why did she murder Chesterton?"

"He got too greedy." He shrugged. "Who knows? The point is you have an out."

"But darling, I don't want an out."

"Clara, you have to be realistic."

"Why would I want to do that?"

"I'm serious. Have you thought what it could mean? What it could do to your reputation? Your social standing? It was bad enough that you were planning to lower yourself and marry a copper, but now you're marrying into the family of a murderer. You'll be ostracized."

Clara took his face in her hands and gazed into his eyes. "Darling, you might as well get this through your thick skull right now. I don't care one bloody shilling about what anyone thinks about me. Or you. Or your family. I am a woman in love and I plan to marry you, Detective Inspector Peter Covington. So you'd just better accept that."

"How can you be sure? How can you want to marry into this family?"

Lady Clara snuggled closer. "You silly goose. You can't honestly believe that would make a difference. Besides . . ."

"Besides what?" Peter said.

"You've only met a small fraction of my relatives. When you've had a chance to meet the rest of the bunch you may decide that a little bit of murder in the family may be the least of your worries."

After a few moments Peter pulled Clara close and kissed her thoroughly and completely.

Chapter 50

There was nothing more satisfying than typing those two words. THE END. I stretched, gathered my things together, and took the elevator upstairs to my suite. I made sure the door was closed behind me and sat down and put my feet up on the ottoman. I didn't realize how tired I was until I sat down.

I must have dozed off. When I woke up the room was dark. I was wrapped in a blanket and Frank was asleep on the sofa. I glanced over at the man who meant so much to me. Like Lady Clara in my book, I was shamelessly in love. Regardless of what the future holds, I was thrilled to know that I was going to be facing this next chapter of my life with Frank Patterson. With any luck, our story would have a happy ending.